CW0068919Z

KIND RELATIONS

By the same author

Fiction
Stepsons
The Last Enchantments
The Deep End
Unreal City
The Aunts

Non-fiction
Twin Spirits
Elizabeth and Ivy
A Mind at Ease

Robert Liddell

Kind Relations

LnA

Peter Owen *London & Chester Springs*

PETER OWEN PUBLISHERS
73 Kenway Road London SW5 0RE
Peter Owen books are distributed in the USA by
Dufour Editions Inc. Chester Springs PA 19425–0449

This edition first published in Great Britain 1994
Copyright © the Estate of Robert Liddell 1939, 1994

A catalogue record for this book is available
from the British Library

ISBN 0–7206–0947–X *(cased)*
ISBN 0–7206–0951–8 *(paper)*

Printed in Great Britain by Biddles of Guildford and King's Lynn

TO
MY BROTHER

PART I

1914

I

When the War broke out Colonel Faringdon had to return immediately to Egypt. Mrs. Faringdon stayed on at Folkestone with Nandy and the children until the end of August, and then they all went to her sisters, Mrs. Graves and Miss Milburn, at Handborough Regis.

It was at once evident that Mrs. Faringdon was seriously ill. On fine days she could still sit in the garden, or go out in a bath chair with Stephen by her side, while Andrew pretended to pull; but her strength was rapidly failing. Andrew heard her say to his Aunt Anne: 'I know I am going to die.' Mrs. Graves had answered 'Nonsense', and Andrew was reassured for the moment, but that night his mother found his pillow wet with tears, and he only shook his head when she asked why he was crying. When he was finally forced to answer, he said that he was crying because Nandy had lost her prayer-book. His mother told him that he was a little goose, and was satisfied.

A few nights before Andrew had been found crying bitterly over the prayer-book which Nandy had lost ten days ago at Folkestone; it was a pretty little prayer-book, fastened with a clasp and carried by a handle, and it had been a birthday present to Nandy from Mrs. Faringdon. Andrew used to save up sad things and cry over them at night, often long after they had happened, and long after grown-up people thought he had forgotten them. Mrs. Faringdon said they would buy another prayer-book just like it; they would go together to choose it as soon as she was well again. Andrew had to pretend to be comforted, as he could not tell his mother

9

or anyone else the real reason why he was crying: they would not understand. Of course he was sorry for Nandy, who had lost a prayer-book of which she was fond; but the source of his tears was an overwhelming pity for the lost prayer-book itself. He had been taught to be kind to 'dumb animals' who could not tell their wants; but they could at least cry out in pain, or make some noise to say where they were. How much more should one be kind to dumb objects, such as prayer-books, which could utter no sound at all.

They had gone back to the church to look for the prayer-book; perhaps they had passed quite close to it, but it could not speak to them. In the end they gave up the search; Nandy said that it was time for tea, and they had to go home. Andrew had begged for another few minutes; the prayer-book would think that they did not love it any more if they did not come to find it. Now it was gone for ever. It was perhaps in the hands of rough and dirty children who were unkind to it. It would never be happy again. In his pity Andrew embraced all lost things, children and dogs, and cried suffocating tears into his pillow.

Nandy's prayer-book was the first sad thing that Andrew could think of when his mother asked him why he was crying; and having said that he was crying about it, he naturally began to think about it again, and so cried himself to sleep. He knew by experience that even the kindest grown-ups were strangely callous about the sufferings of Things, and he had given up hope of enlisting their sympathy.

That was the last night that Andrew slept in his mother's room; after that he was moved into the night-nursery with Nandy and Stephen, and his bed was taken by a nurse. That day Nandy took the children out on the Heath and sat down on her camp stool;

Stephen was in his push-cart, and Andrew was made to sit on a rug and write a letter to his father in Egypt. Nandy and he composed it together.

'My dear Daddy, — Thank you so much for your lovely postcard.'

'You must say that Mummy isn't so well, dear,' said Nandy.

'Oh, Nandy, but he will be so sorry! Can't I say that she is a little better? I really think she is to-day. She said her head was better.'

'No, dear, the doctor doesn't think she is quite so well; and that is why the new nurse has come to make her better. Say: "I am sorry to say that Mummy is not so well."'

'But he will be so sorry, Nandy! Must I say that?'

'Well, what is the good of writing if you don't tell Daddy the news, just as it really happens?' said Nandy firmly.

'Well, shall I say: "I am very sorry to say Mummy is not so well to-day," and then I could say, "but the doctor has sent another nurse to make her better"? Then you see Daddy wouldn't mind so much her not being so well, because he would know that the new nurse was going to make her better.'

'That's a very good idea, my love.'

' "I am very sorry to say that Mummy is not so well, but the doctor has sent a new nurse to make her better. The new nurse sleeps in my bed, and I sleep in the night-nursery with Stephen and Nandy." Is that all right, Nandy? What shall I say now?'

'You'd have plenty to say to Daddy if he were here, love. Can't you write some of it?'

'I know! "As soon as Mummy is better we are going to choose Nandy a prayer-book like the one we lost at Folkestone." When *will* she be better, Nandy?'

'I don't know, dear. We mustn't be impatient. The doctor said it couldn't be for a long time yet.'

'And shall we stay here for the winter?'

'I expect so, my dear.'

'And I shall see snow! How lovely! Have I ever seen snow before?'

'Only when you were a tiny baby, dear.'

'Patience hasn't seen snow. How angry she'll be when I go back to Cairo and tell her I've seen it.'

'Well, finish your letter, dear,' said Nandy; 'we must be thinking about going home.'

Two days later a third nurse came. Andrew was excited, and was proud of his mother for being so ill that she needed three nurses. He was not allowed to see her all that day: she was so tired, they said. He wanted to ask if she were not excited too. He was woken up not long after he had fallen asleep, and carried on to her bed for a moment; but he was very drowsy, and hardly knew afterwards if he had been dreaming. Mrs. Faringdon pressed Nandy's hand and whispered: 'Nandy — the children — Andrew and Stephen.' She died early next morning.

When Andrew got up he said to Nandy: 'Aren't you going to make Mummy's Benger?'

Nandy sat down on the ottoman. She said: 'Andrew, your Mummy has gone away. She was very ill, so God has taken her to His house.'

Andrew buried his head in her lap, and cried into her apron; Nandy cried, and so did Stephen to keep them company. Andrew thought contemptuously that Stephen was only a baby, and did not know what he was crying about. Andrew knew why he was crying: his mother had gone away to Heaven for a rest cure. Lately they had stayed at a friend's house; his mother had never come down to breakfast, and he was told that she was having a rest cure. He supposed that God had invited her for the same purpose; it was kind of Him, but He might have asked Andrew and Stephen and Nandy as well, as Miss Philpotts had. After all, He must have room for them, as Nandy said He had many mansions. Andrew wondered when she would come back. He thought of asking Nandy, but something prevented him. He felt at the back of his mind that this might perhaps never be, but he did not want anyone to tell him so. He was afraid of being told for certain that she would not return. He wanted so much to be able to believe that she would.

Nandy, Andrew and Stephen were invited to spend the day at Great-uncle William's house. This shewed that it was not an ordinary day, and Andrew felt that they were important people as he walked beside Nandy and the push-cart. He was proud that they were important, sad people always had something distinguished about them; but at the same time he was shy, and hung his head whenever they passed anyone. Everyone must see that they were important people that morning, and everyone would look at them.

They only said good morning to Uncle William. They spent the day with his housekeeper, Mrs. Pulker. Mrs. Pulker sent Andrew and Stephen into the garden, each with a long crinkly finger of shortbread, while she and Nandy sat in the kitchen and talked about 'poor Mrs. Faringdon'. They were very kind to the children at lunch, and afterwards Mrs. Pulker gave Andrew a large slice of plum cake.

Next day the Aunts came to the nursery soon after breakfast. 'We have two invitations for you, Andrew,' said Aunt Margaret. 'Miss Philpotts wants you to go to stay with her again, and thinks you would enjoy her lovely garden; and your Aunt Emma wants you to

13

go to Quenby and play with your cousins. You are to choose which you would like best.'

'I should like Quenby,' said Andrew promptly, 'because we've been to Miss Philpotts quite lately.'

It was the more daring choice, and he felt a little afraid of it. Quenby was about ten miles away; he had never stayed there, but his mother and the Aunts had sometimes taken him over to tea with their brother's family. He was not sure about Aunt Emma, whom he did not know very well; she seemed kind, but he knew that his mother and the Aunts did not like her at all. Perhaps they were right; he did not like her silly way of talking to him as if he were a baby. And there were so many cousins; he could hardly tell any of them apart except Tom, a year younger than himself, whom he detested.

But Quenby attracted him very strongly; it was a paradise into which he had only glimpsed, and he longed for an opportunity to sample all its delights at leisure. Few grown-up people would have thought the house beautiful, or even comfortable; none would have thought the large ill-planned garden comparable with Miss Philpotts's well-kept lawns and flower-borders. For a child, however, Quenby possessed infinite attractions; the house had cupboards full of toys and books and fancy dresses, and the garden was full of hiding-places and had a pond with a punt and an island in it. A summer afternoon had never been half long enough to explore these marvels.

Aunt Anne did not seem to approve of his choice. 'Are you sure you want to go to Quenby?' she asked. 'You don't like Tom, you know.'

'Don't put the child off, Anne,' said Aunt Margaret. 'You agreed to leave it to him. Are you quite sure which you want, dear?' she asked Andrew, 'because I

14

shall have to write to Miss Philpotts and to your Aunt Emma.'

'Yes, I should like to go to Quenby,' said Andrew firmly.

'Well, perhaps it's just as well,' said Aunt Anne with resignation.

II

UNCLE AUBREY came over in his car to fetch Nandy and the children. They arrived at Quenby at tea-time. At the sound of the car all the cousins poured out of the house to watch their arrival, and stood in a row at the front door. They looked unreal, stiffly grouped like a family photograph, with staring faces and fixed smiles.

Cynthia was eighteen, four years older than any of the others; she stood apart from her brothers and sisters, and welcomed her cousins with a pleasant smile. The younger children were huddled round the little governess, Miss Hunt. There was Gladys, an unattractive and sullen-looking girl of fourteen, shortly to return to school at Roedean. Flora was twelve, and Mabel eleven; both were dark and sallow, but Flora was plump and good-natured, while Mabel was excessively thin, and blank stupidity was written upon her inexpressive face. Philip was nine years old, Arthur seven, and Tom five; they were all dressed exactly alike in grey flannel knickers and grey jerseys, and stared anxiously at Andrew and Stephen, who had just lost their mother, and to whom they had been told to be kind. Andrew's heart sank; they seemed so overwhelmingly many.

After tea, while Nandy and Stephen were taking possession of their room, Andrew sat at the school-room table playing Prince's Quest with Miss Hunt and the cousins. It was a lovely game. You played it with dice, and it was only a variation on Snakes and Ladders, but much more romantic. Each player had a 'prince' of cardboard, who set out on the quest of a sleeping beauty across a board chequered with accidents and adventures: you might light upon a cloak of darkness or a fairy godmother (go on six moves), or you might fall into the clutches of a wizard (miss three turns), or meet a wicked stepmother (go back to the start). After passing through all kinds of vicissitudes the winning prince, the lucky seventh son, scaled the Crystal Mountain on shoes of swiftness, and pierced his way through the enchanted briar which surrounded the bower of the Sleeping Princess.

This was the first time that they had slept at Quenby. Nandy, Andrew and Stephen had been given for their nursery a vast room, known as the store-room on account of the many trunks, work-baskets, disused sewing-machines, lay figures and other mysterious and useless articles shrouded in brown holland, which encumbered the corners of the room, and assumed gigantic and terrifying shapes by lamplight. They went up to bed by a series of passages and staircases with brown and shiny wallpaper, lit by oil-lamps, which gave a feeble light and a powerful smell. The store-room itself was almost entirely lined with cupboards; one of these opened behind Andrew's bed and revealed a miscellaneous collection of books: *The Scarlet Pimpernel*, *Magnall's Questions*, *The Poems of Peter Pindar*, and *The History of the Fairchild Family*.

Andrew lay looking up at the ceiling, and thinking how strange everything was. He supposed that his mother must be finding things strange in Heaven, with an angel to put her to bed instead of a hospital nurse. He hoped God was kind to her; he thought she would probably get on very well with Jesus. He was afraid that there was something cold and unhomely about Heaven, probably there would be clean sheets there every night; it might be very grand, without being really comfortable. He wondered if they still gave her Benger's Food there, and when she would be well enough to come back; perhaps she would be back at Handborough Regis before he left Quenby. The Aunts and Andrew had agreed that he must be back in time to see the sycamore tree cut down in the garden in November; it would be a pity if she were not back too, as she would enjoy that. Probably God would send her back in time.

Aunt Emma came up to look at the children. Stephen was fast asleep, clutching his beloved rabbit 'Old Bun'. Andrew looked up and smiled. Aunt Emma took his hand and said that she hoped he would be happy at Quenby with his cousins, and that he was to tell her everything when he was unhappy, just as he would have told his mother. She added that she had always been so very fond of his mother. Andrew did not think that his mother had ever liked Aunt Emma at all, but he could not think why, as she seemed very kind. He decided that it was perhaps better not to mention it, and he kissed his aunt good night in silence.

The garden was so large that Andrew easily persuaded Nandy that there was no need to go outside it for their morning walk. They explored the kitchen-garden, with Stephen in his push-cart. There was a large green-house, in which one of the gardeners was busy making a wreath with white flowers and maiden-hair fern. Andrew wanted to watch, but Nandy did not like to stay there; she suggested that they should go to look at the cousins' bicycle-shed, where their large collection of bicycles and tricycles and pedal-cars was kept. It was a favourable opportunity, as the cousins had gone for a walk to the village with Miss Hunt.

At Quenby Nandy felt herself more her own mistress than at Handborough, where in many little ways the Aunts had interfered with her management of the children, and often came into the nursery. Mrs. Milburn

18

and Miss Hunt very seldom came into the store-room at Quenby, and then only to fetch one of the household articles kept in the cupboards there. Miss Hunt and the Milburn children formed a separate establishment from Nandy and Andrew and Stephen. They all took their meals together in the school-room; but Nandy retained an absolute and independent authority over her children. When the cousins took their morning walk to Duckwold, where Miss Hunt executed commissions for Mrs. Milburn and gossiped with the tradespeople, Nandy and the little boys walked into the country, or round the farm and the gardens. Miss Hunt and Nandy were very friendly. They often sat together on the terrace on warm afternoons, and talked about 'poor Mrs. Faringdon' and the children; while the children bowled hoops or rode up and down on their tricycles. Mrs. Milburn sometimes asked Nandy into the drawing-room for a few minutes, or took several paces with her in the garden. Nandy thought her less stiff than the Aunts, and was glad to talk to her about the Faringdons.

The children did not see very much of Mrs. Milburn, who always seemed to have a great deal to do; now and then she would bustle into the store-room, and when she had found what she wanted she would bustle out again as quickly, saying cheerfully: 'We're all busy now there is a war on.' Uncle Aubrey came back from London after bedtime, and only entered their lives when he carved the chickens for Sunday luncheon.

Stephen was too young to have much contact with the cousins, and Andrew was almost as little affected by their company. Arthur was the nearest to him in age, and they did not mind each other. They found it convenient to play together various games which neither could play alone, and they never quarrelled; but they could not have been called friends. Flora and Philip treated him with the kind condescension which elder children often shew so charmingly to 'babies'. Andrew was fond of them, and thought they were very clever. Philip could draw extremely well, and Flora had a gift for telling long and elaborate stories that never came to an end. Tom and Mabel were always fighting, and never united in anything except to tease Andrew and Stephen, who detested them. One day they heard Andrew calling to Nandy on the stairs: 'Oh, Nandy, wait for me!' On every possible occasion afterwards they would call after Andrew in whining voices: 'Oh, Nanny, wait for me!' Stephen soon provided them with a phrase to use against him; when Berthe, the Swiss nursery-maid, urged him to eat up his milk pudding at lunch one day, he scowled at her severely and said: 'Oh, but I don't want to.'

Andrew kept very much to himself. He had always been a solitary child, but he never felt lonely, at least not when he was alone. Stephen was still too young to be much more than an audience for whose benefit he could think aloud. The chief bond between them was a toy rabbit. 'Old Bun' had belonged to Andrew at first, but had held quite an unimportant position in his menagerie; he far preferred Teddy bears. Just before they left Egypt in May, Stephen had fallen in love with Old Bun; Andrew had quite willingly ceded his rights in him, and Old Bun was chosen as Stephen's travel-companion. Stephen and Old Bun were inseparable by day and night. Through Stephen's adoration for Bun, Andrew had learned to appreciate Bun's supreme qualities. It was recognized that Stephen was Bun's friend, master, or slave; the exact nature of the relationship was not determined. Andrew had a lesser share in the ownership and service of Bun. Both children loved Bun better than anyone or anything in the world, and loved each other for Bun's sake. Stephen placed absolute faith in his oracular powers; 'what Bunny says' was law. Like priests of other religions he worked his oracle to advantage. 'Bunny doesn't want to go out this afternoon' was a frequent utterance of the god; but in this matter Nandy opposed the will of Bun with ruthlessness, and frequently incurred his displeasure.

Andrew had a more passionate faith in Bun, because he already had temptations to scepticism. He clung to his idol in the face of all evidence. Bun was not only a sentient being like 'real rabbits', but was also endowed with a wonderful wisdom and goodness, and with omniscience. There was one thing that Bun lacked; Mummy had told him that Bun had no soul, and would never go to Heaven. Andrew had accepted this as an authoritative statement, and was very unhappy about it. He had often cried about it, but now he had hit upon a plan for getting Bun a soul. He often prayed: 'Please God give Bun a soul, for Jesus Christ's sake.' He sometimes made secret prayers like that to God, and hoped that they would get there, although detached from his official evening prayers which he said into Nandy's lap. He felt rather mean when he talked to God behind the back of Nandy, His representative and priest upon earth, but after all there were some things that she did not quite understand, and he thought God might. There seemed no reason why prayers whispered into a pillow should not get to Heaven just as well as prayers said aloud in a special voice (which Nandy called a 'reverent voice'), into a starched white apron.

The form of evening prayer authorized by Nandy to be said daily, kneeling, was as follows: 'Pray God bless dear Daddy and Mummy, Stephen and Nandy, all Uncles and Aunts, all kind relations and friends. Bless me, and make me a good boy, for Jesus Christ's sake. Amen.'

21

This formula was never changed, though sometimes a clause was added at Nandy's command: 'And please God forgive me for telling a lie.' This was not often, as Andrew was truthful. Once he was sadly embarrassed; he had not told a lie, but Nandy was convinced that he had, and he was unable to prove his innocence. She insisted that he should pray to be forgiven. It seemed so silly, because God must be perfectly aware that he had told no lie. In the end he said the clause to save argument, mentally adding: 'But I didn't tell a lie, you know.'

Andrew's loneliness did not oppress him; it seemed almost that he had elected it. He was a romantic child, and already familiar with stories of chivalry. In these he had always chosen for himself the hermit's part. He had a horror of violence, even if used against dragons and wicked knights. It was therefore impossible for him to become a Paladin. He would not have minded being a damsel in distress, praying by a tree while her knight cut off the dragon's heads; it would be an exciting life, and how pleasant to ride home clasped in the strong arms of the Red Cross Knight! Unfortunately boys could not become damsels in distress. There only remained the role of the holy hermit, who lived in the wood and gathered simples and told his beads. It was a lonely life, and uneventful, but for the occasional excitement of tending a wounded knight, or of sheltering a damsel in distress. All the same, it was a life that would suit him very well.

His vocation as a hermit increased Andrew's natural piety. He had very seldom entered a church, and never understood what happened there, so religion for him naturally meant private worship. In Cairo his mother disliked taking him into the town to church, as she feared infection. He had attended Stephen's christening; and once at Handborough Regis he had been to a children's service, and greatly disliked it. There were a number of little children — and he hated other children — all dressed in Sunday clothes and taken to church to meet God; just as one was washed and fetched down to the drawing-room to meet the Vicar. He had twice come into contact with more exotic forms of religion, and found them far more attractive. In Cairo the Mohammedan funerals went by his house, with women wailing, and they haunted his imagination. Quite near where he lived there had been a Catholic convent; he used to hear the little bell with its foolish tinkle. He passed by the small white chapel with his mother one morning; it was a hot glaring day, and from the cool dark church a delicious smell stole through the open door. 'That's incense,' said Mrs. Faringdon, 'because it's a Roman Catholic church.'

Andrew decided that he must have an oratory. He thought that a small disused aviary would do very well; it was carpeted with moss, and comfortable for kneeling. He broke two sticks, and inlaid them in the form of a cross in the moss; then he knelt down and thought that he might begin being a holy hermit. It suddenly occurred to him that he could easily be seen by anyone who passed, as the sides of the aviary were made of wire netting. He felt shy of making his vocation known, and went in search of a more hidden sanctuary. There was a low stone bench in a secluded grass walk at the end of the garden. This he made his altar. He would go there, when he could creep away unobserved, and kneel against it, with his head resting on the moss-grown stone. Sometimes he would bring a flower or two, and lay them on his shrine. His meditations bore no relation to his ordinary prayers, and he asked for nothing; it was as though they were addressed to a different god.

23

He knelt still, and felt that the cousins and the world of Quenby were very far away and did not really matter. He was alone, he was Andrew, a separate person enclosed underneath his skin; not Tom, nor Mabel, nor even Stephen. He could hear Himself breathe and notice Himself think; he knew just how much it hurt Himself if someone were unkind to him. He could be unkind to Himself; he sometimes refused, when offered a thing which he intensely wanted. Nobody else knew that He was there. His mother never even suspected it; and he did not want anyone to find out. God knew.

For an anchorite Quenby had advantages over anywhere else where Andrew had ever lived. The garden was larger, and if he vanished for a few minutes Nandy did not worry: probably he was with an older cousin and quite safe. At Handborough and Cairo there was no possibility of evading vigilance, and other people were a nuisance when all this was going on inside himself. Once while he was walking beside Nandy and kicking a stone, it suddenly occurred to him that other people might be like *that*, too. This was a discovery of immense importance; his breath was taken away, and he stood still in a wild surmise. The world was more full of mystery than he had supposed. He had lately found out that he was Andrew; perhaps Nandy was Nandy, and Stephen was Stephen. Perhaps they had independent secret lives of their own, as he had. It might be that Nandy, as she tied her apron or lit her spirit-lamp, was not thinking of him, but was also thinking of herself and of God.

Andrew had only made one other discovery of comparable importance. When he was four years old his grandmother was still alive. He was in her room; she made the musical-box play for him, while Aunt Margaret sat by with her sewing. The lid was open, and the prickly roller of the musical-box slowly turned, as it played its tinkling tunes. He thought that Grandma was very old, and would die; he knew that people did die. Andrew himself would grow older and older, and would one day die too. And little babies would be born to take Grandma's place, and his place. So that the world would go on and on, with different people, but roughly the same number; just as they sometimes had different maids at Handborough, but always three. And he thoughtfully placed a finger on the prickly roller.

III

LIFE passed smoothly at Quenby; unpleasant contact with Tom and Mabel was easily avoided. Andrew kept close to Nandy's side. They wandered about the farm and the gardens with Stephen in his push-cart. Often they sat under a cedar tree on the lawn, and Nandy wrote interminable letters to her sisters with a stylo which Mrs. Faringdon and Andrew had chosen for her last birthday present. Andrew was greatly interested in Nandy's family; she had a sister who was maid to an old lady in Scarborough, and a brother and sister who lived at her old home in Somerset, a thatched cottage covered with roses. One day she was going to take Andrew and Stephen to stay with them.

Andrew drew sketches of Quenby from different aspects in a bold impressionist manner. He thought it a most picturesque house, and filled pages of his sketch-book with studies of its french windows and gables. Sometimes he would distract Nandy's attention from her letter-writing with the question: 'Do you think I've got the perspective right?' He had learned the word from Aunt Margaret, who once gave him a drawing lesson, and he was fond of using it. The landscape part of his sketches never caused him any trouble; anyone could draw trees. His only concern was to do the background as quickly as possible, and his father had taught him a labour-saving device:

> Turn your pencil round and round
> And trees appear upon the ground.

Andrew turned his pencil, and thought trees crowded into a perfectly satisfactory shade.

Nandy was a true countrywoman, and had spent her childhood on a farm. She took great pleasure in initiating Andrew into country sights, and he rewarded her with an insatiable curiosity. They visited the dairy, his hands were inspected, and he was allowed to dip the tip of a very clean finger in the cream which had collected at the top of the cool white pans of milk.

A quiet cow was found for his first attempt at milking. Nandy shewed him the way. It seemed so easy, and the milk fell with a pleasant rattle into the pail. Then it was his turn. He grasped the horrible slippery udders and pulled, but only a mean intermittent trickle came. He did not think that he much cared for milking. It was so unpleasant to touch other creatures' bodies, especially their more private parts. From his own body, even, he had an instinctive shrinking. He was told that it was 'fearfully and wonderfully made'; but much of it seemed to him superfluous and rather disgusting.

Quenby had not proved a disappointment to him, although before his visit Andrew had regarded it as an earthly paradise. Now he still compared it with Heaven. This was a natural comparison; his mother was in Heaven, and he was at Quenby. His knowledge of poetry was confined to the Hymns; he knew nothing of a Golden Age or of El Dorado, but he knew all about the 'home for little children above the bright blue sky'. The hymn said that no home on earth was like it, nor could with it compare; but Andrew thought that Quenby might compare with it very favourably, and he decided that he had no reason to envy his mother.

His faith in her return was of the same nature as his faith in the 'realness' of Bun. It was better supported by grown-up authority; Nandy had told him that he would see her again. He did not talk much about Mummy; there was a grown-up mystery about her, he fancied,

27

and he did not wish to seem inquisitive. He missed her, and in his thoughts continually referred things to her judgement. Grown-ups were awkward when they mentioned her, and this prevented him from speaking of her naturally to them. He thought that she must be feeling the cold, as Heaven must be so very high up, and so exceedingly bracing. Once he said thoughtfully to Nandy, as they returned from a walk: 'What a good thing Daddy and I chose those furs for Mummy last Christmas!'

'Why, dear?' asked Nandy.

A sudden shyness prevented Andrew from explaining; he said he did not know. Nandy said he was a funny child and did not press him. Andrew was glad to change the subject; he had a secret fear of being told more about his mother's present state. No one had definitely said that she would come back, perhaps Andrew would have to go to Heaven to find her; and there was no talk of his going there just at present.

After four weeks at Quenby came Andrew's sixth birthday. Miss Hunt wished him many happy returns, and said that it was sad for him to spend a birthday for the first time without either of his parents, but that everyone at Quenby would try to make it up to him. In the end Andrew enjoyed it as much as any birthday he had ever spent, except perhaps his last. He had spent his fifth birthday on the *Mongolia* on his way out to Egypt. His mother was not there, she was in London in a nursing home and followed later with Aunt Margaret, but he had had a letter from her. (She never wrote from Heaven; he thought that she was probably not yet well enough.) The steward on the *Mongolia* had discovered that Colonel Faringdon would be forty-five on 21 October, and that Andrew would be five on 23 October (they never knew how he had found out).

28

On Andrew's birthday there was an enormous cake for both of them, with the initials O. R. F. and A. R. F. It was the best cake that he had ever had; it was large enough for everyone in the ship to have a slice, and it was decorated with shells made of toffee. Andrew handed it round at the children's tea, and the remains were given to the grown-ups. He and Nandy took some of it to the second-class dining-saloon. The second-class grown-ups were ever so nice, but some of them were rather common. One second-class lady said: 'Thank you for the lovely *kike*.'

At Quenby everyone chose his own luncheon on his birthday; even Miss Hunt chose hers when it was her birthday. When Andrew had once asked her how old she was, she had replied 'Seventeen'; which was ridiculous, as Cynthia was eighteen. Andrew chose a rabbit and orange jelly for his birthday luncheon. He chose a rabbit, because he wanted to see it being skinned. He seldom had a chance to indulge his taste for the macabre. Only lately they had killed a pig and cut it up, and had even made some of it into sausages, all behind his back. His rabbit was not going to escape him in the same way; he made an appointment with the cook at half past ten.

The rabbit lay on the table in front of Cook; it was limp but lifelike. In spite of his dread of all dead creatures, Andrew ran a finger along its back, and made a small furrow in the fur. If he were God he would tell it to rise and run away, while Cook had turned her head. Even as it was, he might be able to do something; lots of people had worked miracles. He might raise the rabbit to life; but Cook would be surprised, and it would need some explanation. And perhaps he might fail; that would be humiliating. On the whole it was wiser not to try. Cook seized the rabbit and began her work;

29

it was too late now. The skin rolled back like a glove. Soon the rabbit was a pink shapeless thing, unpleasant to look at. Andrew turned his head and blinked; he had a terribly strong inclination to cry. He did not think that he cared for rabbit after all; and was there not a kind of treachery to Old Bun in this? A wave of darkness passed over him, blotting out the sun; and all the world seemed bad and senseless. This quite often happened to him, though it never lasted long. This time he was sufficiently recovered by luncheon-time to eat two helpings of rabbit.

After luncheon he went into the drawing-room to undo his presents. There was an enormous box of bricks labelled 'for Andrew, with love from Daddy and Mummy'. His heart leapt for joy; here was definite proof that his mother had not gone away for good. It was the first time that she had communicated with him since she went away. There was still no letter from her, but Colonel Faringdon had written from Cairo. He said that he missed them so much, so did Abdulla the cook, and Mohammed the house-servant, and Said the hippopotamus at the Zoo. Andrew felt sorry for his father, all alone in the house in Cairo. He did not miss him very badly; the children and Mrs. Faringdon always returned to England for the summer months, and he was used to separation from him. He was fond of him, but he hardly minded leaving him every May as much as he minded leaving Aunt Anne and Aunt Margaret in October. He always embarked at Port Said with pleasurable excitement, but wept bitterly every time he left Tilbury.

Uncle Aubrey and Aunt Emma gave Andrew a clock-work train, with a station and a signal-box. The Aunts had each sent him a book, and had written to him from a hotel at Lyme Regis. There were funny little presents

from the cousins, tied up lumpily in thick brown paper
and odd pieces of string, and labelled 'Andrew, with
love and best wishes from Arthur', or 'Andrew, with
love and best wishes from Tom'. He had to kiss everyone, which was most disagreeable.

As it was his birthday, he was allowed to stay in all
the afternoon and look at his presents; that made up
for everything. He never cared for going out at the best
of times. While it had been warm it was pleasant
enough to potter about the farm; but now the weather
had broken Nandy insisted on a 'brisk walk'. Often
they had to wait, looking out at the weather through the
window. Nandy would say: 'I think it may clear up
in time for our constitutional before tea', or 'I think
we shall manage to get out between showers'. Andrew
hated going out between showers.

Their time at Quenby was now drawing to a close.
Andrew had thoroughly enjoyed himself, but he was not
sorry that it was nearly over. The pleasures of winter
belonged more to the nursery than to the garden, and
at Handborough Regis he would have undisputed
mastery over the nursery. At Quenby the variety of the
cousins' toys, and the wealth of their dressing-up cupboard, was more than counterbalanced by the en-
cumbering presence of the cousins themselves. He was
younger than any of them, except Tom, and could
therefore only expect a subordinate role in their games.

Nandy was less pleased at the prospect of returning to
Handborough. Her authority in the nursery there was
always liable to be overridden by a command from the
Aunts: she had resented taking orders from them during
Mrs. Faringdon's illness, and now they were to stand
in the place of the children's parents for an unlimited
time. Of all the charges she had ever had, Andrew and
Stephen were more peculiarly *her* children than any of

the others. Their mother had in a way commended them to her when she died. She was jealous of sharing their affection with their aunts; she had even grudged Andrew's adoration for his mother, although she had accepted it as inevitable. Her jealousy was needless; her position in the children's lives was unique, and could not be undermined by the Aunts or by anyone else. The children loved their aunts more than anyone, except Old Bun, each other, Nandy, and their mother; but Nandy was nearer to them, and a more present force in their lives. She made the weather fair or foul for them, and they would always ultimately have chosen her when there was a conflict of loyalties. This was only fair; she would without hesitation have died at the stake for them, and would have thought she was doing no more than her duty.

She began to say: 'We must make the most of it; there aren't many days left. Soon we shall be back at old Handborough, trapesing over the Heath, I expect.'

Andrew said that it would be rather fun to see the sycamore being cut down, and that he should like to see Handborough in winter for a change.

Nandy was rather cross. She said no doubt he would be glad to get back to his dear Aunt Anne, and to be her little tell-tale again. This was not quite fair, and not at all kind; and she knew it. If she had not been a good woman, she would have been angry with Andrew for making her feel ashamed of herself, as he looked up with sad and puzzled eyes.

She bent and kissed him. 'I'm sorry, my love,' she said humbly, 'Nandy's a little out of sorts to-day. Don't mind too much what she says.'

Andrew was comforted in part, but it did not make it quite right. The most unjust reproach never failed to set up a painful train of self-examination in his morbidly

32

sensitive conscience. He wondered if he had always been loyal to Nandy under the rapid fire of Aunt Anne's cross-examination. It is improbable that he had. Aunt Anne was apt to suspect him of preparing a prevarication if he hesitated to reply to any question. Even if he replied at once, she would look at him suspiciously, if his answer differed from that which she had expected. It would have been easier to have taken the line of least resistance, and to have said exactly what Aunt Anne wished him to say. This was generally obvious from the way in which she framed her questions.

1915

I

AT Handborough they soon settled into a way of life which was to be unchanged until Andrew went to school. Stephen and Nandy slept in the nursery. Andrew had a small bed in Aunt Margaret's room. Aunt Margaret had a long low room, whose walls were covered with wedding groups and holy pictures. Andrew was put to bed at six o'clock by Nandy, and when he had had his supper he lay on his back and gazed up at the ceiling until Aunt Margaret came in to dress for dinner. It was like being in Cairo again, except that at Handborough Regis there was no need to sleep under a mosquito net. When he slept in his parents' room in Cairo, he used to love watching his mother moving about at her dressing-table, especially when she was going out to dinner and had put on a pretty dress and, on grand occasions, her pearl tiara. While Aunt Margaret was dressing Andrew used to ask her for information on every kind of subject, and she usually acquitted herself very well under his examination.

Andrew dressed himself in the morning, and if anything was not very tidy Nandy would put it right when he went into the nursery. He ate his breakfast there, with Nandy and Stephen. First they had a kind of porridge prepared by Nandy, and sometimes as a treat they had golden syrup with it. You let it trickle from the spoon, and wrote your name with it on the porridge, with a flourish at the end.

After breakfast Nandy made their beds, and the children played. Often Andrew was seized with educational zeal, and tried to teach Stephen to read. Stephen repulsed his efforts with such passion and determination, that Andrew seriously feared he would remain for ever illiterate. *Reading without Tears* had no charms for Stephen. Andrew himself secretly thought that A was not much like 'a house with one window', nor B like 'a house with two windows'. He did not think much of *Reading without Tears*; he had had a more interesting book in Cairo, which made the astonishing statement:

W. Y. W.
Means Water why bubble you?

All the same Stephen must be taught. Sometimes the lesson ended in an unseemly scuffle in which, as often as not, the pupil got the better of his master. Nandy might manage to check this at an early stage by the dogmatic and irrelevant statement that 'Birds in their little nests agree'. At such moments the children sobered down, but hated the self-righteous birds. When open warfare had started, Nandy forcibly restored order and usually quoted:

Let dogs delight to bark and bite,
For God has made them so;
Let bears and lions roar and fight,
For 'tis their nature too.
But children, you should never let
Your angry passions rise:
Your little hands were never made
To tear each other's eyes.

This rhyme was peculiarly hateful to Andrew; he winced as soon as anyone began 'Let dogs delight'. Often he begged Nandy not to go any further, and she left off. He hated it for two reasons. Firstly he thought it silly; he did not think dogs ought to be allowed to delight in barking or biting. Nobody thought so really. When Aunt Anne's dog Nigger barked, Aunt Margaret scolded him; and what would happen if Nigger started biting? If God had made dogs so, He had made them very badly; and the same applied to bears and lions. There was no doubt that the rhyme was silly; and if anyone said anything silly, he always felt ashamed. But it was the last line that was really horrible. As soon as Nandy began 'Let dogs delight', he had a dreadful vision of torn eyes. It hurt so very much if something went into your eye. He could not bear to think of any-one's eyes being touched. A small girl in Cairo called Barbara Jacob had an operation on her eyes. Andrew overheard another nurse telling this to Nandy in the gardens. He felt uncomfortable all over, and turned red. Nandy had to punish him for 'having an accident in his trousers'. From that day on he used a hundred wiles to persuade Nandy not to take him for a walk by Barbara Jacob's house. For the very name of the child, to whom this terrible thing had happened, he con-ceived an almost superstitious horror. He did not like Nandy to read to him about Jacob from the *Child's Bible*, and asked her to sing something else when she began to sing *Jacob's Ladder*. Of course he could not mention the cause of his distress, and had to hug it in silence.

They usually walked on the Heath in the morning; this was better than Cairo, because Andrew knew no children at Handborough, and Nandy knew no nurses. Friends were such a nuisance; it was far more agreeable to be just themselves. They took biscuits to eat for what Nandy called 'elevenses'. When it was warm enough, they would sit on a seat to eat their biscuits; and Nandy would read *Home Chat*, or write a letter. Andrew would read *Home Chat* too. There were shelters on the Heath where they could sit, except on the very bitterest days in winter; but sometimes they found their favourite seat already occupied by a tramp, and were robbed of their morning's rest. Kind old ladies often came up to share their seat, drawn by the children's golden hair. The children divided their attention very fairly between them. Stephen in his push-cart naturally enjoyed the homage of baby-worshippers. Andrew was shy, but he was a very successful conversationalist when he was sure that he was being appreciated. He was quite pretty, in a way that was both pathetic and quaint; and when he told his admirers that his father was in Egypt and his mother in Heaven, his sentimental attraction was irresistible.

The afternoon was passed in much the same way as the morning; though they usually went further, and did not sit down. Sometimes the Aunts sent them to buy eggs at a farm. This was a pleasant walk, and they enjoyed their little talk with the farmer's wife, Mrs. Everdale. There was however a perpetual anxiety lest her old mother should appear, a poor old woman who had been wandering in her wits since she had had a stroke a few years before. She was in no way repulsive, but had indeed a strikingly beautiful and gentle face, and her ramblings were not alarming. She would only murmur: 'I must be packing up soon, I'm going back to Hereford.' In time Andrew became used to her; he grew very fond of her, and was disappointed when Mrs. Everdale managed to prevent her from coming to the door.

When they went to 'the Egg Farm' they came back through a dark little wood which they called 'the Dingle'. It lay in a hollow, in one of whose rocky sides there was a cavern, where a venerable tramp had made his home. This elderly and picturesque person, who gave his name as 'Bristol Jack', was at first, like Mrs. Everdale's mother, an object of terror, but was soon accepted as a friend. The children asked to be allowed to give him a Christmas present, and Aunt Margaret said that they might ask him to choose whether he would like a warm vest or a pair of woollen gloves. Bristol Jack chose the vest, but after he had worn it for a week or two he told the children that he had come to the conclusion that he would rather have the gloves, if their aunt would kindly change them. Aunt Margaret gave him a pair of gloves, but did not accept his offer to give back the vest.

Bristol Jack was a philosopher and a hermit, though perhaps not a very holy one. Sometimes he would stop them on their walks and make them listen to his philosophy. 'Some people are so selfish,' he was fond of saying, 'that you'd never think the stars was looking at them night and day.' It made one feel quite creepy to think that the stars were there watching always, though they were at the moment hiding behind the dull grey sky of a winter afternoon.

The children felt the awed respect that simple people generally feel for madness: Bristol Jack and Mrs. Everdale's mother were not ordinary three-dimensional people like the Aunts and the maids, but something greater. They were important powers whose friendship was valuable; and there was, after all, no more reason to be frightened of them than of God, or Old Bun, or the Fairies, who were all probably far more powerful. At this point Andrew's theology was a little confused; he would have hesitated to say for certain that God, or Bristol Jack, or Old Bun was a kind of fairy, and yet it was difficult to see what else they could possibly be.

AFTER tea Nandy dressed the children to go down to the drawing-room to the Aunts. The Aunts were genuinely fond of children, and had been used to look on Andrew and Stephen almost as their own, even while Mrs. Faringdon still lived. The descent to the drawing-room was therefore not awe-inspiring, as it often is to small children — like going to church, only worse. Grown-ups have all the fearful attributes of a Calvinistic deity, with the added terror of being visible. It is no use pretending they are not there, because they insist on being talked to and kissed. God, on the other hand, can easily be pretended away. Of course you know He is there all the time; but He does not obtrude Himself, as grown-ups do. It is always possible, if you are terribly bored in church, to press your fingers on your eyelids, and to watch the colours that come and go. Of course you ought to be saying your prayers, but it is far more amusing to play with this natural kaleidoscope. God is not petty enough to mind about a little thing like that. And after all it is no one's business but His.

The Aunts were what Andrew thought grown-ups ought to be. They were an audience for whom he could be clever. Younger children were a very good audience too, but somehow Andrew's friends had nearly always been older than he, and rather superior. Stephen sometimes thought he was quite clever; but Stephen was really too young to understand everything, and when he understood he did not always admire. He had already a streak of irony in his composition. The Aunts thought highly of Andrew's abilities, and he knew it.

Grown-ups, if they take the trouble, are better company for a child than other children, because they are usually more appreciative. They have also the advantage of being far more unselfish. If two people are building houses with bricks, they generally have no trouble until they are ready to put the roof on. When they come to the roof, there are never enough long bricks in the box to roof two houses. If Andrew and Arthur had been building together, they would have made a compromise and halved the bricks. This saved a quarrel, but it did not really satisfy either of them. They could only roof half of their houses, and pretend the other half of the roof. If Andrew were with Tom, they would no doubt quarrel. Tom would probably smash down Andrew's house and snatch at his bricks. Grown-ups never behaved in so undignified a way. Aunt Margaret or Aunt Anne would cheerfully forgo her share of the long bricks, and Andrew could complete his roof. Sometimes he would refuse the sacrifice, and insist on giving up his long bricks so that Aunt Margaret or Aunt Anne might complete her roof.

It is pleasant to make sacrifices for a grown-up, but bitterly hard to give up anything to another child. Andrew once played with a little Italian girl, who took from him one after another of his playthings. He was out to tea and on his best behaviour, and was so deeply shocked by her undisguised selfishness, that he did not lift a finger to stop her. He was praised for his courtesy and unselfishness in 'giving way to a little girl'; but he hated her ever afterwards, and stigmatized her for ever as 'the horrid little Italian girl'.

Andrew particularly hated to be told to give way to little girls. Of all grown-up superstitions, he thought the privileged position of little girls the silliest and the most annoying. The only difference between them and boys was that they wore more stupid clothes (and incidentally thought far too much about them), and that they were worse tempered. Grown-ups sometimes gave as their reason that little girls were not so strong, which did not seem to be true; or that they were prettier, which was an obvious lie. Andrew knew that grown-ups made far more fuss over him than over many little girls; this must be because he was prettier, since prettiness was about the only quality in a child that seemed to appeal to them.

When he thought of the children in Cairo, Simon seemed to him incomparably the most beautiful. Simon was a tall, fair, delicate boy, a little older than Andrew. He was once invited both to lunch and tea; Andrew had him all the afternoon, and it was a great day in his life. Simon sat opposite to him at lunch, and Andrew said to himself: 'And he'll be there at tea, too.' They rested together afterwards in the darkened night-nursery and, though they were not allowed to talk, even resting did not seem dull with Simon near him. Andrew had heard someone say that Simon was delicate, and he was always in terror that he would die. He would often shiver when he heard the wailing of an Arab funeral (he did not know that Europeans were not buried in the same way), and he would cautiously try to find out from Nandy if Simon were quite well.

Andrew of course did not realize that Simon was his first love. Grown-ups quite often had the bad taste to pretend that he shewed some partiality for this or that little girl, whom he had met at a party or in the gardens. Such mischievous teasing hurt him, and made him feel uncomfortable; and his own discomfort was mingled with a vicarious shame for the older person, who had said a stupid and cruel thing. There was a small girl called Patience, his elder by a year, with whom he played every day in the gardens in Cairo.

44

She was his most intimate friend, and his preceptress. He looked up to her as to an elder sister, for she could blow her own nose at a time when he still had to run to Nandy for assistance in that operation. Once when they had had a fight, and were being taken home in disgrace, Patience's nurse said that it was a shame that 'little sweethearts' should quarrel. Andrew was very angry, but soon forgot about it. When he remembered it again he hated Patience's nurse, and did not feel very fond of Patience. Had anyone teased him about Simon, he would have suffered far more. No one could have been completely forgiven after such an insult; and months afterwards the recollection would have made him cry into his pillow at night. Simon was different, he was precious and secret. He did not talk much about him. He did not want other people to *know* about Simon; his discovery must be kept to himself.

Andrew was never disposed to gratify his relations by shewing chivalry to little girls; he saw no point in it, and he was right. Chivalry is aroused by someone of a different kind from oneself; Andrew could have felt it for an elder person, for a very small baby, or for a half divine person like Simon or for the Angels. He could have entertained an angel with singular grace and courtesy. He did not feel a difference between girls and himself: the best of them were the same as boys, and the worst of them were only rather unpleasant little boys. The only reason he admitted for giving way to little girls was that otherwise they often cried. His mother often teased him for his misogyny, and never failed to make him furious by chanting in a sing-song voice:

> Sugar and spice and all things nice:
> That's what little girls are made of.
> Frogs and snails and puppy-dogs' tails:
> That's what little boys are made of.

Andrew had a secret wish to be a girl; not that he liked them, but they grew into women, while boys grew into men. Ladies were smooth and soft when they kissed you; they smelt nice, and their voices were gentle. Men were rough and bristly; they smelt of smoke, and their voices were harsh. Besides, men were expected to be strong and brave. At the present moment vast numbers of them were being compelled to fight. Andrew tried to find out why they had to do this; he could not suppose that any of them liked being hurt, or that all of them liked hurting other people. Nandy and the Aunts said that the Kaiser was a very wicked man, and that he and his Germans were being cruel to a poor little country called Belgium. They thought it was the duty of the English to help the Belgians; which meant that his cousins Paul and Richard had gone off bravely to kill Germans.

Andrew could not see how events in Belgium could affect Richard. Aunt Anne explained to him by an unconvincing analogy. 'What would you do if you saw a big boy bullying a little boy?' she asked.

Andrew recognized her didactic tone of voice: it was clear that Aunt Anne thought there was something that he ought to do in the circumstances. Had she asked in an ordinary tone of voice, he would have answered promptly: 'Nothing, of course', and would have marvelled at the stupidity of her question. It appeared that Aunt Anne thought he ought to do something when he saw a small boy being bullied; this was a novel point of view. He thought he had better first discover what course his aunt thought he ought to take, and then say that he would take it. Meanwhile he said cautiously: 'What would *you* do?'

Aunt Anne said she would give the bully a thrashing, and so, she was sure, would Andrew. Andrew was perfectly sure he would do nothing of the kind. It was quite a different matter for Aunt Anne. She was a grown-up person, and if she wanted to smack a child, it was unlikely to offer resistance. Besides, grown-up people had the right, or rather acted as if they had the right, to interrupt quarrels between children and to restore order. This right they frequently exercised both capriciously and unjustly: they were apt to assume that the child whom they liked the better was always in the right. Still, there you were; they were grown-up people, and had different standards. They must not be judged with too much severity. If any child began behaving like that, and started punishing bullies and restoring order, he would be acting as if he were a spy set amongst them by the grown-ups. Aunt Anne thought that Jesus would have behaved like that as a small boy, but she could produce no evidence that He had so behaved. Andrew had always been fond of Him, in spite of what he considered His odious precocity among the Doctors, and he did not believe his aunt.

THE War raised another moral problem which Andrew felt more keenly. Everyone said that it was splendid of Richard to have enlisted. But they knew perfectly well, and so did Andrew, that Richard had told a lie. If he had said that he was seventeen when they asked his age at the recruiting office, he would not have been allowed to go to France to kill Germans. Andrew had always been told that it was wicked to tell lies, or even to exaggerate or to pretend in any way. Once he had spilled some jam, and then slipped his plate over it to hide the stain. 'That's a sin,' said his mother.

'I'm sorry,' said Andrew, 'what's it called?'

'Deceit,' she said; and she told him that he must always be completely honest, even in the smallest things, or God would be deeply grieved.

Yet here was Richard being dishonest in quite a big thing; and everyone was calling him splendid for it. Andrew asked Aunt Margaret if she did not think that Richard had been naughty to tell a lie; but she said it was quite different from an ordinary lie. Andrew did not press her. Grown-ups disliked being driven into logical corners. When hard pressed by the ruthless reasoning of a child, they were apt to take refuge either in bad temper, or in the weird world of make-believe, in which they seemed habitually to dwell.

Andrew could not understand why Richard should be exonerated for his lie; still less could he understand why he should have been tempted to tell it. No nice person could want to go and kill Germans. Paul was a soldier; it was quite different for him. Soldiers had to do what the King told them. If King George told Paul to kill Germans, he would have to kill them; just as Andrew had to do what Nandy told him. Richard had however gone of his own free will to kill Germans, when he ought to have been still at school doing his lessons. And Richard was a very nice boy; Andrew loved him.

The Aunts told him that the Germans had made a lot of Belgian babies into sausages. Well, what if they had? That had nothing to do with Richard. Andrew felt grateful to the Germans for behaving like the ogres in a fairy story. If there really were a great many ogres about, he was living in stirring times; he might hope to fall in with wizards, dragons, fairies, wicked step-mothers, and the rest of the cast.

He was determined never to be a soldier. At Cairo people used to pat him on the head, and ask if he would like to be a soldier like his father when he grew up. When he felt bold, he protested; but more often he hung his head and blushed. He was afraid that he would be made into a soldier against his will. His mother once put a penny into a fortune-telling machine on the pier at Folkestone. The machine whirred round, and the gipsy's finger pointed to a sentence on the dial. His mother would not read him the sentence; and when he pestered her for his fortune, she said he was going to be a soldier. He did not want to be smart, to wear a red coat, and to march to the sound of a drum; all these things were beautiful in a way, but horrible. They were splendid and cruel, like the lions in the Zoo. Andrew told his friends that he would rather be the 'pig-tub man', and so he would.

The Aunts talked more and more about the War, a subject which Andrew hated. They tried in particular to elicit his sympathies for the poor little Belgian children who had been turned out of their homes and had come as refugees to England. He would rather be expected to shew sympathy for homeless children, than to hate the Germans. He pretended to be extremely interested in Belgian children, and found them a useful subject for conversation with his aunts and with their friends.

The Belgians soon forfeited his affections. The Aunts thought it would be a 'good deed' if he made a scrap-book to amuse a Belgian child at Christmas. Odd moments, when he had nothing to do and was feeling cross, were pressed into the service of the little Belgians. Pictures were cut out and put into a box; but he hated pasting them in. They lay neglected for days, until someone said: 'Poor little Belgians!' in the reproachful voice which always made him feel wicked, though he did not know why.

The scrap-book was never finished, and he never heard the last of it.

'You were so keen on it,' They said. 'You are always taking something up, and then getting tired of it. Aren't you ashamed to drop a thing, when you have begun it?'

Andrew said that he had never really liked the little Belgians much; and though this was perfectly true, no one would believe him.

They said: 'You're fickle.'

'I'm not,' he said; 'and I wish the Germans had made everyone of them into sausages.'

They were very cold indeed after this outburst, and told him that it was a wicked thing to say. 'We shan't punish you.' ('I should think not,' thought Andrew, 'seeing that I haven't done anything at all.') 'We shall leave you to your conscience.'

Andrew's conscience seldom had the courage of its convictions; it always capitulated to grown-up people in the most contemptible way. If anyone thought he had been wicked, and told him so, in a few minutes he was all tears and contrition; genuinely sorry, often for a fault which he had never committed. Sometimes his accuser had to apologize, after making him repent in tears for a misdemeanour of which he had been innocent. When They apologized They usually said: 'But after all, you had the comfort of knowing you were right'; and They wondered why he was so difficult to console. They did not realize that it felt exactly the same whether one were guilty or not, if other people thought one guilty. If other people were quite sure that Andrew had done something wrong, in the end he almost believed them. His memory still held out against them and maintained stoutly: 'I know I didn't do it.' His conscience promptly went over to the enemy and whispered: 'I feel I have been naughty.'

They had told him that his conscience was the voice of the Holy Ghost, and so was theirs. They really believed this extraordinary doctrine. They did not deliberately inculcate it in order to secure a theocratic power over him. Of course it had this effect; when Nandy's conscience forbade her to grant him a perfectly harmless indulgence, he knew that it was quite useless to argue. He would have thought that they might have delayed bedtime for ten minutes; but the Holy Ghost said that they must not, and it would never do to commit the sin against the Holy Ghost, for which there was no forgiveness.

Nandy could sway him completely by her claim to divine inspiration. It would have been difficult for her had the 'still small voice' in Andrew given contradictory oracles; but fortunately it never did. Andrew's conscience was in the pocket of his elders and betters. It never occurred to him that under their persuasion the 'still small voice' within him not infrequently told lies, and bore false witness against him. Had he fully analysed the tergiversations of that 'voice', which he was taught to identify with the Holy Ghost, he would soon have lost all respect for that person of the Holy Trinity.

In any case the Holy Ghost was rather misty and unreal. Andrew could not take much interest in Him, and
Nandy and the Aunts felt on less firm ground than
when they were discussing God the Father or Jesus.
Andrew connected the Holy Ghost with his arrival in
England every summer about Whitsuntide. He was involved in the appearance of gooseberry tart, just as the
Infant Jesus was inevitably associated with plum pudding. There was a hymn about Him with a tune of the
sugary quality that appeals to Nurses. It was not
Nandy however who had taught Andrew to sing *Our
Blest Redeemer, ere He breathed.* He had learned it from
old Wace the gardener, who took the children into his
potting-shed sometimes and sang to them. Wace's
repertoire was limited, and consisted mainly of hymns.
There was also a temperance song of which Stephen
was inordinately fond; the chorus ran:

> Take away the wine-cup,
> Take away the beer!
> Water, give me Water,
> Fresh and clear!
> Water, as it dances
> On the lily vale,
> Water is the drink for me!

Stephen used to drone it away in a tuneless monotone
at all hours of the day, especially in his bath. The old
charwoman, Mrs. Crump, was enraptured by his singing, when she was once deputed the task of bathing him.
'Master Stephen had been singing that lovely,' she said,
'that she wished his poor mother had been there to

hear him. It was a fair treat, it was.' Stephen always sang the words as 'water is a dansis', and was extremely annoyed if anyone asked him what a 'dansis' was.

Old Wace the gardener was a great friend of the children, though the Aunts did not like him, because he stole their fruit and vegetables. He gave Andrew and Stephen each a little plot of their own in the kitchen garden. Stephen never attempted to do anything on his property; and Andrew seldom worked on his except when he wanted to try one of old Wace's marvellous experiments.

Wace said that if you planted a primrose upside down, it would come up as a polyanthus. Andrew tried, and found that old Wace had spoken the truth. Next morning there was a polyanthus, where he had planted a primrose upside down. Wace said that if you planted a big flower-pot, you could dig up a lot of little flower-pots after a day or two: flower-pots were grown more or less in the same way as potatoes, but they rarely flowered. Andrew could not believe this for a long time; but at last he was persuaded into planting a large flower-pot in his garden to try the experiment. Two days later his garden was full of small flower-pots, and he had to confess that he had been foolishly sceptical.

The most lugubrious of Wace's songs was a kind of dirge which began: *In Trinity Church I met my doom.* Wace did not know any more words, so he endlessly repeated the first line, with a refrain of *Boom, Boom, Boom!* He explained that at Holy Trinity he had married Mrs. Wace.

Mrs. Wace was always sending messages by her husband to say that she would be honoured if 'the young gentlemen' would call on her, and one Sunday afternoon they went, each tightly gripping Nandy's hand.

The Waces lived over some stables; when Grandma had kept a carriage it was housed there. The Aunts said that they never opened the window in their parlour; and indeed it would have needed a serious upheaval of their furniture before they could have done so. The window was heavily curtained with lace; at the top there was a deep valance of crimson velvet, and at the bottom a table stood against the window supporting an enormous aspidistra. It was with genuine admiration that Andrew said to Mrs. Wace: 'How lovely it is where you live!' Mrs. Wace said to Nandy that she could see the young gentleman had the artist's eye, and she hoped that he might be spared to use it; thereupon she shook her head sadly, as if she did not think this likely.

Mrs. Wace was a remarkable woman. 'Dear young gentlemen,' she said, 'how I should love to nurse you if the dear Lord sent you a fell disease, as He sometimes does for our good. Many's the fell disease I've nursed before I gave up nursing to set up house with Wace. He was that ardent that I had to give way; but I feel I'm wasting my talents, as I often tell him. Don't I, Wace?'

'Yes, Martha, that you do,' said her husband submissively.

'I often tell him that if I saw a fell disease that needed my care, I should hear a voice saying: "Martha Wace, come over and help us." And then I should have to go. Wace, he says I must be a good wife to him, and cleave to him till Death do us part. He don't understand my call. But some people is not large-minded; their minds is not expansive.'

'Are you a trained nurse, then, Mrs. Wace?' asked Nandy.

'No, Nurse, I don't hold with this hospital training

55

and this massage' (she pronounced it to rhyme with 'passage'). 'What I give is just good old English *rubbing*. Many's the poor soul that I've rubbed; and they've all felt some relief from their afflictions. Of course it ain't everyone that can rub. It's a gift. I'm that spiritual, I am. You see, my father was the seventh son, and I'm his seventh child. There were two brothers, two sisters, and two miscarriages. You don't understand, do you, young gentlemen? Never mind, I won't go into it now; you'll learn all about Maternity at school, I daresay.'

Nandy became very uncomfortable. 'I don't think we'll talk any more about that, if you don't mind, Mrs. Wace,' she said; and to change the conversation she suggested that Andrew should recite.

Andrew loved being asked to recite, and went through the ceremony of mock reluctance very convincingly. He said he knew nothing, and hung his head with fascinating bashfulness, feeling quite certain that Mrs. Wace would press him, and that Nandy would suggest a poem which he knew perfectly well. Not till he had started did genuine stage-fright attack him; then it came surprisingly and overpoweringly. He turned fiery red and forgot his words, amid the tactful applause of his hostess. Mrs. Wace then gave a rendering of *The Burial of Moses*, by Mrs. Alexander; she put a great deal of expression into it, and Nandy thanked her warmly for giving them something so suitable to Sunday.

Mrs. Wace then suggested that they might all put up a short hymn, as none of them had gone to church. Nandy was a very good churchwoman, but she was only free to go to church on alternate Sundays. Mrs. Wace was pious, but lazy and valetudinarian. Despite her zeal to relieve 'fell diseases', she was herself, on her own confession, a 'dead thing' until Wace had brought

56

her an early cup of tea in the morning; and she rarely left her house.

They sang the twenty-third psalm, and *Loving Shepherd of thy Sheep*. Then, all aglow with goodness, the children went home with Nandy to nursery tea.

V

THERE were currant buns because it was Sunday, but
they did not really compensate for the sabbatarian re-
strictions which Nandy rather severely imposed. She
had strict notions about 'Sunday toys'. No kind of dice
or card game was permitted; at the best of times she
had a puritanical mistrust of them. It is true that she
gave Andrew a board for Snakes and Ladders; but once
when he and Stephen quarrelled over it, she was pained
to an extent quite unwarranted by the circumstances,
and said that it was dreadful that they should quarrel
over dice; as if the occasion of their quarrel had given
it a deeper and more shameful significance.

A Noah's ark was a Sunday toy, but their Noah's ark
was in Egypt. Once in desperation Andrew took out his
soldiers; he did not like them at all, but they were better
than nothing. Nandy asked him reproachfully if he
thought them quite suitable for Sunday. He answered
that he was pretending that they were 'Christian
Soldiers, marching as to War'. Nandy was pained; she
told Andrew that he was being irreverent, and that she
hoped he would soon be sorry. After a few minutes'
uncomfortable silence, Andrew said that, for his part,
he was sorry; and was she still cross?

'I wasn't cross, dear, only grieved,' she answered, in
a voice which always moved him to the deepest contrition. Of course he had no idea of what Nandy meant
by 'irreverence'. It was so awkward; his acquaintance
with literature extended only to the Bible and the
Hymns. From these alone could he draw when he
wished to make a literary allusion, and often as not
They told him solemnly that he had been irreverent.

Sundays were rather dull; there were no very active games to be played. It was permissible to spell out easy texts such as *God is Love*, with coloured letters; this was not a very amusing occupation, but Nandy liked to see Andrew so engaged. Fortunately no picture books were forbidden, and he was always willing to sit quietly in a corner with a book for as long as They would leave him alone.

When he had to go downstairs to the drawing-room he always clamoured to be given the 'dear old book'. The 'dear old book' was an album, started by Great-Grandmamma, and continued by Grandma. It was full of lovely pictures. There were a great many family photographs: of Great-Grandmamma in her pony chaise outside the grocer's shop, and of all the great-aunts and great-uncles, as young ladies in crinolines or young men in whiskers. The most fascinating were the pictures of Andrew's mother, of the Aunts and of Uncle Aubrey as children. Uncle Aubrey was a fat little boy in a sailor suit, with sausage-roll curls creeping from underneath a broad straw hat; he was gripping a toy yacht. The Aunts could easily enough be recognized, but Andrew could never have told that his mother was the doleful little girl in a check dress, fingering her necklace and looking as if she would like to cry.

Great-great-aunt Georgiana, who went into a decline and died at the age of twenty-three, had written several poems in a thin pointed hand adorned with flourishes; but these had as yet no interest for Andrew. He was more interested in the water-colour sketches of Great-great-aunt Susanna, which generally represented a romantic landscape, with a river, autumn tints, and a picturesque wood-cutter. By far the most interesting part of the album was the artificial flowers; they were cut out of rice paper and carefully gummed on to the

59

page; and there were crosses plaited out of strips of pale blue and pink paper. They had been made after tea on winter evenings, to serve as markers in prayer-books. A few had been overlooked, and had failed to be given away, or had been preserved as an example of the great-aunts' talent; and they lay loose between the pages of the album.

From this album, so full of family history, Andrew first gained a sense of the past. He had first come to realize the facts of birth and death, and of the continuity of the world, as he laid his finger on the prickly roller of the musical-box in Grandma's room, and thought that she was old and would soon die. The album made this more concrete for him, and supplied him with evidence that there had once lived people who had died long ago — 'before you were born or thought of, dear,' said his aunts. The album illustrated the dress and tastes of a by-gone age. At the time when Uncle Aubrey had sausage-roll curls, or further back, when Great-great-aunt Susanna used to wear a crinoline, Queen Victoria (whose head was on the coins) was on the throne. The Victorian Age was not very remote to Andrew, who had always loved his mother's old books far better than his own. It was for him a time when people dressed differently, when Mummy was a little girl, and when the old books in the school-room were new. The 'school-room' really had been a school-room then; now it was just a comfortable little sitting-room where the Aunts sometimes had tea. Once they really had done lessons there with a formidable Miss Jowett, before they went to Lausanne to be 'finished'.

Before Queen Victoria, King William IV had been on the throne. That was a time of legend, before History began. History began when Queen Victoria had to come down in her night-gown to see the Archbishop of Canterbury, who told her that she was Queen. There were no living witnesses to say that William IV had been King; Grandma had remembered him, but she was dead. King William was not on sixpences any more: at least if he was, they were 'coins' and kept in a bag as a collection of rarities; they were not 'money', to be spent in shops.

People who had lived under William IV were legendary figures; they were mostly known to the Aunts only at secondhand. Such was Great-great-aunt Stanfield, who had no left hand, but only a wooden stump into which a fork was screwed at dinner-time. Another family ogre was Great-great-uncle Henry Ley, who was a miser; he used to eat his egg-shells, and to blow his nose on tissue paper.

Some things which the Aunts remembered were already mythical enough; there were Grandma's dinner-parties at which there used to be ice pudding, or people like Great-aunt Bertha, who had been eccentric while they lived and were long since dead. Aunt Bertha did not like the Lower Classes; if she passed one of the maids in the passages she would explode a small scent-bomb. 'Our social inferiors, my dear,' she used to say, 'exhale such an unpleasant odour.'

VI

THEY felt the cold intensely after Egypt, but their first snowstorm was greeted with wild joy and excitement. When the ground was covered with snow, they all joined in making a snowman. Wace stopped sweeping the paths to help them; and they built a huge and uncouth figure. Someone christened it the Kaiser, and they all vindictively hurled snowballs at it.

Winter was pretty, with its red berries and its silver frosts. The children loved to crumble bread for the hungry robins, and to watch the eager swarms of birds on the garden path, tamed by hunger into coming almost within reach. Andrew and Stephen often brought a little salt in their hands, because Wace told them that the way to catch a bird was to put salt on its tail. Stephen complained that he could easily have caught a great many birds, but for Andrew's impatience. Andrew was clumsy and frightened them, but they would have let him take them.

'Birds love Stephen,' he said proudly, 'birds don't like Andrew.'

'Well, what would you do with them if you caught them?' asked Andrew.

'Nothing,' said Stephen, 'but I want birds.'

Yet winter in England had its disadvantages. Andrew had determined to like it, because everyone in Cairo used to tell him that he ought to be thankful that he was escaping a cold winter in England. Andrew hated being thankful. He had always longed for a really cold winter; and now that he had it, he had to like it. However, there were drawbacks; Nandy made them wear gloves and scarves and gaiters, so that it was a long business dressing to go out for a walk, and when they came in it was ages before they could be ready for tea.

Then they were ill. One night Andrew woke from a dream in which someone was trying to smother him. It was not only a dream; when he was awake he still felt choked. He tried his voice. He liked trying his voice when he was alone, to hear what it really sounded like, and whether it sounded the same as when he was with other people; he often did this in the lavatory. He tried to say his name: Andrew Ralph Faringdon; but something had stuck in his throat. He stood up on his bed, with the bedclothes falling about him, and clasped his hands over his throat. Aunt Margaret came upstairs to bed; through the creak at the top of the door her lamp sent a zigzag of light across the ceiling. When she came in Andrew tried to cry out, but he could only make a whooping noise. Aunt Margaret picked him up and put him back to bed. 'I'll fetch Nandy at once,' she said.

Nandy came in in her night-gown. She poured out a teaspoonful of brown medicine from a tiny bottle, and told Andrew to swallow it. Then he was wrapped round with blankets very tightly and carried to the nursery, where they put him in Nandy's bed. He was very sick, and then he felt better.

Nandy put on a woollen jersey and an old thick dressing-gown; and she began to heat water on the fire. She took a scalding hot piece of flannel out of her saucepan, and clapped it on to Andrew's chest; then over it she spread a piece of green oilcloth to keep the flannel from wetting his pyjamas.

It was very late at night; Andrew heard the clock strike eleven, twelve, and one. Tired though he was, he felt proud of being awake so late.

Every now and then, Nandy would get up from her

63

deep basket chair, and would bend over him; she took away the cooling flannel from his chest, and brought him a fresh flannel scalding hot from her saucepan.

'Try to bear it, my love,' she said; 'the hotter it is, the more good it will do you.'

In the end he felt easier, and could speak without much difficulty.

'After the next flannel, we'll both go to sleep,' said Nandy.

She made herself a cup of tea, and gave Andrew a glass of hot lemon and water. Stephen stirred uneasily in his sleep; he rolled over on to his back, and gnashed his teeth and opened his eyes.

'Hush, darling,' said Nandy; and she hung up his dressing-gown to shade his cot from the light.

VII

DURING their first year at Handborough Regis the children saw no more of their Quenby relations. They had once been asked over to a party, but Andrew had croup and Stephen had refused to go without him. The Aunts saw their brother alone when they could, but had as few dealings as possible with his family.

One afternoon, shortly before their second Christmas at Handborough, Gladys the parlourmaid shewed Mrs. Milburn into the nursery just before tea-time.

'What a delightful surprise!' exclaimed Nandy.

'How do you do, Nandy?' said Aunt Emma briskly. 'Now, children, I'm sure you don't remember who I am,' she added, in the tone of someone who confidently expects to be contradicted.

'No, I don't,' said Stephen solidly, to Nandy's shame and to his aunt's discomfiture.

'But I do!' said Andrew, 'you're Aunt Emma.'

'Yes, dear, and may I come to tea with you? I do love a nursery tea, Nandy.'

'You must be sorry to find Miss Milburn and Mrs. Graves out,' said Nandy. 'But we're in luck. If they were in, we shouldn't be having you upstairs.'

'And very nice it is to pay you a surprise visit like this,' declared Aunt Emma, in what Nandy called her 'jolly voice', a voice which always made Andrew feel mildly uncomfortable.

Nandy made tea, and began spreading butter on the loaf. 'Andrew,' she said, 'go and ask Gladys for another plate and cup and saucer for your aunt, there's a love.'

He ran downstairs obediently.

Nandy and Aunt Emma were whispering mysteriously by the fire as he opened the door and entered with the tea things. 'Careful, dear!' cried Aunt Emma, making him tremblingly nervous. He gripped the tea things very tightly with both hands, and set them down firmly, as far as possible from the edge of the table.

'Well, how are we?' said Aunt Emma jocosely, as they sat down to tea.

'Quite well, thank you,' answered Andrew demurely.

'And when are you coming to see us at Quenby?'

'I don't know,' he whispered shyly.

'You know you'd love to go to Quenby again,' said Nandy. 'Tell your Aunt Emma how disappointed you were to be ill for Tom's birthday party.'

Stephen had so far been eating bread and butter with the silent and remorseless activity of a machine, biting and masticating as if automatically. Bread and butter had to be eaten before there would be bread and jam. The process was neither pleasurable nor disagreeable in itself, and Stephen was going through it in the most practical manner, glancing neither to left nor to right. He rather despised Andrew for fidgeting nervously, and for trying to make conversation. They had sat down to eat their tea; and the appearance of a strange aunt was not going to disturb him from eating, which was his proper business at the moment.

'I'm sorry I had croup, and couldn't go to your party,' Andrew was saying obediently, but untruthfully.

Stephen put down his bread and butter and spoke slowly and deliberately: 'I hadn't got croup. I didn't want to go. I hate parties.'

He took up his bread and butter again, and continued to munch it, oblivious of Nandy's scolding. He had said what he thought; people ought to say what they thought, and ought not to tell lies like Andrew.

Andrew had never wanted to go to Tom's party, and should have said so. God would be vexed with him.

'But, Stephen, surely you like to play with other children?' said his aunt.

'No,' he answered with decision, 'I hate little children, I only like grown-ups.'

'Dear, dear, what a funny old gentleman! What do you say, Andrew? Which do you like best, grown-ups or other children?'

'Oh, grown-ups,' said Andrew shyly. This was quite true, and Aunt Emma ought to be pleased, because she was a grown-up herself.

'Well, I suppose Andrew and Stephen see many more grown-ups than children here,' said Mrs. Milburn to Nandy. 'I do think a child misses so much in being kept without the companionship of other children of its own age. The give-and-take which goes on in a large family is so good, such a training for school and for after life. I am afraid that Andrew and Stephen are going to be unhappy little boys later, if they cannot get to like other children better.'

Andrew lost interest in his tea, and was filled with sad perplexity by his aunt's words. He had combined truth with politeness in saying that he preferred grown-up people to children, and then had returned with a peaceful mind to his bread and butter, expecting to receive approbation for his preference. Instead of this Aunt Emma had talked about him in a pitying tone to Nandy, ending with a sad and reproachful smile in his direction.

'Never mind, dear,' said Aunt Emma soothingly, 'you'll come over to Quenby again one of these days and play with your cousins, won't you? We are always *so* pleased to see you; and do you know Miss Hunt has often wondered when you would come?'

'I should rather like to see Miss Hunt,' said Andrew without enthusiasm.

Aunt Emma wanted to see inside their toy-cupboard, and they had to shew her their latest acquisitions. These were mostly of a patriotic and bloodthirsty description. There was a set of ninepins called 'the Boches', caricatures of German soldiers designed to be bowled over by British children. Each had his name printed on a label and stuck at his feet. 'Otto' was a stout creature with a gaping mouth; someone had said he was like Stephen, who in consequence adored him. Andrew's affections were divided between 'Hermann', who had a squint, and 'Ludwig', who had a name which he could pronounce correctly, but which the maids pronounced as it was spelt. The Aunts infuriated the children by calling the Boches 'disgusting creatures'; and Aunt Emma seemed equally insensitive to their charms.

There was a complicated game called 'Bombardment'. Two tin aeroplanes were made to revolve round a stick, which was planted in a map of Germany. You hit them as they spun round, and made them drop bombs into holes labelled 'Hamburg', 'Cologne', 'Frankfort', etc. The bombs usually missed their mark. Aunt Emma gave the aeroplanes a twirl, and succeeded in bombing 'Dresden'.

'There!' she cried. 'And now Nandy has finished clearing up, she and I must have a chat. And you and Stephen can play with those nice soldiers of yours.'

'Yes, Aunt Emma,' said Andrew dutifully; though nothing bored him more than playing soldiers.

'Oh, but I don't want to,' said Stephen stubbornly.

Andrew looked at him with imploring eyes, dreading that he might make a scene in front of Aunt Emma, whom he did not quite trust. 'Do come along, Stephen,'

68

he begged. 'I'll be the Germans, and you shall be the Allies.'

'But I want to be the Germans,' said Stephen.

He had his way; and the children lined up their opposing armies, and fired in turn. It was a most decorous battle, conducted according to strict rules and entirely without enthusiasm. The temper on either side was perfect, until their boredom got the better of them, and the shooting became erratic. Nandy and Mrs. Milburn were talking in subdued voices by the fire.

'Is it nearly quarter to six?' asked Andrew wearily.

'Why a quarter to six?' said Nandy.

'Oh, only because Aunt Margaret and Aunt Anne said they would be in then, and we are to go down and say good night.'

'Why didn't you tell me before?'

'Oh, I don't know,' he answered; 'I never thought of it.'

'Dear me,' exclaimed Mrs. Milburn, 'what a pity! I shall just miss my sisters-in-law. I really can't stay any longer. The car will be waiting for me in the High Street as it is; and Cynthia will be wondering what has become of me. It *has* been so nice seeing you. Good-bye, Nandy . . . oh, are you going to see me downstairs? How kind of you! Good-bye, children!' — and Aunt Emma hastily gathered her things together, and disappeared.

Andrew and Stephen picked up their soldiers and threw them carelessly into a box. When Nandy returned they were peacefully drawing. Stephen was engaged on a spirited and ambitious picture; it represented Master Hutton, the doctor's nephew, a child who combined all the natural virtues in a prodigious degree, if the Aunts were to be believed. Stephen detested ' 'orrid little 'Utton', as he called him, though

69

he had not seen that paragon above three times. He had depicted Master Hutton as strapped into a push-cart, which was running down an incline of forty-five degrees into the sea. The careless nursemaid stood at the top of the hill, weeping into a spotted handkerchief; she did not look to see whether her charge were more likely to perish by drowning, or in the jaws of one of the horrible monsters which infested the sea. Stephen inclined to the latter alternative. It was one of his happiest compositions. He continued to fill the sea with creatures of ever-increasing frightfulness, while Andrew, occupied with a sketch of Salisbury Cathedral from memory (he had once seen it from the train), pains-takingly made the spire more and more finely pointed.

From this pleasant occupation they were called by Nandy. 'Quarter to six, children. Put your books away.' Their hair was brushed, and they were sent down to the Aunts.

On the stairs Andrew began to feel uncomfortable. It was almost certain that someone would talk about Aunt Emma's visit; and then the Aunts' faces would turn hard, as they always did when she was mentioned, and he would feel an uneasiness, without quite knowing its cause. It was odd that when the Aunts talked about Aunt Emma, it always sounded as if he were being scolded for something; it was not fair, she was not his fault. He resolved not to open the subject.

The Aunts were feeling tired. 'What have you been doing, dears?' they asked perfunctorily.

'I've been drawing,' said Andrew quickly, to turn the conversation into a safe channel.

'So have I,' said Stephen. 'I've drawed 'orrid little 'Utton in his pram. We saw him to-day. The pram ran right away, and right away down a hill — down, down, down. And 'orrid little 'Utton went SMASH!'

'*Is* that true, Stephen?' asked Aunt Anne.

'Nope,' answered Stephen regretfully; 'but I wish it was.'

'And I drew Salisbury Cathedral,' said Andrew, talking as fast and as cheerfully as possible; 'and I think I got the spire quite well. But I'm not sure if the perspective is quite right. You must look at it, Aunt Margaret.'

Aunt Margaret suggested that he should look at the photographs of cathedrals in Grandma's album, to see if there were a view of Salisbury. He knew that there was not, but he gladly took the album into a corner. The evening passed peacefully, without allusion to Aunt Emma. Fortunately their visit to the drawing-room had to be very short that day. At quarter past six Nandy appeared; the children rose without even a formal protest, and went up to bed.

Their next visit to the drawing-room was far less agreeable. When Andrew went up to kiss his aunts, Aunt Margaret said in a reproachful tone: 'Aunt Anne and I are not at all pleased with you.'

'Why, what's the matter?' he asked, too perplexed even to feel unhappy.

'You know quite well what the matter is,' said Aunt Anne sharply; 'you told us a deliberate lie yesterday.'

Andrew knew that he was innocent, but he felt strangely uncomfortable; that feeling was called a 'guilty conscience'. However, he did not know what the exact charge against him was, so he was forced to deny it. The Aunts were only making trouble for themselves. If they had charged him outright with any crime, he would have promptly admitted it.

'I don't know what you mean,' he faltered.

'You know perfectly well what we mean,' said Aunt Anne. 'When we came back from the bazaar yesterday, did you or did you not tell us that nothing had hap-

71

pened in the afternoon? You never thought of mentioning, I suppose, that your Aunt Emma had come to tea with you?'

'How did you know she had come?' asked Andrew, who was always unfortunate in his attempts to defend himself against Aunt Anne.

'There, you see!' she said to Aunt Margaret; 'he was deliberately keeping it from us. It was Gladys who told us, Andrew; you might have known you would be found out. It was stupid to tell that lie, as well as being wicked.'

'But I didn't say Aunt Emma hadn't come,' he protested.

'But you said nothing had happened,' said Aunt Margaret.

He had a good memory for detail. 'No, I didn't,' he answered. 'You asked what I had been doing, and I said I had been drawing Salisbury Cathedral; and so I had.'

'Very well,' grudgingly admitted Aunt Anne; 'I suppose you didn't actually tell us a lie. But the fact remains that you deliberately kept from us that your Aunt Emma had been to tea with you. Why did you?'

'I don't know,' said Andrew, hanging his head.

'You must know,' cried Aunt Anne impatiently, 'only idiots don't know why they don't do things.'

'But I really don't know; perhaps I didn't think of it.'

'Was it something Nandy said?' asked Aunt Margaret. 'Did she tell you not to say that your Aunt Emma had come?'

'No,' he answered, blushing deeper, because he felt that Aunt Margaret had expected him to answer yes.

'Andrew,' said Aunt Margaret severely, 'I don't need to tell you that it is very wrong to tell lies. You know that as well as I do. Are you quite sure that Nandy didn't ask you to say nothing about Aunt Emma?'

'Quite,' replied Andrew firmly.

'Well, perhaps she didn't ask you directly,' said Aunt Anne; 'did she say anything about its being better not to mention it to us?'

'No,' he answered.

'Then for what reason did you say nothing about your Aunt Emma?' persisted Aunt Anne.

'There wasn't any reason,' said Andrew despairingly, wishing he could say something to put an end to this torture; but after all there was nothing that he could make concrete enough to give to the Aunts as a reason.

'That's just foolish,' said Aunt Anne, 'you can't expect us to believe that.'

He burst into tears. 'But it's true. How can I say why I didn't tell you, when I don't know?'

'Are you really telling the truth, Andrew?' said Aunt Margaret more gently.

'Yes,' he sobbed.

'Are you quite sure?' asked Aunt Anne.

'Oh, leave the poor child alone, Anne,' said Aunt Margaret. She wiped his face and kissed him.

Stephen looked up from the floor and remarked diplomatically: 'Look at my lovely house I'm building.' Peace was restored; both Andrew and the Aunts were feeling slightly ashamed, and they were glad to forget their argument.

VIII

Shortly after Christmas Uncle William sent a note to the Aunts to say that the Quenby children were coming over to lunch with him and going to the pantomime, and that he wanted Andrew to come to lunch to meet them. Aunt Margaret told him about this invitation.

'Must I go?' he asked, without much hope of reprieve.

'Of course you must go,' said Aunt Margaret. 'Anyway, your cousins are going, and I suppose you would like to see them; you're always talking about Quenby.'

'Well, I wish I hadn't got to go,' he complained.

'Nonsense, you'll enjoy it when you get there,' said Aunt Anne — an annoying piece of grown-up wisdom which forced Andrew to protest: 'Everyone says that; and I never do.'

Aunt Anne looked solemn, and told Andrew that there were a great many poor little children who had no kind uncles to ask them out to luncheon, and who very seldom got any luncheon at all.

'Well, they're lucky not to go to parties,' he said.

Aunt Margaret admitted that it was often tiresome to have to go out when one would rather stay at home; but she said she thought Uncle William might perhaps take him to the pantomime. Aunt Anne frowned at her. 'You must not depend on it, my dear,' she said. 'So often one builds up hopes, and then one is only disappointed.'

Andrew was annoyed with her, and turned to Aunt Margaret. 'Do you really think he will take us?' he asked.

'Well, I'm not sure, but it's quite likely,' she said.

For the next few days his thoughts were entirely taken

up with the pantomime. He drew upon every source of information about the theatre. There was an illustrated Shakespeare in the drawing-room, with photographs of Irving or of Beerbohm Tree in famous parts; and there were bound volumes of *Punch*, full of harlequins and columbines, of clowns, policemen and red-hot pokers and strings of sausages.

The Opera House at Handborough Regis was an imposing edifice with a sea-green cupola, from whose external magnificence Andrew argued even greater splendours hidden inside; and the maids had told him that it was lovely, all white and gold and red plush. The story of Aladdin promised many delights: a handsome young Aladdin, rather like Henry Irving, and a beautiful princess like Ellen Terry, in a magic palace of superb gorgeousness. He waited for Wednesday with blissful expectation mingled with nervousness. Uncle William might be the friendly enchanter, who would throw open to him the magic world that lay under the sea-green cupola of the Opera House; but he looked far more like a malignant gnome.

On Wednesday morning Andrew was sent into the dining-room tightly buttoned into a thick overcoat, and further protected with a muffler and gaiters. Aunt Anne delivered a charge, and he stood on the hearthrug and promised not to eat more than was good for him, and to say thank you to Uncle William before he left.

'Nandy will call for you,' said Aunt Anne.

'But won't she be there all the time?' he asked.

'No, your Uncle William said you were to go by yourself.'

'Oh, but why?'

'Well, you're old enough, I suppose,' said Aunt Anne. 'You don't need to be tied to Nandy's apron-strings, I should think. If you're going to the pantomime, I daresay there's no room for Nandy as well.'

'Well, I wish Nandy was going,' said Andrew plaintively.

'Don't be a baby, Andrew, or I shall be very cross,' his aunt threatened.

Andrew thought she had been cross enough already, and he went thankfully back to Nandy for a few kind words before his ordeal. She accompanied him to Uncle William's house, and delivered him into the care of Mrs. Pulker in the hideous coloured glass porch. He smiled back at her bravely and she turned away, and the heavy green door with its heavy brass letter-box was shut between them.

'Come in here, Master Andrew,' said Mrs. Pulker, 'there's a nice fire in the morning-room. Your uncle isn't down yet, but he will be soon, I expect. There now, give me your things; you'll be nice and warm there. I mustn't stay; I have to be back in the kitchen. There's *Punch* if you'd like to look at the pictures, Master Andrew, my dear.'

Andrew sat on the edge of his high carved chair and idly turned the advertisement pages of *Punch*; then he leaned on his elbows and gazed at the black marble clock with its gilt dial, or looked through the window at the damp grey lawn and the dreary pruned rose trees. It was not very comfortable and not very pleasant to have to wait in Uncle William's solemn, stuffy morning-room ; but at least this inactivity, this silence save for the ticking of the marble clock and for the sparrows hopping about on the steps of the french window, was better than hand-shaking and the noisy cheerfulness of human beings.

There was a rumble; it might be the Milburns' motor-car — but no, the car did not turn in at the gate, and he saw it pass the end of the garden. At the same time his breath had caught, and his heart continued to rap out an extra beat. Then there was the unmistakable sound of a car slowing and turning; the tyres drew slow furrows in Uncle William's drive, crunching the damp gravel. And the bell rang. There was the noise of Mrs. Pulker's bustling footsteps; then loud and cheerful voices sounded through the open door.

'Well, here we are, Mrs. Pulker.'

'What a cold day, ma'am.'

'Come back for us at half past five, Thomas.'

'Mr. Stanfield is just coming down, and Master Andrew is waiting in the morning-room.'

Andrew stood in the corner and clenched his hands. 'Don't let them come,' he whispered; 'oh stop, stop, STOP!'

It was no good; the door-handle turned, and the cousins seemed to pour in. They formed a solid block facing him. He looked from Tom to Arthur, from Arthur to Philip; on each face was the same bleak absence of expression; each was dressed exactly alike, each had the same colourless hair stuck down with water. Their sisters were no better; Gladys, Flora, and Mabel stood in a row, scrupulously neat, with hair tightly twisted into plaits and mouths hanging foolishly open. Andrew timidly interpreted their herd stupidity as hostility towards himself.

Aunt Emma came in with Uncle William.

'Well, well, this *is* nice,' she exclaimed; 'all the happy family together. Say good morning to your uncle.'

One by one the cousins filed by Uncle William and bade him good morning in a toneless voice, smearing flabby kisses on his cheek, which he wiped off impatiently with the back of his hand. Andrew felt he would be intruding if he joined in their queue, and stood aloof while the Milburns performed their ritual.

'Aren't you going to say good morning to your Uncle William? Or to me?' said Aunt Emma in a gentle voice, which failed to rouse Andrew from his abstraction.

'Come, come, boy!' called Uncle William sharply, and thumped the floor with his stick.

Andrew turned very red. He came up and whispered: 'Good morning, Uncle William, good morning, Aunt Emma.' The cousins turned on him a cold, incurious and concentrated stare.

Mrs. Pulker beat on the gong.

'Well, how are we to sit, Emma?' asked Uncle William. 'You will take the end of the table, of course?'

'Yes, and may I have little Andrew next me?' she said. 'We don't meet often enough, and we're great friends, aren't we?'

He blushed uncomfortably.

Aunt Emma continued: 'And if Gladys sat on his other side, she could help Andrew with his dinner. I daresay we get into difficulties when we are out to lunch, and haven't got Nandy or the Aunts to look after us.'

Gladys was a conscientious child; she paid no heed to Andrew's scowls. After giving him one superior and annihilating glance through her spectacles, she attended to her appointed duty, and laboriously removed every morsel of flesh from his chicken bone.

'Thank you, Gladys, that's a good girl,' said Aunt Emma; 'say thank you, Andrew. And what have you and Stephen been doing with yourselves? Have you had nice presents? Careful, dear, not too fast. *There* now, and on your *nice* trousers . . .'

Gladys mopped up the spilt gravy with her napkin.

'Never mind, darling,' murmured Aunt Emma. 'Ac-

78

cidents will happen. You haven't told me yet how you
and Stephen have been amusing yourselves. Do you
bowl hoops like my children?'

'No, never.'

'Perhaps you play about with a football, like your
cousins?'

'No, we haven't got one.'

'I *wonder* what you do?'

'Oh, I don't know,' murmured Andrew uncomfortably.

'But you must know, surely,' Aunt Emma pressed
him.

'Well, we go out for walks with Nandy, of course.'

'I suppose you have plenty of little friends at Handborough, who play with you on the Heath?' she asked.

'No, we just go with Nandy as a rule.'

'That doesn't sound very interesting for you,' said
Aunt Emma.

Andrew lapsed into silence; it was so uncomfortable
of grown-ups not to let children be happy in their own
way.

Mrs. Pulker brought in a plum pudding. The older
children pretended not to see it; but an unrepressed
cry of 'Ooh' went up from Arthur and Tom.

Uncle William stuck in a spoon and fork. 'Who says
pudden?' he cried jocosely.

'I do,' said Andrew.

'Tut tut, ladies first,' snapped Uncle William; 'plum
pudden's too good for little boys.'

Andrew winced; and he ate his pudding wretchedly
when at last it came to him. He wished that Uncle
William would not ask questions that he did not want
answered, and would not serve Tom before him. He was
nearly a year older.

'Well, well,' said Uncle William, 'we must be moving

79

soon if we don't want to miss half the pantomime. Give me your arm a moment, Flora, my dear. You'll be stiff when you get to my age.'

Mrs. Pulker opened the door. 'I've come to help the young ladies and gentlemen into their coats,' she said.

'Oh, Mrs. Pulker,' said Uncle William, 'will you please take Master Andrew downstairs with you, till someone comes to fetch him? Good-bye, my boy.'

Andrew's hope of seeing the pantomime had been cruelly disappointed. He turned his back miserably upon the others and went down to the kitchen. He heard the sound of voices and of bustling footsteps up above. There was the noise of a car in the drive, and the bang of a door; and then the steps of Mrs. Pulker coming downstairs, and the quiet of the empty house.

He sobbed quietly. It was nearly over when Mrs. Pulker came; only red eyes betrayed him. She tactfully ignored them. 'Master Andrew, my dear,' she said, 'I think we'll have a nice cup of tea, shall we?'

She put on a kettle, and warmed a little brown teapot; then she brought a tin out of the cupboard and gave him a long finger of shortbread.

They were chatting comfortably in front of the fire when Nandy and Stephen called on their way out for a walk about three o'clock. Mrs. Pulker was telling Andrew about the dinner for twenty people, which she had suddenly been called upon to cook when she was a young girl, just gone out to service, and the cook had had a fit. They had just come to the ice pudding, and he was listening with enthralment, when Mrs. Pulker had to answer the bell.

Nandy said: 'We thought we would look in, in case Andrew was still here. But I suppose he has gone with the others to the pantomime?'

'No,' said Mrs. Pulker, 'and I do think it's a shame.

80

All the others went off with Mr. Stanfield, and poor Master Andrew was left behind in the kitchen with me. He was so good, poor lamb; but when I came down from seeing the others off I found him crying. Of course he wanted to go to the pantomime too; it was a shame to ask him to luncheon, if he wasn't to go. Well, I made a cup of tea; and we've been sitting down there as comfortable as you please, having our tea and talking about old times, when I was a girl and just gone out to service. He's such a funny old-fashioned child; and he's been sitting there listening to me, as quiet as a mouse.'

Andrew went home with Nandy and Stephen in that lovely calm that comes after tears; there remained only a small, almost unpainful pang of disappointment. It would keep; he would cry about it when he was in bed, but not till then.

PART II

1916

I

THEY spent their Easter holidays in Devonshire, by the sea. The children came back to lunch with pails full of treasures gathered on the shore, shells, star-fish, and seaweed. In the afternoons they walked in the lanes, and came back with hot hands full of withering flowers; they preferred the most evil-smelling that were to be found — wild parsley, lords and ladies, and wild geraniums. Stephen would cram their pathetic drooping bunches into a vase in their room. Aunt Anne once asked him smilingly who had taught him to arrange flowers so beautifully. 'It just comes to me,' he answered, with careless pride.

One thing clouded Andrew's pleasure: when he returned to Handborough, he was going to a day-school in the town. Everyone was agreed that it was time that he started lessons; he could read, but he could scarcely write at all and he could not do sums. The Aunts had wished to engage a governess for two or three hours every morning, and had found a pleasant, sympathetic woman to whom he had taken an instant liking. Unfortunately, Colonel Faringdon wrote firmly from Cairo that Andrew was to go to school, and to mix with other children. The Aunts had protested that he was delicate and shy and not yet ready for school. Colonel Faringdon had written them an unpleasant letter in reply, suggesting that if Andrew were still too much of a baby to go to school, now that he was seven and a half years old, it was their fault; and that the sooner he grew out of his timidity, the better it would be. Colonel Faringdon added that he had not heard very favourable reports of his development.

The Aunts at once decided that their sister-in-law was attempting to make mischief between them and Oswald. Mrs. Graves did not wish to let the matter drop lightly; but her sister convinced her that it was useless to argue with Oswald, because the War had rendered the post to Egypt both long and insecure. Moreover, she readily admitted that he was always as weak as wax in Emma's hands and, when once persuaded by her, very obstinate in maintaining his opinion.

The Aunts had acquiesced in their defeat, and had visited most of the schools in Handborough Regis. They rejected the best and most modern school in the town, because the Head Mistress was suspected of pro-German sympathies; she had been an active member of a Peace Society and had refused to dismiss her German Fräulein. It was decided that Andrew should be sent to a small old-fashioned school in Northumberland Lane, run by the Misses Low, who took boys up to preparatory school age, and girls until they were finished.

They returned to Handborough before the term began at Selborne House. The Aunts looked out their old lesson-books and found a large atlas which they lent to Andrew, who used to lie on his stomach on the drawing-room floor, poring over the map of England. He grew to love the straggling coast of Essex, which was coloured a delicate pale brown; and pink Norfolk, which bulged; and Kent where they lived; and Northumberland, after which was called the lane where Selborne House stood.

Andrew looked forward to his lessons; he thought he would be good at them. He did not like the prospect of meeting a great many other children, but he would only be at Selborne House in the morning, and Nandy would fetch him home to luncheon at half past twelve.

On the whole he was excited and pleased that he was going to school, and rather wondered that the Aunts were sometimes sad. He was a little frightened at the idea of spending every morning with strangers, and sometimes wished that his father had allowed him to have a governess. It would have been a pleasant and important feeling to hear the bell ring at a quarter to ten; then the parlourmaid would come up to the nursery and say: 'Will Master Andrew please come down to the school-room? Miss Brown has come.' Andrew would say good-bye to Nandy and Stephen in a superior way and walk downstairs with books under his arm. This was such a delightful picture, that he shed a few tears of regret.

He caught a cold and could not go to school until a week after the term had begun. This made it worse; there was more time to think over it. When he was well enough, Aunt Anne said that she would take him to school. It was a bright sunny morning. Aunt Anne wore a light summer dress, white and lavender, and carried a parasol. They went into the garden and cut a few flowers to take to Miss Low.

'You shall give them to her,' she said.

'No, you, Aunt Anne,' he begged.

'But it's you who ought to.'

'No, please, Aunt Anne, you give them.'

'Very well, dear.'

She was very kind to him, and said that she hoped he would be happy at Selborne, and that he must not expect life to be all a bed of roses.

'What's it like?' he asked her for the hundredth time; and again she told him: 'It's a tall house with a verandah, and the outside is all little pebbles.'

'What colour are they?'

'Grey, dear,' she said; 'and inside there is a long

school-room, with tables on trestles and maps hung up on the walls.'

They walked up the narrow flagged Northumberland Lane, which led up from the town behind Saint Saviour's church. They both walked slowly, unwilling to arrive. Too soon they reached an iron gate, with 'Selborne House' painted on the stone gate-posts; and they walked up a few steep steps to the school.

They had come late; morning prayers were already in progress. The maid shewed them into a little cool drawing-room with a powder-blue carpet and chintz-covered chairs. A solemn rococo clock was ticking on the mantelpiece, on either side of which hung portraits in pastel of a lady and a gentleman with powdered hair. From across the passage came the sound of a wheezy piano, which had suffered its youth to be worn out under the heavy hands of Miss Low's pupils; and children's voices sang:

> 'Eternal Father, strong to save,
> Whose arm hath bound the restless wave,
> Who bidd'st the mighty ocean deep
> Its own appointed limits keep . . .'

The piano gathered its forces for a last assault:

> 'O hear us when we cry to Thee
> For those in peril on the Sea.'

The mistresses were being patriotic, singing to God about the British Navy, which patrolled the Seas in their defence, and in His cause — as He was frequently reminded in collects authorized to be addressed to Him in time of War. The children sang rapturously; this hymn always fired their imagination, and they thirsted to be 'in peril on the sea'. Andrew made a confused and silent prayer for himself; it was true that he was not on

the sea, but he did not know what perils might await
him in this drawing-room with the soft blue carpet, or
in that unknown school-room full of children's voices.

The door opened and Miss Low came in. 'They are
still at prayers,' she said, 'but I was told that you had
come, so I came to be introduced.'

'This is Andrew,' said Mrs. Graves; 'and he is so
excited at coming to school.'

'Well, dear, I hope you'll be happy,' said Miss Low;
'you will be in my sister's class. When prayers are finished I will take you to her. She is called Miss Fanny;
she is very tall, but you mustn't be frightened of her,
because she is very kind.'

'May I come too, and see the children?' asked Mrs.
Graves.

'Oh, do, Mrs. Graves,' said Miss Low; 'I think we
might go now. I hear a noise, so they must have
finished prayers.'

Mrs. Graves shook hands with Miss Fanny, then
smiled at Andrew and left him. The older children had
filed out of the class-room to their own form-rooms
upstairs, and it was time for the first lesson. Miss Fanny
said that she would read to her class, as it was Andrew's
first day. She read them a poem called *Casabianca*, and
shewed them a picture of a handsome, dark Spanish
boy on a burning ship. Then she read a story about a
girl called Grace Darling, and shewed them a picture
of a large fair girl in a rowing-boat. The children had
to say which of the two they preferred. Andrew was
glad that he did not have to speak first. Obviously
Grace Darling, who had saved other people, was a far
more useful and intelligent person than Casabianca,
who had stupidly and unnecessarily refused to save himself. On the other hand, he was dark and slim and
beautiful and had a romantic name. He lived on the

continent, and was no doubt a Roman Catholic; and he was connected with things which Andrew inevitably thought exciting and adventurous, because the Aunts disapproved of Roman Catholics and of people who lived on the continent. Grace Darling was fair and fat and lived in England; and her rowing-boat could hardly be compared with Casabianca's burning deck; and he didn't like girls. Yet, although he was beautiful and was probably a Roman Catholic, Casabianca's stupidity filled Andrew again with resentment: he hated fools. It was annoying that for a piece of typically grown-up silliness Casabianca had been turned into the hero of a poem, and was held up to the admiration of other children. He preferred Grace Darling; but he would not say so. The boys would think him silly to like a girl better than a boy. The boy next to him, who looked about with such a bold and assured air, would certainly despise Andrew for his choice. He would copy him if he could; and if Miss Fanny asked him first he would say he preferred Casabianca.

She did not; he was relieved to hear her say: 'Denys, which do you like the better?'

'Casabianca,' he answered, without hesitation or enthusiasm.

'Andrew, which do you like the better?'

'Casabianca too.'

'Why, dear?'

He had not expected that, and hung his head shyly. 'I don't know,' he answered. It might sound silly to say: 'Because Denys likes him best.'

One or two girls chose Grace Darling. Miss Fanny said that they were both so brave and fine, that there was not much to choose between them.

Miss Low took the second class, and wanted to see how Andrew could read. He had to stand out of the class and read a few sentences out of *Reading without Tears*, over which he stumbled several times.

'Thank you, dear,' said Miss Low, 'I am sure you will read very nicely when you are more used to us.'

He sat down and blushed, but not unhappily.

At half past twelve they put their books away. The day-boarders, who stayed at school for lunch, went out for a walk with Miss Clements; the others were fetched by their nurses. Nandy was there waiting for Andrew, and Stephen was with her. He walked back beside Stephen's push-cart full of importance, telling them how he had got on at school.

Next time Nandy took Andrew to school. They started early and arrived in time for morning prayers. All the children stood in their places round the class-room wall; Miss Clements sat down at the piano, and the baby-class was asked to choose the hymn. *'For those in peril on the sea,'* said Charlie.

'No, dear, we had that yesterday,' said Miss Low.

'Loving Shepherd of thy sheep,' suggested Andrew timidly.

'No, that's a baby hymn,' said Eleanor scornfully, 'can't we have *Crown Him with many crowns*, Miss Low?'

'That's rather difficult, my dear,' answered Miss Low; 'I think we'll have Andrew's hymn, we all know that. Are you ready, Miss Clements?'

They all sang. Then Miss Low read a few verses from the Bible, looking up to frown at Eleanor; one of Eleanor's curls had blown into her mouth, and she spat it out and giggled.

After prayers there was catechism. 'What is your name, Denys?' asked Miss Low. 'I asked you to learn it for this time, and I hope you know it at last.'

'N or M, Miss Low,' answered Denys with a puzzled look; but he knew it must be right, because it was in the Prayer Book.

91

'That's not at all funny, Denys,' said Miss Low severely. 'You know perfectly well that your name isn't N or M. What *is* your name?'

'Denys Monro.'

'Not *that* name,' said Miss Low, with a patient sigh; 'in catechism your name is Denys Hugh. Do try to remember that, please. And who gave you that name, Mabel?'

'My godfathers and godmothers in my baptism; wherein I was made a Member of Christ, the Child of God, and an Inheritor of the Kingdom of Heaven,' replied Mabel promptly.

'Very good, much better than last time,' said Miss Low. 'What is your duty towards God, Rosamund?'

Rosamund told her.

'Very nice, dear; and now we'll run through a few commandments,' said Miss Low. 'Philip, what's the third commandment?'

'Mm . . . Miss Low . . .' stammered Philip.

'No, Philip, I am not the third commandment,' said Miss Low facetiously. 'Try to think what it is,' she said. 'It's the one Eleanor broke during prayers.'

'I know, Miss Low! Thou shalt not commit Adultery,' cried Mary triumphantly.

'No, Mary, I didn't ask you. Eleanor didn't commit Adultery during prayers. She was irreverent, and irreverence is forbidden by the third commandment. Will you tell us what it is, Hilda?'

'Thou shalt not take the Name of the Lord thy God in vain,' chanted a demure little girl, and concluded, with a spiteful glance at Eleanor, 'for the Lord will not hold him guiltless, that taketh His Name in vain.'

SATURDAYS and Sundays were whole holidays, and even on week-days Andrew only went to morning school. Nursery life, therefore, continued as a parallel to school life, in almost undiminished importance. Andrew walked every afternoon by Stephen's push-cart; sometimes he talked about school, but more often he preferred to forget Selborne, and to return to the fictitious world which he and Stephen shared. In this world Bun was the chief actor, and they were never tired of elaborating the legends with which they had surrounded him.

'Every year Bunny goes mad,' Stephen would say, 'quite mad.'

'Yes, every March,' Andrew would add.

'And then he drives an engine as fast as he can.'

Andrew would try to vary the saga: 'No, an aeroplane, Stephen.'

'No, he drives an engine,' Stephen would insist; 'faster and faster and faster.'

'Yes. And he bumps into everything on the line, and smashes up trains and makes enormous railway accidents, doesn't he, Nandy?'

'Yes, dear,' she would say, 'but doesn't he hurt a lot of people?'

'He kills hundreds of people,' they would reply triumphantly.

'But how do they stop him?' Nandy would ask.

'They don't,' Stephen would answer; 'but you see at the end of the month he isn't mad any more, and then he stops.'

Poor Old Bun was growing more and more shabby

and dirty. One of his ears was coming off; Nandy had sewn it up, but it still flopped pitifully. Aunt Anne said that the best-bred rabbits had flop-ears, and the children were delighted with this explanation. Then Bun's chest began to moult. At first his eczema was entirely delightful to the children, who put him to bed and kept him on a milk diet. Andrew gave instructions before he went off to school: 'Don't let Bun get up, and don't let the Teddy bears or the Boches or the other children go near him — eczema is *dreadfully* catching.'

When he came back from school and ran upstairs to get ready for luncheon, the first thing Andrew asked was: 'Is Old Bun better?'

'No, much worse,' Stephen answered gloomily.

They did everything they could. Bun spent four days in bed and was given gallons of medicine. He was rubbed with imaginary embrocations, and poulticed with dock-leaves, carefully collected on their walks; but he would not recover. Andrew printed WORSE on a piece of paper, and this unchanged bulletin hung at the end of Bun's bed.

It was so dull with Bun in bed, when they were tired of playing hospital with him. Andrew suggested that they should pretend that he was better. Stephen pointed dismally at his chest. 'But he isn't,' he said solemnly, 'he's worse.'

Nandy had a brilliant idea; she took a piece of red and blue ribbon, and sewed it on to Bun's sore place, so as to hide it completely. She then announced that the King had given Bun the D.S.O. Nandy had gathered Bun's skin together under the D.S.O., and he stopped moulting.

Everything that Andrew learned at Selborne was pressed into the service of the nursery world: fresh from a geography lesson, he would come home and

94

draw an island which he called Bunland, exhibiting all the features that he had just discovered in the map of England, though far more pronounced. There were tortuous rivers, sharp promontories, and semicircular bays. It was a very picturesque country. History was put to the same use. Stephen was not much interested in the history and geography of Bunland; but it was better than the real history and geography lessons, which Andrew was only too ready to give him.

When Andrew returned from school he frequently repeated his lesson to Stephen, and was hurt and amazed at his lack of interest. He should have thought that even a baby like Stephen would be interested in such stories as Bruce and the Spider, or Alfred and the Cakes. Poor Stephen was not taught in an encouraging manner; Andrew always hurried through his instruction, in haste to arrive at the best part of playing School, the questions. It was always enjoyable to ask strings of questions: 'Who was Alfred? Why was he hiding? When did he live?' — even if he had to answer them all himself.

Stephen was a tiresome pupil: Andrew preferred playing School with the Boches, and the Teddy bears and the other children. Sometimes they answered questions right; in all cases they at least said something, and he could move them up and down. Stephen said nothing and was always at the bottom of the class.

III

THE Aunts had less and less time for playing. Even Handborough Regis, the most peaceful town in the kingdom, had been transformed by the War, and everyone was 'doing his bit' — especially the clergy, the retired colonels, and the invalid ladies.

There was no longer a band in the little pavilion on the Parade, playing Gilbert and Sullivan, and sometimes 'something classical'. In the upstairs tea-rooms overlooking the Parade there were fewer and fewer ladies in white and lavender summer dresses drinking their cups of coffee and reading novels with yellow labels from the circulating library. Everyone was in a hurry, and most people were in a bad temper.

'These times of suffering are bringing out the best in all of us,' said the Low Church Vicar of Saint Saviour's, and the High Church Vicar of Saint Simon Zelotes's, and Father Penfold at the Roman Catholic Church, and Mr. Pilkington at the Baptist Chapel; and their congregations all agreed with them. 'Yes,' they said, when they went home to lunch, 'what the Vicar says is so true. These times of suffering *are* bringing out the best in every one of us.'

The clergy of Handborough may be presumed to have known the hearts of their people: who had a better opportunity? A more superficial observer, however, might have lamented the ever-increasing growth of hatred, envy and all uncharitableness in the town since the beginning of hostilities.

At first there had been an outbreak of organizing. By a rapid working of the laws of natural selection the most brutal and overbearing women in the town had filled all the committees; and the heavy and inglorious routine work was left for the humble and meek. The war-workers talked bitterly of their superiors behind their backs, and before their faces changed the conversation to another favourite topic, the slackness of women who would not work and the cowardice of men who would not fight. If they were men, the war-workers of Handborough were convinced, they would all enlist, to a woman, and go out to France thirsting for German blood.

Some of the men of Handborough were less enthusiastic; for example, Mr. Finch, a near neighbour of the Aunts. His mother said it was his duty to look after her, now that his poor father had entered into rest, and there was no one left her but Johnny. His neighbours intimated to him with increasing rudeness that they considered that he ought to enlist. The Vicar invited him to take a walk one afternoon and marched him to the very door of the recruiting office; and before Johnny Finch knew where he was, he had begun to appeal to his better nature.

'Mother is expecting me home to tea, I must hurry,' said Mr. Finch rather lamely. The Vicar sighed, and preached next Sunday from the text: *Jesus looked upon him sorrowing, for He loved him.*

Johnny Finch decided to offer himself for duty as a Special Constable, a safe and useful way of serving his country. His country, as exemplified by the ladies of Handborough Regis, remained ungrateful. The Aunts took a charitable view of Mr. Finch. He was a pleasant-spoken young man who had often come to tea; they could not therefore conceive that he might be unwilling to kill Germans. He would be all right, they said, if his mother did not fuss him so. Mrs. Poltimore-Robinson was less kind. Mr. Finch, in his office as Special

Constable, called upon her one night to request her to draw down her blind, as her hall light was shewing. She told him that she could not understand how an able-bodied young man could prefer skulking about, extracting fines from respectable citizens of Handborough Regis, to wallowing in trenches and disembowelling Germans. She hinted that Mrs. Finch's ancestry would not bear examination: 'There was a German streak somewhere.'

Johnny Finch forced Mrs. Poltimore-Robinson to pay her five shillings, and she continued to persecute him with increasing animosity. She called on Mrs. Finch to speak to her as woman to woman; but Mrs. Finch had a headache, and was not receiving visitors. Finally Mrs. Poltimore-Robinson took an ostrich feather from the trimming of an old hat. Ostrich feathers were not likely to 'come in' again, so many people thought it cruel to ostriches. She enclosed it in a large envelope and posted it to her victim, as a final insult addressing it to 'Mr. Johnny Finch'.

When the possibility of conscription was debated, Handborough society could only see it in terms of Johnny Finch. The choir-boys sang after him: 'Johnny get your gun, get your gun, get your gun'; and the Vicar preached an inspiring sermon at Mattins on the parable of the labourers who came to the vineyard at the eleventh hour, and at Evensong on the text: *Go out into the highways and hedges, and compel them to come in.* The Vicar had just 'given' a son to his country, and his sacrifice was much appreciated in the parish. He had never thought that it would be in the poor boy's power to give him such satisfaction. The Vicar's wife mourned, being poor in spirit.

Immediately after conscription had been proclaimed, Mrs. Poltimore-Robinson called on the Aunts. She was a little out of breath, she had paid so many calls that afternoon. She gave Andrew a rapid kiss, and began to pour out her story to the Aunts. He pretended to be intent on his picture puzzle.

'Well, Margaret, what do you think?' exclaimed Mrs. Poltimore-Robinson. 'That young Finch has blown off two of his fingers, so that he'll be useless for the army!'

'Is that really true?' asked Miss Milburn. 'One hears such extraordinary stories nowadays.'

'My dear Margaret, would you have me disbelieve my own eyes?' cried Mrs. Poltimore-Robinson.

'You don't mean to say, Phyllis, that you actually *saw* it?' said Mrs. Graves.

'Well, not exactly,' Mrs. Poltimore-Robinson admitted; 'but I have it for a fact.'

'Tell us the whole story from the beginning,' Mrs. Graves demanded.

'Well, where was I?' said Mrs. Poltimore-Robinson. 'Let me see . . . yesterday evening I was going to my window to stick a pin in my pincushion about seven o'clock; no, it must have been half past seven because it was Thursday. Thursday is Susan's day out, and we always have supper later on her day out. No, yesterday was Wednesday, of course — and I remember it wasn't Susan's day out because I had just spoken to her. The butcher had sent such a tough little shoulder of lamb, and so I said to Susan, I said . . . Where was I? Yes, I said to Susan that she must speak to him when he came next. "You leave it to me, ma'am," she said, "I'll *sort* him!" Her funny Scotch expression, you know; an English girl would simply say: "I'll give him what for!" Not nearly so picturesque, don't you think?' She paused and took breath.

'But what about Mr. Finch?' asked Mrs. Graves impatiently.

Andrew pricked up his ears; he had been in torment during Mrs. Poltimore-Robinson's digressions.

'The young slacker!' cried Mrs. Poltimore-Robinson vindictively. 'The dirty little sneak! I hope they conscript him just the same and put him in the front line. After all the trouble the poor Vicar has taken too! The Vicar is bearing up splendidly after his bereavement; but poor little Mrs. Tomlinson is still rather low, don't you think? Well, where was I?'

'Sticking a pin in your pincushion,' said Miss Milburn.

'Why, so I was!' exclaimed Mrs. Poltimore-Robinson happily, 'and I heard a shot. I thought it might be one of the Jacomb boys shooting rooks. So dangerous, I always think. Mrs. Jacomb is a perfect fool.'

'And what was it?' Mrs. Graves interrupted.

'Why, young Finch shooting his fingers off, of course!' said Mrs. Poltimore-Robinson with triumph.

Andrew turned deep red and felt rather sick.

'But how do you know it was that?' Miss Milburn asked.

'Well, five minutes later Mrs. Finch's parlourmaid came in. I hate that girl, I'm sure she's dishonest, and she's so flighty. I don't like Susan making such a friend of her. But at any rate she asked to use my telephone to ring for a doctor, as Mr. Finch had met with an accident. I couldn't well refuse.'

'Did she say what had happened?' asked Mrs. Graves.

'No, but when Susan called me this morning she told me that he had blown off two fingers. Of course they *say* it was an accident, and that he was only cleaning his gun. But I must say it's a funny sort of accident to happen just at this time. And what do you think? His dog found the remains of his fingers and brought them in in his mouth and laid them on the door-step. The maid found them when she took in the newspaper. Hullo, what's that?'

It was Andrew being violently sick. They asked him what he had eaten, and put him to bed, and hoped he was not sickening for any infectious illness. He waited until they had all gone away, and then wept bitterly. No tragedy of the War ever affected him as much; when he heard of his cousin Richard's death, he only felt a sinking feeling. The story of Mr. Finch rent his heart. The War was wicked and horrible; he decided to forget that it was there. He would never again let Nandy take him past Mr. Finch's house if he could help it; something too horrible had happened there.

Handborough grew more and more militaristic. The Vicar, preaching from the text: *Blessed above women shall Jael the wife of Heber the Kenite be,* demolished the case for conscientious objection to the complete satisfaction of himself and of his congregation of women and old men.

'If Christ were among us to-day,' asked the Vicar, 'where would He be?' and answered himself: 'With our brave boys in France, using His bayonet.'

The congregation thought this a little irreverent, not quite in the Vicar's usual good taste. Our Lord would of course not be with those dreadful conscientious objectors in Wormwood Scrubbs. He would be doing war-work on the right side; but they were rather vague about its character. He might be an army chaplain. It was a pity that He was not a woman; He would have made such a lovely V.A.D.

Handborough Regis now had a hospital full of wounded soldiers in blue coats. Aunt Margaret worked there at the cost of great sacrifice; she had to rise very early in order to arrive there in time, and then had to work under the supervision of a woman whom she particularly disliked. Andrew sometimes came in the afternoon, when he had been given chocolates or cigarettes to give to the soldiers. He did not like visiting the hospital, but he never ventured to say so, because it was supposed to be a treat for him.

It was unpleasant to be reminded of the War, now that he had sent the War to Coventry; and the hospital reminded him of the War in a particularly unpleasant way. He hated to see bandaged heads and arms in slings. Then he was told that he ought to be grateful to the soldiers, who had been wounded in his defence. This prejudiced him against them. In the first place it was silly to say that they had been wounded for his sake, because they had never heard of him before; and it was annoying to owe anyone gratitude — it was as uncomfortable as having a guilty conscience. When grown-up people said: 'You ought to be grateful to those poor soldiers who have been wounded in defending you,' there was always a note of reproach in their voices, as if they had said: 'Are you not ashamed of wounding those poor soldiers?'

It was so awkward if some of the soldiers came to tea. More often than not, they came from the Lower Classes. They were the sort of people whom one would not have dreamed of asking to tea if they had not been wounded soldiers. Now they were privileged people; they were treated as if they did not drop their aitches — and all because there was a war on. Andrew resented their privileges; it was wrong that the War should be made so important as to upset all the conventions that always had been sacred. He was kind and polite to the soldiers. They did not see him wince when they called him 'Sonny'; and he pretended to laugh at their rude jokes, for example when they offered him cigarettes or asked when he was going to join up.

He was terribly afraid that the War would go on and on, and that he would have to fight unless he did something to himself like poor Mr. Finch. Aunt Anne used to tease him by pretending that the age limit was rapidly being lowered. One day she shewed him a small boy dressed up as a soldier walking about in Handborough.

'I do think it's absurd, don't you, Aunt Anne,' he said, 'for little squits to dress themselves up like that?'

Aunt Anne said that she understood that a juvenile regiment was being formed, and that no doubt they would come round to Selborne to recruit. She was rather cross when he said that in that case he would copy Mr. Finch.

IV

GERMAN spies became an obsession both with Andrew and with Aunt Anne. She made up exciting stories about any funny-looking people whom they happened to see; Handborough is always full of eccentric-looking people, and if anyone looked queer Aunt Anne and Andrew decided that he was in disguise. It was an exciting experience to take a walk with Aunt Anne on Nandy's Sunday out. An old clergyman with flowing white locks might go by, muttering to himself, and stabbing the asphalt path with an alpenstock. As soon as she supposed him out of hearing (and Aunt Anne took for granted that he was rather deaf), she said: 'Would you have thought that he was a dangerous character? The police know all about him; he's an Austrian Arch-Duke, and the centre of all the trouble here. But he's so clever that they can never prove anything against him.'

A melancholy creature, with watery-blue eyes and a drooping moustache like that of the White Knight, was occasionally to be seen on the Heath placing little pieces of paper on top of the gorse bushes. Once they went up to a bush and found a little piece of paper, like a motto out of a Christmas cracker, rolled up and wedged between the prickles. Aunt Anne unrolled it and read: *Christ Jesus came into the world to save sinners.* 'Disgraceful,' she said; 'he's pretending to be scattering texts from the Bible. Of course they are really messages in a secret code to other German spies. A good thing we picked up that one, I shouldn't wonder if we had prevented an air-raid.'

'German Spies' was a lovely game, but sometimes a

little embarrassing for Aunt Anne; Andrew had a shrill and penetrating whisper, and often a respectable old lady passing in a bath chair was startled to hear him telling Aunt Anne: 'I'm sure she's a German spy.'

He was naturally observant and inquisitive, and it was difficult to distract his attention from any sight considered 'unsuitable for children' which had interested him. The German Spy game increased his natural acumen. Once he distressed Aunt Anne by trying to hunt after a drunk woman, whose rolling gait and horrible blasphemies convinced him that she was a spy; and on several occasions he darted into the bushes after concealed spies, and found himself standing beside two trippers sprawling on the ground in amorous abandonment.

Andrew was vastly delighted when a real spy was detected in Handborough. She was a Hungarian girl whom Aunt Anne had once met. A bomb was found in her room, among her handkerchiefs. Aunt Anne was pleased too. With this encouragement they continued to people Handborough with spies, and on his return from school Andrew would commonly announce: 'I saw three German spies on my way home.' He seldom saw any on his way to school; it was too early for them.

When people did not look like spies, Aunt Anne discovered that they had German names, so their cunning did them no good. Mrs. Hutton, for example, looked like anyone else; but Aunt Anne had heard of a Baroness von Hutten, and Andrew added that he had seen advertisements for van Houten's cocoa. 'There the mystery thickens!' exclaimed Aunt Anne; and Mrs. Hutton went down on their black list. Their black list was kept in their heads; Andrew had wanted to keep it in a little black note-book, but Aunt Anne said it was too dangerous.

Aunt Anne and Andrew seldom disagreed over the diagnosis of a spy; but they often argued about the fit punishment for spies when they were caught. Aunt Anne thought they were 'fiends' and ought to be shot. Andrew liked them because they were romantic, and because he admired their courage in going about Handborough in disguise, and their ingenuity in disguising themselves. He thought they should be put in prison, and sent back to Germany when the War was over. She complained that it was very obstinate of him to defend these wretches, when he knew that there was really nothing to be said for them.

V

DURING Andrew's second term at Selborne the Aunts
heard from their brother-in-law that he expected to
come home on leave during November. He also told
them that he was engaged to be married; which would
in any circumstances have caused them anxiety on the
children's account, and now made them exceedingly
indignant, because his fiancée was unfortunately a
German. Elsa von Blankenheim was the daughter of
German parents long settled in Edinburgh; she and her
brothers and sisters preferred to spell their name 'Blankenham' and to drop the particle. Elsa had met Colonel
Faringdon some years previously, and a long correspondence had at last issued in their engagement. It
seemed obvious to the Aunts that Oswald had weakly
allowed himself to be 'caught'.

The Aunts lost no time in collecting what information
they could about Elsa. When Andrew came in to lunch
that day, Mrs. Graves asked him: 'Do you remember
seeing a Miss von Blankenheim in Cairo, my dear?'

'I think so; why, Aunt Anne?'

'Oh, nothing. I only wondered. When did you see her?'

'The day Stephen was christened she came to tea, she
and Mrs. von Blankenheim, and another lady. They
didn't come to the christening; they didn't know it was
that day.'

Andrew was unsuspicious of Aunt Anne's questions;
his memory had carried him back to a pleasant afternoon in the garden in Cairo, and he thought only of
that day. He and Nandy were sitting in the garden by
the sand-heap, and Stephen was in his pram. He was
only a little baby then. Andrew had been to church;

he had sat in a pew with Mummy, while Nandy and Daddy and one of the neighbours and a clergyman were christening Stephen at the font; so he had his best clothes on, and could not play with the sand. He had a big heap of white sand and a small green can, with which he fetched water from a tank. The tank was cool and green, and maidenhair fern grew round the edges; but the stones round the sides were slippery, and he was always terrified of falling in.

He remembered that afternoon perfectly well. Mummy had visitors to tea upstairs in the balcony. She had leaned over the side, and lowered a piece of Stephen's christening cake each for him and Nandy. She let it down to them in a cardboard box on a string, and the visitors looked over and smiled. He told the Aunts about it.

'Were the Blankenheims nice?' asked the Aunts.

'Yes,' he said, 'they were rather nice. They gave Stephen and me two india-rubber frogs to play with in our baths. They had tubes with bulbs at the ends, and if you pressed the bulbs the frogs swam. I bust mine, and then I asked if I could have Stephen's; because you see he was only a baby and didn't need anything to play with in his bath. Then they gave me his frog, and I bust that too.'

Colonel Faringdon's return from Egypt was now soon expected. The Aunts now no longer looked forward to it; Oswald was in disgrace with them. Andrew was excited and pleased. Stephen asked continually if Mummy would come back too; this made Andrew flustered and anxious, and he always talked very rapidly about something else. The Aunts helped him; they did not at all like to be asked if Colonel Faringdon were going to bring Mummy back to Handborough Regis with him.

At Nandy's dictation Andrew laboriously wrote an appalling letter of welcome to his father, on behalf of himself and Stephen.

'My dear Daddy,

Your two little boys are just longing to have their Daddy home with them again, and are praying God to send him a safe journey back to them. We cannot say how dearly we love our Daddy, or how happy we shall be when he is with us once more.'

Fortunately this letter never reached its destination; the ship which carried it was sunk by a submarine.

Then there was a telegram to say that Colonel Faringdon had reached Marseilles. The nursery now expected him at once, but the drawing-room did not anticipate a very prompt visit. Mrs. Graves suggested to Nandy that it would be better not to allow the children to excite themselves so much; it would be several days before their father landed in England, and perhaps a further week before he came to Handborough. Nandy was indignant. '*I* know Colonel Faringdon,' she said; 'of course he'll come straight home to his little boys.' The Aunts had told her about Miss von Blankenheim, but she could not think that she had charms to keep Colonel Faringdon from Andrew and Stephen.

However, Miss von Blankenheim prevailed. The Aunts received a letter from London saying that Colonel Faringdon was going first to Edinburgh, and then a letter from Edinburgh saying that he and Miss von Blankenheim were going to be married as soon as possible. They had nothing to wait for, and while the War lasted, they never knew when they would have another opportunity.

Andrew was given a holiday from school for the few days of his father's visit to Handborough, and immensely enjoyed it. He was very proud of Colonel Faringdon, who came home in uniform; and he took him to shew to everyone. He had not liked soldiers before, but it was thrilling to have a soldier of his own. Colonel Faringdon came with him to Selborne to beg for a holiday from Miss Low; she was very kind, and said some pleasant things about Andrew. They even went to call on Mrs. Wace. She met them at the door, dressed in a nurse's uniform, and explained proudly: 'As the Colonel was in his regimentals, I thought I ought to wear mine.'

Then Colonel Faringdon suggested that they should go over to Quenby. Andrew was delighted at the chance of shewing the cousins how far more interesting his father was than Uncle Aubrey. In the car Colonel Faringdon pulled out a pocket-book and shewed him some photographs; Andrew was not much interested in them.

'That's Miss Blankenham,' said his father, 'and she's coming to live with me. There she is again; and there is her sister Miss Bessie Blankenham.'

He received this statement without much concern. He was bored by his father's friends; there were so many of them. Since he had left Egypt various people had lived with Colonel Faringdon in the house in Cairo; there had been a Mr. Grey there, and then a Mr. FitzGerald; his father hated living alone. Now Miss Blankenham was going to live with him.

They had a lovely day at Quenby; the cousins were suitably impressed by Colonel Faringdon, and were quite kind to Andrew. He was allowed to choose what game they should play after tea, and of course he chose Prince's Quest. That was the best time of the day, when the lamp had been brought in and the dark red curtains had been drawn, and they were all sitting round the school-room table playing — rattling the dice and dropping it on the board, and following their cardboard princes through dangers and enchantments. It was a pity that one so soon had to go away, back to bed at Handborough, under Aunt Margaret's wedding groups and holy pictures.

Another day Colonel Faringdon took Andrew and Stephen up to London to have lunch with Great-aunt Isabella. Aunt Isabella was a kind old lady with white hair, who dressed in purple and wore a little gold watch with a monogram engraved on it over her left breast. She lived in a tall house in Eaton Square and was rich and had a butler. She was very placid and talked amiably about the weather. She liked making conversation, but never minded saying or hearing the same thing over and over again; and Andrew was embarrassed when she asked him for the third time if he were Andrew or Stephen. She did not seem to him to be very much interested in them; but she kissed them frequently and almost tearfully when they went away, and asked plaintively when they were coming to visit her again. Andrew felt very sorry for her; but he was relieved to put on his hat and coat with the assistance of her butler, and to find himself standing with his father and Stephen on the pavement of Eaton Square.

They took a taxi to the Savoy Hotel; Colonel Faringdon told them that they were going to see the Blankenhams, and explained whom they were to expect to meet. There would be old Mr. Blankenham, Miss Blankenham who was going to live with Colonel Faringdon, and Miss Bessie Blankenham. Mrs. Blankenham was not there; she was ill in Scotland.

They arrived at the Savoy before they were expected, and were shewn into the restaurant, where the Blankenhams were sitting over the end of a late lunch. They professed great disappointment that the Faringdons would not begin their lunch over again, but they consoled themselves by ordering coffee for Colonel Faringdon, and offering sweets to Andrew and Stephen from a little silver dish on the table. The restaurant gradually emptied, but the Blankenhams still sat lovingly over their luncheon table. Andrew was more and more bored; of all things he most detested sitting at a table when the meal was over. At home, directly he had swallowed his last drop of tea, he always leapt to his feet and hurried through his formula: 'Thank God for my good tea; please Nandy may I get down?' He could not think why grown-up people, who were old enough not to say grace or to ask leave to go, should so obstinately sit on at table; but grown-up people never seemed to realize their advantages, or to profit by them.

Andrew was very much afraid of the Blankenhams; he was always shy of strangers, and he had been told that the Blankenhams were Germans. At home it had been amusing to be pro-German, for the sake of differing from the Aunts; but when one was brought face to face with some Germans, it was difficult not to be frightened. He would not have known that Miss Bessie Blankenham was German, if he had not been told so: she looked and spoke just like anyone else, and was very kind and pleasant. Miss Blankenham was whispering to Colonel Faringdon all the time; Andrew had been told that whispering was very bad manners, but Colonel Faringdon did not seem to mind. It is true he did not encourage her by whispering himself, but he nodded and grinned amiably. Andrew was embarrassed, and did not like Miss Blankenham.

Mr. Blankenham was a fierce-looking old man with a beard; Andrew usually could not understand what he said, and therefore concluded that he was talking German, and was rather alarmed. All the same he was proud of sitting with three Germans. It was a distinguished thing to do in the middle of the War; one did not have the chance every day. It was all the better that one of them should talk real German.

Mr. Blankenham was really an extremely kind old man, despite his ferocious appearance; but unfortunately the more kindly and conciliating his manner became, the more did it terrify Andrew. He said something quite unintelligible to a waiter, who presently returned with a large envelope on a salver. Mr. Blankenham cleared his throat terrifically, and opened the envelope.

'Here, my dear boy, are two diaries,' he said in a terrifying voice; 'one is for you, and one for Stephen. I will first write your names in them.'

He produced three fountain-pens and a gold pencil from his breast pocket, then choosing a pen he wrote in a hideous angular hand: 'Andrew Faringdon from Grandpapa Paul, November 1916. Stephen Faringdon from Grandpapa Paul, November 1916.'

'You will call me Grandpapa Paul, will you not, my dear boys?' he asked; a request which seemed to them both terrifying and ridiculous, but they promised to call him so.

He opened Andrew's diary and said: 'At the beginning of this book is a table, to tell you when the sun rises. In the other part write you everything that you do. For instance, Monday you will write: "Played for England cricket," and Tuesday: "Played for England football," *und so weiter.*'

Andrew thought it unlikely that 1917 would be such an eventful year for him, but he said thank you very pleasantly.

'You are at school?' asked Mr. Blankenham. 'You will be a clever man. You shall be a great inventor or a great discoverer; should you not like that?'

Andrew acquiesced shyly.

At last the Blankenhams began to rise. Mr. Blankenham was rheumatic and had to be helped to his feet by a waiter. He refused any further help. 'I will be supported by my new grandson,' he said. 'May I lean on your shoulder, my dear boy?'

He put his right hand heavily on Andrew's shoulder. With slow steps they walked across the shining polished floor. Andrew was certain that he was going to slip; and then this terrifying old man would fall with him. He would be dreadfully hurt, because he was so old; and he would be extremely angry. He would shout at Andrew in German and perhaps hit him with the stick which he was holding in his left hand; and Daddy would be angry, and so would that black-looking Miss Blankenham who was going to live with him. She would turn and whisper something nasty to him, and even the nice Miss Blankenham would desert him.

There seemed an immense stretch of polished floor. He could not think how they would ever cross it safely. Stephen was walking behind, holding Miss Bessie Blankenham's hand; he was safe and happy. It was unfair that Andrew always had to be the elder, and always had to do the dangerous and uncomfortable things, while Stephen was spared them. He did not dare look up; there were so many lights, and the blurred faces of waiters. And he dared not look at Mr. Blankenham. He looked down at the shining floor, and that was worse still.

At last they reached the door of the restaurant, and walked along a safe thickly carpeted passage, and went up in the lift. Mr. Blankenham went away to rest, the others went into a small sitting-room where they seemed to spend an interminable time. Andrew and Stephen sat on the floor with Miss Bessie Blankenham doing a picture puzzle. None of them was really very much interested in the puzzle, but it was better than doing nothing. From the corner of his eye Andrew could see his father and Miss Blankenham. They were behaving very strangely indeed. They were sitting at the window with a small table between them, and they appeared to be counting silver spoons. At intervals they would break off from this extraordinary occupation to bend forward and kiss across the table. He was horribly embarrassed; and he was in terror lest Miss Bessie Blankenham should see them and should say something. He turned very red, and talked quickly about anything that came into his head, so that he might engage her whole attention.

Somehow or other the day in London came to an end; they came back tired and sleepy to Handborough to be bathed and put to bed. Andrew had not long been in bed when Aunt Margaret came into her room to dress for dinner. This evening she made no attempt to check his loquacity; she was far too anxious for news of his day in London.

'Where did you go, dear?' she said.

'Well, we had lunch with Aunt Isabella, and then we went to the Savoy Hotel to see the Blankenhams.'

'Whom did they consist of?'

'There were two Miss Blankenhams, and Mr. Blankenham.'

'Are they *very* German? The daughters, I mean. I know the old man is.'

'I don't know about Miss Blankenham, I didn't notice particularly. Miss Bessie is just like an English person. But Mr. Blankenham is *very* German; he talked in German to the waiter.'

To his great satisfaction, Andrew found that the shot

115

had not missed its mark. Aunt Margaret was quite indignant. 'How dared he?' she cried.

Aunt Margaret did not seem to like the Blankenhams at all; Andrew was made to feel that he had been spending the day in company of which he ought to be ashamed. He often had that feeling; in the drawing-room he was ashamed of having been in the nursery with Nandy, whom the Aunts did not like; and in the nursery he was ashamed of having been in the drawing-room with the Aunts, whom Nandy did not like. He thought that he had better say something conciliatory. 'Aunt Margaret, isn't Mrs. Blankenham Scotch?' he enquired.

This innocent and well-meant remark had an unexpected effect. 'No,' said Aunt Margaret decidedly; 'she's just as German as Mr. von Blankenheim — *more* German. Has Nandy been telling you that she was Scotch? How did you get the idea?'

'I don't know,' said Andrew.

'Andrew, are you quite sure you're telling the truth?' asked Aunt Margaret severely. 'If Nandy didn't tell you she was Scotch, who did?'

'I don't know, I suppose no one could have said she was Scotch, I just thought she might be,' said Andrew in bewilderment. What did Mrs. Blankenham's nationality matter? He had merely asked if she were Scotch; because if she were, Aunt Margaret might not mind so much that Mr. Blankenham was German. He vaguely hoped that she might be; the Blankenhams lived in Scotland.

'Well, if anyone tells you that Mrs. von Blankenheim is Scotch, you must contradict it,' said Aunt Margaret firmly. 'She's German.'

Aunt Margaret was anxious to know which of the two Miss von Blankenheims Andrew preferred. Without hesitation he said that Miss Bessie was far nicer than Miss Elsa. Aunt Margaret seemed to think that this was a pity.

Colonel Faringdon went away a few days later; before he went, Andrew was allowed to polish his buttons, and brought them to a brilliant shine. Ordinary life was promptly resumed, and he went back to school. Colonel Faringdon had been a glorious interlude, but now he was gone the children went back to the serious routine of everyday things without sorrow. Their father did not belong to the world of Handborough, and was out of place there; they had enjoyed his visit, but they did not miss him when he went. He was something special, like Father Christmas or a conjuror; one could not keep him always, and one did not wish it.

V I

ANDREW and Stephen were taken ill only a few days after Colonel Faringdon went up to Edinburgh. They both had high temperatures, and when the fever subsided sore places broke out on their necks and faces.

Andrew had been moved into the nursery; he sat up in bed reading *A Child's History of England* by Charles Dickens. He had bought this book with three and sixpence of his own money (he seldom had any money of his own, and when he had, he was hardly ever allowed to spend it). He loved this more than any other book. It was beautifully bound in half-calf; he had bought it as a remainder, a real bargain for three and sixpence. He always read it in a paper cover, and he knew it exceedingly well.

Sometimes it puzzled him. Charles Dickens wrote of Henry III: 'He was as much of a King in death as he had ever been in life. He was the mere pale shadow of a King at all times.' Andrew could not make this out. In the small note-book in which he recorded the chief characteristics of the kings of England, together with other pieces of useful information, he set down that Henry III was as much a king in death as in life. But it still worried him. How could Henry III be a king in death? History books said silly things — for example, the chief characteristic of Charles II was a propensity to have natural children; but surely all children were natural phenomena.

When the doctor visited him, he entertained him with descriptions of the sufferings of the Protestant martyrs under Mary. 'They watched the executioner burning their own bowels,' he said dramatically.

'They couldn't,' said the doctor. 'They'd be dead first.'

'But they did,' insisted Andrew, exasperated at the doctor's scepticism. 'The book says so.'

Nandy lent him *Pears' Encyclopædia*, and from this wonderful shilling book he quickly gathered a vast store of general knowledge. He learned that if you wanted to help someone who had been poisoned, you should keep him awake until the doctor came; and you should make him take a great deal of coffee and raw eggs. He learned suitable menus for dinner-parties at different seasons of the year, and the doctrines of the Greek Orthodox Church; and he read, without much comprehension, the table of precedence of the nobility and gentry.

One day Nandy came in joyfully and said they must make haste to get well. What did they think? Daddy wanted them to go to stay with him and Miss Blankenham in London; would not that be delightful? Stephen was not much impressed; Andrew's heart sank, and he had a prompt relapse.

Stephen returned gradually and complacently to health; and he and Nandy went to London, despite protests and floods of tears from Andrew. They could not wait for him; Colonel Faringdon was beginning to be impatient. It was terrible to be without them; Andrew wished he had been well enough to go with them, though he would have infinitely preferred them all to stay at Handborough. He sat alone in the nursery, very pale and red-eyed, with a sore place on his cheek, and wished he were back in bed again. But They said he must sit up in his room, otherwise he would never become strong enough to go up to London.

Aunt Anne was very kind to him. After the first day he was not so unhappy without Nandy and Stephen, and his only anxiety was not to be sent away from

Handborough. He and Aunt Anne decorated a screen with scraps; and one day they spent a lovely afternoon looking at all the jewels and silver in the safe.

Aunt Margaret was very kind too; though she was busy at the hospital most of the day, and had less time to spare. She gave him a drawing lesson, and she searched in a cupboard and found a pile of old picture-books for him. Best of all, she lent him a copy of Shake-speare. This was better even than Charles Dickens's history-book; and he read *Richard III* with great pleasure.

His convalescence was gradual, but it was quicker than he wished. He knew that he would have to go up to London as soon as he was well enough. Nandy and Daddy had written to say that they were sorry he was making such a slow recovery. Aunt Anne was sym-pathetic, and kept him at Handborough as long as she could; but at last she told him that he really must go to London.

She took him up herself. At the station her heart smote her when she looked at the pale-faced little figure at her side, holding the cardboard box in which she had packed his possessions, and looking so tired and so re-signed. A thought of the second Mrs. Faringdon came into her mind, and she put sentiment aside. 'Andrew,' she said sternly; 'I hope you won't ever call that Ger-man woman "Mummy", as you called your mother. If she wants you to, ask if you can call her something else. You could call her "Aunt Elsa", or "Mamma" if she insists.'

'Yes, Aunt Anne,' said Andrew dutifully. He felt very uncomfortable. People were always talking about Miss Blankenham nowadays; he was beginning to un-derstand her significance, and he did not like it. He knew, though no one had ever told him directly, that she had married his father. Therefore she was his step-mother. Stepmothers were always wicked; and Miss Blankenham was not only a stepmother, but a German into the bargain. He was afraid that she would there-fore be extraordinarily wicked, even for a stepmother; and the Aunts did not speak of her in an encouraging manner.

Then, by drawing the simple inference that if his father were married again, his mother must be dead, Andrew first fully realized the fact of his mother's death. It did not come as a shock to him. He had deliberately refused to examine the theory that she would come back from Heaven, because he secretly felt that it would not stand examination. Yet it had spared him the necessity of saying good-bye for ever; he had never faced the fact that he must go through life — and for all he knew, he might live for hundreds of years — without ever seeing her again.

His mother was dead; he said it to himself quite dully. She was dead like thousands of people who did not matter, because their lives did not touch his at any point. Like all the soldiers who had died in France lately, she was just dead. When Nandy said she had gone to Heaven, she had not told him a lie. People who died went there, unless they had been wicked and had gone to Hell. But Nandy had misled him. 'Your Mum-my was ill, so God took her to His house,' she had said. If God only took her because she was ill, he had natur-ally concluded that she would return when she was better. Now she would never come again; she was dead. She would not send a letter to say that she was coming; nor would she come in suddenly, and kiss him just as he was going to sleep. That was how he wanted her to come; he would see her first. Stephen would be asleep already, because he was only a baby still; he would not see her till the next morning. Andrew would fall asleep knowing that she had come, and would wake next day warm with happiness; at first he would only know vaguely that there was something to be happy about, and then with full remembrance would come a flood of joy because she had come back.

He resented Miss Blankenham, and felt that she had killed his mother; he was glad that Aunt Anne did not like her either. It was with great nervousness and reluctance that they left their taxi at Prince of Wales Terrace, and climbed the stair of the dingy house where the Faringdons had taken apartments. Aunt Anne's heart beat faster, and Andrew felt sick.

Colonel Faringdon was not in the room when they entered. Miss Blankenham was there wearing a green hat; she was playing with Stephen on the floor. Andrew had a dazed feeling of being very far away looking on, while Miss Blankenham and Aunt Anne stood wide apart looking at each other. Then his father entered, and there was some rapid conversation. Colonel Faringdon went out with Mrs. Graves to find her a taxi, and Andrew was left with his stepmother and Stephen. They were both rather cross.

VII

Life in Prince of Wales Terrace was interesting, but rather uncomfortable. The children had no nursery to themselves. Their bedroom was too small for them to play in, and they had to share a sitting-room with their parents. Fortunately Colonel and Mrs. Faringdon were often out.

Nandy took Andrew and Stephen for walks in the Park. Andrew did not care for this. The Park was a stupid imitation of the country, they had far better country at home at Handborough Regis. It was silly to pretend to be in the country when they were in London; it was much better to walk in the streets. Sometimes Nandy was persuaded into taking them for walks in Kensington; she avoided crowded streets and they walked through quiet residential squares, full of houses to be let or sold.

There was far more romance in a London street than with Peter Pan in Kensington Gardens. Sometimes they saw a battlemented and turreted mansion, built in the most flamboyant period of the Gothic Revival. Andrew would accept it as a genuine mediæval castle, and would decide that it had often been besieged. Nandy agreed that this was most probable.

It was something to be in a street in London: scenes in Shakespeare often happened just in 'a street in London', and why not in this street in which they were walking, as well as any other? It might have been in Ennismore Gardens or in Exhibition Road that Anne, passing through London with the murdered body of Henry VI, had met Richard Duke of Gloucester. Even at the present day, though the murdered body of the

King was not likely to be carried by on a bier, one might be fortunate enough to see an accident or an air-raid. The Germans were continually dropping bombs on London; they had aimed at Aunt Anne when she left Prince of Wales Terrace, and only narrowly missed her.

Sometimes Andrew went out with his father to see the sights of London. They went one morning to Westminster Abbey. Andrew said solemnly that he wished first to see the grave of Charles Dickens, who had written his history-book, and a kind verger found for him the plain slab of stone in the nave inscribed CHARLES DICKENS. They went with another verger and a party of tourists to see the Royal Tombs. Pressing close to the guide and hearing every word of his discourse, Andrew was taken through the chapels on the south side of the ambulatory until they arrived at Henry VII's chapel. He flung back his head and gazed in astonishment at the roof, forgetting the guide and all the other people, until the kind voice of the verger brought him back to earth. His neck was stiff, and his head swam.

'Little boy, did you ever hear of Oliver Cromwell?' asked the verger.

Andrew drew himself up. 'Of course I've heard of Oliver Cromwell,' he answered.

'And what do you think of him?' said the verger.

'He was a very wicked man,' said Andrew, a staunch Royalist.

'I'm so glad to hear you say so,' said the verger. 'I was just telling those people there that there used to be stained glass in that window, before Oliver Cromwell broke it.'

'Yes, and he stabled his horses in Ottery St. Mary church in Devonshire,' said Andrew indignantly.

They passed into St. Edward's Chapel: it was a dismal sight. In the middle was a great pile of sand-bags protecting St. Edward's shrine from bombs. On one side of him lay Eleanor of Castile, and Henry III whom Charles Dickens had described as 'the mere pale shadow of a King at all times'. They were both smothered in sand-bags. Only one tomb in the chapel was completely exposed to view — the long stone coffin of Edward I. The verger pretended to have forgotten his date, and invited Andrew to prompt him.

Andrew and his father were very happy together; Colonel Faringdon liked to talk to him about his mother, and was pleased that he remembered her so well. As if he could have forgotten! She had only been away two years, not quite so long as his father; he remembered all about her.

There was one obstacle to pleasant conversation; Colonel Faringdon had told Andrew, rather diffidently, that he would like him to call Miss Blankenham 'Mummy'. He thought of Aunt Anne, and blushed; but yielded to his father. It made things very uncomfortable; he never knew whether his father meant Mummy or Miss Blankenham when he said 'Mummy'. Andrew was talking about Mummy once, and Colonel Faringdon did not understand and thought he meant Miss Blankenham. 'Which Mummy?' he asked confusedly. It was with difficulty that Andrew refrained from bursting into tears.

He still said the same prayer that he had always said every night: 'Pray God bless dear Daddy and Mummy, Stephen and Nandy, all Uncles and Aunts, all kind relations and friends. Bless me and make me a good boy, for Jesus Christ's sake.' Now when he prayed for Mummy into Nandy's lap, he saw a blurred and composite image: there was his own mother, standing at her dressing-table, putting on her ear-rings and smiling at him; and there was Miss Blankenham in a green hat. He could never bring himself to pray for 'Mummy and Mummy'.

It came as a shock to Andrew that Miss Blankenham was now Mrs. Faringdon; of course he could have reasoned that she must be, but he never had. The children were having tea alone with Nandy one day, and Nandy said: 'Isn't it sad that Daddy and Mummy are going back to Egypt so soon? Don't you wish we could go with them?'

There was nothing that Andrew wished less. He would not care for Cairo without his mother, and Miss Blankenham would be much worse than no mother at all, if she were going there.

'Is *she* going too?' he asked resentfully. He never called her 'Mummy' unless it was necessary; he did not want to acquire the habit. He was already wondering what he would be able to call her in front of Aunt Anne. Probably 'that German woman' would please her better than any other name.

'Of course Mummy is going,' answered Nandy with a laugh. 'You didn't think she was going back to Edinburgh to be Miss Blankenham again?'

He had not yet fully realized that Miss Blankenham was going to live with his father for always, and every fresh confirmation of his secret fears was a pang.

One day Miss Blankenham asked him to come into her room to take some medicine. On the floor was a new green cabin trunk with ELSA FARINGDON painted right across it in clear black letters. There was no doubt about it. She was Mrs. Faringdon, just as his mother had been. He began to look pityingly at Stephen. 'Poor little thing, he little knows,' he said to himself, but he decided not to tell him. It was difficult to know how to tell Stephen, and what exactly there was to tell.

VIII

Elsa Faringdon was very fussy; she was always examining the children's finger-nails. She had given each of them a nail-cleaner as her first present. The children were constantly being sent to brush their hair, and their stepmother was very cross if Nandy did it for them. She was always trying to make them do things for themselves which they never did at home, and they greatly resented this interference. The Aunts often tried to make Nandy leave them more to themselves; the children disliked this, but acknowledged that it was just. They knew that as they grew older they would have to do up their own buttons, and lace their own shoes, and go to the lavatory by themselves, and that little by little they must learn these things, just as they had by now learned to blow their own noses. It was all very well for the Aunts to interfere; but a stranger like Miss Blankenham ought to leave things as she found them.

Elsa Faringdon was a woman of little sensibility; but she had started with every intention of bringing up the children well. She herself had been brought up with the one idea of becoming some day a good wife and mother; and for fulfilling these functions she had been trained with rigid German conscientiousness. She had been through courses of lessons in cooking and housewifery, and she had served as a probationer in a children's hospital. There was no question but that her house would be well ordered, and that the health of all its inmates would have every care. She had read a book on the care of children in health and in sickness, on their discipline and early education, and on their instruction in the mysteries of sex; she therefore knew

127

how children should be handled. But she did not like them.

She did not know that all knowledge profits nothing without charity; she did not know that no cook without her heart in her work can succeed, however scrupulously she may follow Mrs. Beeton's instructions; that flowers will not grow for any gardener who does not love them; and that children can be made more healthy, happy and good-natured by a simple country girl who is fond of them, than by an advanced student of infant psychology who dislikes them.

She had decided that Andrew and Stephen had been living with people who ought never to have had charge of children at all. She only knew that Mrs. Graves and Miss Milburn had had little experience of children other than Andrew and Stephen; she knew nothing of Miss Milburn's unfailing patience or of Mrs. Graves's imaginative sympathy with children. Their affection for the little boys she did not doubt, but she assumed that it was excessive, and that the children were spoilt. She therefore applied to Andrew and Stephen, uncritically, the treatment which her reading had suggested for spoilt children. She did not trouble to enquire if they were really spoilt, or if her discipline were applied with judiciousness.

To Nandy she had taken an instant dislike; she thought her too old to be with children, she disliked her possessive attitude to Andrew and Stephen, and thought that she did far too much for them. Nandy had been respectful but aloof; she could see that Mrs. Faringdon did not really like the children and therefore withdrew as far as possible from her efforts at co-operation. Elsa would have liked Nandy to tell her about the children's life at Handborough Regis, and about their dispositions and habits; it would be helpful to her if she were to treat them rightly. Nandy was not communicative.

The children saw Elsa Faringdon as one who liked to change things, and had no business to make changes. She had not had the tact to consolidate her position before making criticisms; a wiser woman would have realized that in a fortnight with her step-children all she could hope to do was to win their respect and liking, and that any alterations in their upbringing must be left for another time.

Subconsciously she hated the children, and enjoyed finding fault; she told herself that it was important to start as she meant to continue, to forbid anything that she did not mean to allow later on, and to check any tendency to form a bad habit before it was too far developed.

The children felt as if they were undergoing an inspection whenever she was with them; she watched how they dressed, how they washed, how they played, how they ate, and how Andrew wrote letters to the Aunts. At every point she had some criticism to make. They must not sit on their beds while they dressed; it was lazy. They must wash with less help from Nandy. They must never leave anything on their plates, fat must be eaten as well as lean. Andrew was once rash enough to say that he hated turnips, when he refused them at lunch; she told him that he must never say that he hated anything. 'One should be able to eat all that is going,' she said, and gave him a large helping.

If Andrew read a book, he had to hold it at exactly the right angle. If he wrote to the Aunts his letter was largely dictated, and she made him use many expressions that he wrote with great shame and reluctance. It pained him to write that he was having a 'spiffing' time in London. Elsa Faringdon had acquired from

Victorian school stories a horrible slang vocabulary, which she believed all normal children habitually used. Andrew disconcerted her by his very cold reception of her most idiomatic phrases, and by his own exceedingly pure English.

Andrew resented her implied criticisms of Nandy and the Aunts almost as much as her severity. She would not allow things which they had always allowed. She ought to realize that she was only a 'temporary', he thought. She bore the same relation to the Aunts as the nursemaids, who took Nandy's place during her holiday, bore to Nandy. He looked forward to going back to the Aunts; Miss Blankenham's authority was only for a fortnight, and she was very far exceeding her rights.

Sometimes she talked to him about Handborough. She talked to him in the same unpleasant way as Aunt Emma. She said no doubt he had plenty of little friends there; she expected he had a lovely time there, kicking a football about on the Heath, or climbing trees. He told her that they always went out alone with Nandy, that his favourite amusements were reading and drawing and writing stories, and that the only things he liked at school were the lessons and the mistresses; the games and the other children bored him.

She decided that he was not a normal child, and she had a horror of abnormality; Stephen was still almost a baby, but she feared that he would develop in the same way. Neither of the children responded to her attempts at kindness; and they seemed to be perpetually on their guard against her. Like all people who have forced children to assume a defensive position, she came to the conclusion that they had a secretive and underhand nature.

Colonel Faringdon's sister Mrs. Thompson came to

London with her little boy for a few days. Andrew and Stephen had not seen Aunt Mary for a long time; they were fond of her, and were glad to see her again. They were not so pleased to see Frank. He was a strange child, unused to playing with other children. He had been told by his mother that he was very fond of his cousins, and he believed her. When he first came to Prince of Wales Terrace he kissed them both affectionately and damply on the cheek; this was not a favourable beginning.

Frank, a lonely child like Andrew, also had a dreamworld of his own; but this world was not peopled by Bun and the Kings of England. He had taken it readymade from *Chums* and *The Boys' Own Paper*, and from Sir Robert Baden-Powell's *Scouting for Boys*.

'I've got a scout-kit,' he told Andrew.

'What's that?' Andrew asked him.

'Clothes like scouts wear, of course; and I've got a water-bottle.'

'What do you want that for?'

'To carry water in, of course.'

'But you never want to carry water,' Andrew objected.

'But you might be on a trek in the desert,' said Frank.

'Well, you never are,' said Andrew decisively.

'Well, anyway, real scouts have water-bottles,' argued Frank.

'But you're not a real scout, so why do you want to dress up like one?' said Andrew contemptuously.

'It's a very fine thing to be a scout,' interrupted his stepmother. 'All boys naturally are keen to be scouts, it is something to be proud of. It's such good *training*.'

Miss Blankenham and Frank seemed to like the same things; this increased Andrew's distrust for his cousin. He decided that he was a prig, very unfairly. Frank was

131

a pleasant child, entirely happy in the ridiculous world which Sir Robert Baden-Powell had created for him; and like Andrew himself he was better in grown-up society than with other children. Unfortunately his manners were unnaturally good; and he had acquired several grown-up phrases which are particularly infuriating to children when spoken by another child. If Andrew happened to ask where he had been when he returned from the lavatory, Frank would reply: 'I would rather not say.'

'Why?'

'Because one doesn't talk about it.'

'Why?'

'Because it isn't done.'

'Well, now I know you've been in the lavatory, and you might as well have said.'

Frank would be very cross. 'Mummy says it isn't nice,' he would say, turning away from Andrew in disapproval.

Elsa Faringdon was fond of Frank; she had gone down to Devonshire to visit him and his mother very soon after her marriage. She knew that Mrs. Thompson had been hostile, but was now willing to be friendly; and knowing that Oswald was fond of his sister, she wished to placate her. Kindness to Frank was her best method of approach. He had been taught to thank people charmingly for their presents, and he knew that it was the best way of getting more presents in the future. His new Aunt Elsa brought him a paint-box; he said it was 'jolly decent' and called her a 'ripper'.

Elsa realized that it would be far easier to manage Frank than Andrew and Stephen; and unfortunately she did not confine this comparison to her private thoughts. The children were told *ad nauseam* that Frank never cried; that he ate up everything that was put on

132

his plate, and was truly thankful for it; that he was always clean and tidy, and that he was so brave that he positively liked hurting himself. In consequence they conceived the greatest dislike for him; and when he went back to Devonshire Andrew said that it was a pity that Aunt Mary had to go away, but he didn't mind it so much because at least she had taken Frank with her.

'Do you mean to say you aren't sorry he's gone?' asked his stepmother.

'Yes,' said Andrew. He thought it ought to have been obvious that that was what he meant to say.

She was very cross, and said: 'Would you like him to say that about you?'

'I shouldn't want him to say he was sorry if it wasn't true,' answered Andrew stubbornly.

THEIR visit to London drew towards its end. When Nandy began their packing, they were given two presents, both of an embarrassing nature. One was a large section of their father's wedding-cake; it was a good cake, and they would enjoy it for some time to come at nursery tea, but its presence would certainly be discovered by the Aunts, who would resent it. One could certainly not offer either of them a slice. The other present was not even useful; it was a large photograph in a silver frame of Colonel and Mrs. Faringdon after their wedding. Mrs. Faringdon had a fly on her nose, and an expression of triumph. Andrew hoped that Nandy would allow him to keep this object in a drawer; there was no need for the Aunts to see it.

They left Prince of Wales Terrace without regret on a cold foggy morning. Colonel and Mrs. Faringdon and Nandy and the children were all crowded together in a taxi. From his back seat Andrew tried to get a last view of London; but in the dense fog only dim outlines were visible, and at regular intervals street lamps glowed. He looked forward to going back to Handborough; he would have such a lot to tell Aunt Margaret in the evenings while she dressed for dinner. It would be such a joy to return to the Teddy bears and the Boches and the other children who had had to be left behind. It was only at home that there were enough books and toys; you could never take enough away.

They had some time to wait at the station; their father and their stepmother bought them papers, and stood at the door of their compartment talking. Nandy had discreetly placed herself behind the children, so that she might not interfere with the parting scene. Occasionally Colonel and Mrs. Faringdon spoke to her over the children's heads. Andrew stared at them; he thought that he must try to remember what they were like. They were the people to whom he would have to write a letter every week. Nandy would say: 'If Daddy and Mummy were here, you'd have plenty to say to them, love. Why don't you write some of it?' Now they were still here for a few minutes, and there seemed nothing to say.

It was a pity one could not press a button and make the train start; but that magic power was not his. Aunt Anne pretended to possess it, and had more or less convinced him of her powers. This train seemed very slow. A guard began shutting the doors. Andrew hastily begged his father to give his love to Abdulla the cook, to Mohammed the house-servant, and to Said the hippopotamus at the Zoo. At last they were off; he waved politely from the window and then sat down and opened the *Rainbow*.

Nandy was disappointed at the farewell scene. A parting in war-time, before a sea voyage and an indefinite separation, seemed to her to require a few tears at least. Neither Andrew nor Stephen had recourse to their pocket-handkerchiefs. Their picture papers entirely satisfied their present needs.

'What funny children you are,' she said. 'One would think you didn't mind Daddy and Mummy going right away to Egypt again.' She looked at them, but there were still no signs of tears. She became a little anxious, perhaps they were being brave and controlling themselves because there were other people in the compartment; it would be better for them to give way and cry. She soon had to abandon this explanation; Andrew could not sit quietly reading the *Rainbow* if he were unhappy. If he did not cry, he would be certain to talk very quickly and loudly, with exaggerated cheerfulness.

Nandy had regretfully to decide that the children were glad to go back to Handborough Regis; she did not like Handborough, and her relations with the Aunts were not easy. She had not enjoyed being at Prince of Wales Terrace; but she felt that loyalty to Colonel Faringdon, her employer, required her to pretend to the children that they had enjoyed it, and that they were happier with him and his wife than with anyone else; though she was beginning to fear that the second Mrs. Faringdon was going to be no friend either to herself or to Andrew and Stephen.

The Faringdons walked away from Victoria; they had some shopping to do at the Army and Navy Stores.

'Poor little chaps!' said Colonel Faringdon. 'I was afraid that they would cry, but they were very plucky.'

'H'm,' said his wife, 'I don't suppose they care. They are quite glad to go back to those females at Handborough Regis.'

'Oh, my dear,' he protested, 'they are the most affectionate children.'

'You don't convince me,' she replied.

1917

I

WHEN their unpacking was finished Nandy placed the photograph of Colonel and Mrs. Faringdon in the middle of the nursery mantelpiece. It dominated the small vases, the faded photographs of distant cousins of the Milburn family, and the little china figures of mandarins with nodding heads. It was crude and pretentious and out of place in its vulgar silver frame; and it was continually falling down.

'I don't like it there, somehow,' said Andrew.

'How funny you are, my dear,' said Nandy. 'Where else could I put it?'

'I thought perhaps we might keep it in a drawer, or in the cupboard,' he suggested timidly.

Nandy was rather cross. 'What an extraordinary thing to suggest!' she said. 'Fancy putting your Daddy and Mummy away in a drawer!   What would Daddy say?'

'He won't know,' said Andrew. He thought to himself: 'But if that photograph stays there the Aunts *will* know, and they won't like it.'

'I think it's horrid to do what he wouldn't like, behind his back,' said Nandy; 'with your poor Daddy going a long way away to Egypt too. He gave it you because he thought you would like to have it.'

'He didn't give it me,' said Andrew; 'Miss Blankenheim gave it me.'

'She's not Miss Blankenham any more, dear, she's your Mummy.'

'She's not *my* Mummy, and if she gave it to me it's *mine* and I can keep it in the cupboard if I like.'

'You mustn't talk to Nandy like that; Mummy said

139

when we were in London that she sometimes didn't like the way you talked.'

Andrew boiled with rage at Miss Blankenheim's presumption in criticizing him to Nandy; he often disliked the things she said and did, but he never criticized them. He supposed that like all grown-up people she felt entitled to judge children as summarily as she pleased, at the same time considering herself above their criticism, however she chose to behave. But he was sorry if he had hurt Nandy.

'I'm sorry, Nandy, but mayn't I do what I like with my photo?'

'Why do you want to hide it?' she asked. 'Are you ashamed of your Daddy and Mummy?'

He hung his head.

'Have the Aunts said anything to you about her?' she continued.

'No, I don't think so.'

'Andrew, are you *sure* you're telling the truth?'

'Well, I think Aunt Anne said . . . something. I don't know what she said.'

'Well,' said Nandy sternly, 'whatever anyone says, remember they're your Daddy and Mummy, and the fifth commandment says you've got to honour them; and what they want matters more than what the Aunts or anyone else wants.'

Andrew hated people to talk like that. Aunt Anne had once said: 'You must remember that Nandy is only your nurse. You're very fond of her I know, and she has been very kind to you. But one day you won't be able to keep her any longer, because you'll be too old. But we are your relations, and we hope we shall always know you.'

It was horrible of people to make conflicting claims upon him, to force him to hurt someone whom he loved. He wanted to oblige everyone, but they made it impossible for him. If a choice were forced upon him, he would rather disoblige Daddy and Mummy than anyone else. They were further away, and they mattered less than Nandy and the Aunts.

Andrew could never hold out against anyone for long. 'I'm sorry, Nandy, if you're vexed at anything,' he said.

'I'm not vexed, dear,' she said in her most patient voice, 'only a little grieved.'

He came close to her, and put his face against her apron.

'Don't be grieved, Nandy,' he pleaded. 'Please be ungrieved again. Do whatever you like with the photo. I'd *like* to have it on the mantelpiece.'

Concord was restored in the nursery. Andrew and Stephen drew quietly in their sketch-books, sitting on the floor at Nandy's feet, while she darned stockings in the rocking-chair and sang to them and to herself:

> 'My mother said that I never should
> Play with the gipsies in the wood:
> I said I should, and so she said
> She'd bang my head with the tea-pot lid.'

Andrew loved that song; he hated her to sing sad songs like *There is a Tavern in the Town.*

At tea Nandy got out the wedding-cake; it was going to be kept as a treat in future, but she brought it out that day because it was their first day at Handborough.

Aunt Anne came in just before they had finished tea. 'I've brought you up some cake,' she said; 'I remembered you hadn't any.' She caught sight of the wedding-cake. 'Oh, it seems you have,' she said; 'I needn't have bothered. Is it . . . ?'

'Yes, Aunt Anne,' said Andrew. He knew that she

141

would have difficulty in finishing her sentence, and cut it short. She looked up at the mantelpiece and started. 'You'll be coming down in a few minutes, children?' she asked, after a brief uncomfortable pause; then she turned and left the room.

She and her sister agreed that Nandy had exhibited very bad taste in setting up a photograph of that German woman in their house, but they decided not to mention it to the children.

ANDREW went back to Selborne for the Lent Term as a day-boarder. This meant that he had lunch at school and did not return home until tea. He did not mind the prospect of afternoon school, but he dreaded the walk which the day-boarders took after morning school, and the extra contact with the other children. When he had only gone in the morning he had scarcely spoken to the others except in the ten minutes' break, and when break came he had always felt lonely.

He found that he had been moved out of the Baby Class into the Boys' Class. This was under Miss Clements, a small, round, dark woman with a pointed chin; she was strict and efficient and was immensely respected. She taught in a class-room upstairs. On the other side of the landing was the girls' class-room, where Miss Low herself gave lessons.

On the first day Andrew had not known that he would have to find a partner to walk with him in the crocodile. At the end of morning school he heard Denys and Charlie Green arranging to walk together. He hastily asked Peter Paradise to walk with him. 'I'm sorry,' said Peter politely, 'but I'm engaged to Philip.'

Andrew made two more unsuccessful attempts to find someone disengaged, and then gave it up. He hoped that he would find someone agreeable left over when the crocodile was formed. Later on he discovered that no one agreeable ever was left over: if you trusted to luck, you were invariably obliged to walk with someone dull or disagreeable.

That day no one at all was left over, and Andrew

had to walk with Miss Clements at the tail of the crocodile. It was very dreary, and there was nothing to say. It was a bitterly cold day, and the pavements were covered with ice and snow. He nearly slipped several times. 'Be careful, child,' said Miss Clements irritably. Her chilblains were smarting, and her nose was crimson with the cold. Andrew was terrified of falling; all the boys would laugh at him, and the girls in front would turn their heads and laugh too. His bootlace had come undone; it generally did when he had tied it himself. He walked on in increasing discomfort, hoping that Miss Clements would not notice.

'Andrew,' she said suddenly, 'drop out of the crocodile and do up your boot. Hurry up and run after us, we can't wait for you.'

He stood against a wall for shelter from the wind, laboriously unbuttoned his gloves and took them off, and struggled with his bootlace. He ran after the crocodile and caught it up, just as it was turning the corner.

'Put on your gloves now, or your hands will freeze,' commanded Miss Clements.

Andrew found that he was holding only one glove. 'You must have dropped the other when you did up your boot. Really you *are* a nuisance, Andrew,' said Miss Clements crossly. 'Now we shall all have to wait, I suppose; run and get it quickly, for heaven's sake.'

He ran back to the exact spot and searched; he dared not take off his other glove, but felt among the snow painfully with his bare left hand. There was no sign of his glove, it had vanished. He returned dismally to Miss Clements; she was rubbing her hands impatiently, while the children were stamping their feet and warming themselves with 'Cabman's exercise.'

'You've been a long time,' she said.

'It's gone,' he replied.

144

She was exceedingly annoyed, and said she did not know what They would say when he got home. Andrew thought They would be kinder than she was. He walked beside her in silent wretchedness, sorry for himself because he had been scolded by Miss Clements, and might be scolded again by Nandy and the Aunts; but more deeply sorry for his poor little glove, separated from its fellow and lying in the cold snow, or stolen by some dirty or dishonest person.

The crocodile went round the edge of the Heath; here and there children separated from it to go home to lunch. Andrew watched them enviously. He thought of the warmth and comfort of the Aunts' house, and its peace. To-day he would have lunch at a long trestle table surrounded by these horrible children. He cried quietly; Miss Clements did not notice.

On the Heath the crocodile was dissolved and the children had to play games. They formed a circle for Twos and Threes. Andrew noticed that they had chosen a spot quite near the Aunts' house; in two minutes he could run home. Aunt Anne's dog Nigger always ran straight home if anyone but his mistress took him out, the moment he was taken off the lead. Andrew felt like Nigger; Miss Clements had taken him for a miserable walk on the lead, but now he had been let loose. He whispered to Denys: 'I'm going home.' Denys looked puzzled, but Andrew supposed that he would tell Miss Clements if she asked where he was, and that she would not come after him.

He slipped away unnoticed, and ran home. The Aunts had already begun lunch when he arrived, red-eyed and panting for breath. They were kind, and did not scold him; but they told him that next time he really must go back to Selborne with the crocodile.

Towards the middle of the term Andrew had become

acutely unhappy; he felt that all the other boys had turned against him and hated him, and he could not think why this was. It was difficult to trace the process by which they had gradually begun to ill-treat him. There were few definite occasions which he could remember, on which anything decisive had happened. But there was no doubt that things had been going from bad to worse.

Of course it never occurred to Andrew that the other boys did not dislike him in the least, and that Denys was in fact rather fond of him. They had simply discovered, by the natural instinct of the hunter, that he provided them with an ideal victim, and they tormented him to their utmost capacity whenever they felt in the mood. Their cruelty was without either remorse or malice.

It began one day because Andrew admitted that he had a German stepmother. Charlie Green ingeniously argued that Andrew was therefore half a German and probably a spy, and ought to be kept in a barbed-wire entanglement. Charlie had no malicious intent, and was thoroughly enjoying the elaboration of his theme, when Andrew suddenly turned crimson and protested angrily that he was not a German, and that even if he were, it would not be his fault.

'It isn't the Kaiser's fault either, that he's a German,' said Charlie with ruthless logic.

'But I'm not a German,' screamed Andrew.

'It's easy to say that,' said Denys.

'Well, anyway, someone ought to tell the police,' said Charlie, 'and then they could say whether you're a German or not. I shall tell them.'

'You shan't,' cried Andrew.

'Well,' said Charlie to Denys, 'if he wasn't a German, why should he mind my telling the police?'

Andrew, by this time thoroughly furious, rushed at Charlie, who easily and quickly overpowered him.

'I told you he was a German,' Charlie said to Denys; 'he scratches, so he must be.'

'I'm not,' sobbed Andrew; then he quickly wiped his eyes and swallowed three times, because he heard Miss Clements coming.

They had now discovered that it was easy to tease Andrew into a frenzy, and that there was never any difficulty in overpowering him. Charlie and Denys and Hector, his chief tormentors, felt a sense of power which they had never experienced before and which was extremely delicious. They were undisputed rulers of the Boys' Class, and no one opposed them. John and Peter Paradise and Philip Grey, gentle and colourless creatures, stood aside and took no part. They used to walk with Andrew, but they never attempted to help him with anything more tangible than privately expressed sympathy; secretly they were content that he should be their scapegoat, and felt grateful to him for monopolizing the attentions of his tormentors.

One morning Andrew came into the class-room a little after the others, and found Hector and Charlie bending over the fire. Hector was heating the metal end of a pencil in the grate, hoping to make it red hot before Miss Clements came in. There did not seem to be much chance of doing this. Andrew's entry suggested a new idea.

'I know,' cried Denys, 'let's brand Andrew on the knee with it!'

'Let's!' said Hector, and jumped up and ran after Andrew. Andrew darted behind the table, but Charlie put himself in the way; and Hector touched his neck with the hot metal.

'Not my neck!' shrieked Andrew.

'If you'll let us burn your knee, we won't touch your neck,' said Charlie.

'All right,' said Andrew. He obediently took down his stocking and offered his knee to be branded. He had thought of struggling a little longer in case Miss Clements came in, but he was afraid that he would be overpowered before she came. It was better to give in than to be forced; and probably it would not hurt so much on his knee as on his neck. Hector gave one sharp, firm jab at Andrew's leg, and then let him go. He pulled up his stocking just as Miss Clements entered, and went to his place. Everyone seemed to approve of his quiet and sensible behaviour, and he hardly minded that his leg smarted.

After break Hector asked to examine Andrew's leg: a small circle of skin had been burned away, and there was quite a satisfactory mark. Hector was very much pleased with the success of his experiment and called the others to look. At that moment Miss Clements came in and dispersed the group. 'What's all this, children?' she demanded.

'Please, Miss Clements,' said Charlie, anxious to be the first with the information, 'Hector has burnt Andrew's leg.'

'What's this?' she asked. 'Andrew, come here and shew me exactly what has happened.'

Andrew took down his stocking, and again presented his knee for inspection. 'Poor child,' she said, 'tell me exactly how it was done.'

He began telling his story with great pleasure. He had only got as far as the branding when Miss Low came in.

'What has been happening, Miss Clements?' asked Miss Low.

'Hector has burnt Andrew on the knee with the top

of a pencil, which he heated in the fire,' said Miss Clements.

'Tell me what happened,' said Miss Low; and he had to tell the whole story from the beginning again. He was enjoying himself.

'Come with me, and I'll put something on your knee,' she said. 'I shall tell my sister about you, Hector, and we will decide how to punish you for your particularly mean and spiteful trick; now you will go straight to bed.' (Hector was a boarder, and in consequence the Misses Low had a greater opportunity to punish him.)

Miss Low took Andrew downstairs; she knocked on the class-room door. 'Fanny,' she said, 'I want a word with you. Will you kindly come into the drawing-room?'

Andrew had to repeat the whole story to Miss Fanny; he sat on the edge of the chintz sofa, while Miss Low bandaged his leg. 'But you ought to have told us at once,' exclaimed Miss Low; 'you ought to have had your leg attended to at once.'

'Why ever did you let Hector do it?' asked Miss Fanny.

'Because he'd have done it whether I let him or not,' said Andrew.

'Well, anyway, he shall be well punished,' decided Miss Fanny.

'He shall have the stick,' said Miss Low grimly.

'And no lunch,' added Miss Fanny.

'At any rate, no pudding. And he shall stay in bed for the rest of the day,' concluded Miss Low, fastening a safety-pin in Andrew's bandage. 'Now you had better go back to your lesson.'

Andrew was very popular for the rest of the day. Denys asked to walk with him, and wanted to hear all about his interview with the Misses Low. Andrew said they were going to beat Hector.

'H'm, I daresay Miss Low could swish him quite hard,' said Denys reflectively. 'I shouldn't think Miss Fanny would be much use, though.'

Denys was very amiable, and talked agreeably about his stamp collection. 'I've got a triangular Cape of Good Hope, and a Black Penny too. I couldn't bring them to school, or someone would bag them. Perhaps you might come to tea one day,' he suggested shyly, 'if we ever knew each other as well as that.'

Andrew timidly said that he should love to see them. They were both very shy. Children at Selborne never asked each other to tea if they did not already know each other 'at home,' unless they were very great friends. Denys began to think he had been a little forward, and so did Andrew; to his great annoyance he found himself hanging back timidly. He was afraid that he had discouraged Denys.

Aunt Anne called for Andrew after school that day. Miss Low asked her to come into the drawing-room, and apologized to her for Hector's conduct. 'Hector's an extraordinary boy,' she said; 'he's the son of a clergyman at Oxford, and his mother used to be a friend of mine. He was sent to us as a boarder, I suspect because they found him trying at home; but I was told a lot about his being so highly strung and needing careful attention and so forth. You know what some parents are like; they think their child is unique and needs such special treatment. I often wish all the children were orphans, they would be so much easier to manage. Well, to go back to Hector, he has been a nuisance from start to finish. Always begging to have the light on a little longer at night so that he can read his Bible; and then being such a little ruffian in the day.'

'It was very silly of Andrew to let him do it,' said Aunt Anne. 'I can't think why you didn't defend yourself, my dear child. Fancy taking down your stocking and holding out your knee to be branded. Why, it's just like turning the other cheek!'

Miss Low tactfully interrupted with renewed apologies. Her profession required her to possess a more exact knowledge of the scriptures than that of Mrs. Graves; she seemed to remember that 'to turn the other cheek' was not an expression of blame.

'But what was I to do?' said Andrew on the way home. 'If I didn't let Hector burn my knee, he'd have gone on burning my neck; and that was worse.'

'Well, you might have put up a fight, and shewn that you weren't going to let him have it his own way,' said Aunt Anne, in the pugnacious tone in which good peace-loving women usually discuss other people's combats.

'But everyone was on his side,' complained Andrew.

'Well, they might have helped you if you'd put up a fight,' said Aunt Anne. 'You can't expect anyone to help you, if you don't help yourself.'

'Well, they wouldn't,' said Andrew; 'they wanted to burn my knee as much as Hector did.'

'But, anyway, you had right on your side,' said Aunt Anne weakly. Andrew said no more; by her last feeble argument Aunt Anne had admitted that he was right. It was a pity that grown-ups needed so much argument before they could be brought to see reason.

After the branding Andrew was very much happier at school; unlike Aunt Anne, the other boys thought he had behaved very sensibly; much more sensibly than Charlie Green, who had given the whole thing away to Miss Clements, while Andrew had held his tongue. Hector had not been punished severely, and sympathy had not veered round to his side. Rosamund had seen the luncheon tray which was carried up to

151

him. 'He didn't have only bread and water,' she said indignantly. 'He had the same as everyone else. Even a jam tart.'

When Hector reappeared he was very facetious about his imprisonment. 'Miss Low came up and gave me a *religious* lecture,' he said, 'and then Miss Fanny came and tried to whack me.'

'What did she whack you with?' asked Charlie.

'Only the old family whacker,' answered Hector, irreverently designating Miss Fanny's plump hand.

'Well, *that* can't have hurt much,' said Denys with disgust.

III

In February Uncle William fell ill. On his Saturday
and Sunday walks with Stephen and Nandy, Andrew
often went to Uncle William's house with messages or
enquiries. Mrs. Pulker would come into the glass porch
to talk to them, and she was very miserable because
'the poor gentleman' was usually no better. These
visits made Andrew very unhappy; he had always been
afraid of Uncle William and had never cared for him,
but he was fond of Mrs. Pulker and was upset by her
red eyes and her sad and tired voice. Aunt Emma was
most attentive to Uncle William during his illness;
often Andrew was obliged to tell the Aunts that he had
seen her coming away from Uncle William's house, and
the Aunts' voices when they asked questions about Aunt
Emma became exceedingly severe.

One morning, before Andrew had got up, Gladys
came into Aunt Margaret's room. 'Mr. Stanfield's maid
has come,' she said, 'to say Mr. Stanfield passed away
at six o'clock this morning.'

The funeral was on Saturday, when Andrew did not
go to school. He was told that a lot of people were
coming to luncheon that day, and Aunt Anne asked
him to help her with a few preparations. She gave him
the heavy silver jardinière for the dining-room table to
polish, and they went together into the green-house
to choose a plant to put in it. Then Aunt Anne had to
be busy cutting up sponge cakes and spreading them
with strawberry jam and pouring sherry and custard
over them. Andrew was allowed to decorate the finished trifle with almonds and cherries and ratafias.
He was not allowed to help Aunt Margaret, who with

Gladys's assistance was bringing down the best dinner service of superb old Worcester china from the lumber-room, and was washing it ready for use.

From the kitchen came the sound of a continuous crashing of pots and pans, which served as an accompaniment to the high, cracked voice of little Mrs. Simpkin the cook, who was in a tantrum, and was singing her usual war-song:

> ' 'E said it would be pleasant
> As we went down the hill
> That we should go together,
> _ff_ BUT I DON'T THINK IT WILL.'

'Is Mrs. Simpkin _very_ bad to-day?' asked Andrew sympathetically.

'_Very_,' answered Aunt Anne. 'When I went into the kitchen to order luncheon, I found her in the middle of the room with her arms akimbo, and wearing a velvet toque. When she has that on, it's a sure sign she's on the war-path.'

'Why is she mad to-day?' asked Andrew.

'Don't ask me,' said Aunt Anne; 'she usually likes there to be "company" for luncheon.'

A bell rang; Mrs. Simpkin burst out of her kitchen brandishing a wooden spoon. 'The front-door bell!' she cried dramatically, 'and where is Miss Milburn to answer it, I should like to know!'

Aunt Anne and Andrew giggled nervously when Mrs. Simpkin had retired again to her own kingdom. 'What a trial she is!' sighed Aunt Anne. 'I wish she were only mad in March, like Bunny. And it's going to be such an everlasting day with all these people coming.'

'Who are they?' he enquired.

'Oh, relatives, all relatives,' she groaned. 'To begin with, there's Uncle Aubrey and Aunt Emma and Cynthia,

154

whom you know, of course. And there's Cousin Ponsonby and Cousin Blanche from Eastbourne, whom you've forgotten, I expect. Dear me, I must see if there is enough whisky for them; they get through a vast quantity of the beastly stuff. Then there are the Crawleys, Cousin Ada and Cousin Harriet. I'm not sure if you've met them since you were a baby. How shall we arrange the table? Cousin Harriet must be as far as possible from Cousin Blanche.'

'Why? Doesn't she like her?'

'She can't bear her! She's an awful snob, and of course Cousin Blanche isn't quite *quite*. You must be *frightfully* careful how you behave when Cousin Harriet is there. For goodness' sake don't have hiccups.'

'Can I sit next to Cousin Blanche?' demanded Andrew.

'You can if you like; but you wouldn't enjoy it much. Let's arrange the table. We'll put the mustard-pot there; that stands for Aunt Margaret, and she'll have to sit there. I shall sit opposite; that salt-cellar will do for me.'

'Who's the red pepper going to be?' asked Andrew.

'It had better be Cousin Ponsonby; he's a peppery little man. And you can be the pepper-mill, because you're peppery, too. And we'll have an oil bottle for Aunt Emma, and a vinegar bottle for Cousin Harriet; because they're rather like oil and vinegar. Now we'll begin moving them about; remember Cousin Harriet (that's the vinegar) isn't to sit next Cousin Blanche. I don't know what will do for her; we'll have to use the whisky bottle to stand for her. Remember to keep the vinegar and the whisky separated.'

Andrew and Aunt Anne had a lovely game of permutations and combinations with their relations, until they had finally arranged them as well as possible.

Aunt Margaret came in. 'Are you two still gossiping?' she said.

'We're arranging the table,' said Andrew importantly; 'the oil is Aunt Emma, the vinegar is Cousin Harriet, and the whisky is Cousin Blanche.'

'What a shame!' said Aunt Margaret, and laughed. 'Well, the whisky and the vinegar will be here in a moment and catch us in our overalls if we don't hurry.'

Cousin Ada and Cousin Harriet were the first to arrive. Cousin Ada was a tall woman with a very sharp nose and high cheek-bones, and she wore a very large hat. Cousin Harriet was stout and had a deceitful appearance of geniality; at first sight people usually preferred her to her sister, who was in fact very much less objectionable.

Both sisters were volubly affectionate. 'Deah Anne, deah Margaret, *darling* Andrew,' they cried, sharply pecking each of them on the cheek ; and then, assuming a solemn voice, 'Poor Uncle William!' they said in unison.

'But it was a happy release,' said Harriet.

'May he rest in peace,' said Ada self-consciously; she was High Church.

'One has to resign oneself to old people going,' said Harriet in a tone of deep resignation; 'but there are youngah people who could be spared bettah.' She paused; and Mrs. Graves, Miss Milburn, and Andrew all applied her last remark to themselves. They were relieved to find that she had someone else in mind. 'Are Ponsonby and Blanche coming?' she asked sharply.

'Yes, we're expecting them any minute now,' said Miss Milburn.

'I trust they will be sobah,' said Ada kindly.

'I should *hawdly* think that even Blanche would exceed on such an occasion,' remarked her sister. 'I hope, Anne, that you will offah them nothing strongah than cidah.'

'Oh, we shall have to give them whisky, Harriet,' said Mrs. Graves. 'But fortunately there isn't very much in the house.'

'Perhaps I ought not to repeat it,' said Ada discreetly, 'but someone, whose name I must not mention, told us that Ponsonby and Blanche carry a large supply of whisky with them everywhere in their car, in a petrol tin.'

The Quenby party were shewn in by Gladys. 'Well, here we are, Margaret,' said Mrs. Milburn, 'so good of you, such a large party I'm afraid.'

'Deah Aubrey, deah Emmah, *darling* Cynthiah!' ejaculated the Crawleys, and then with returning solemnity: 'We have had a very sad loss.'

Cynthia and Andrew, overwhelmed by the atmosphere of immense family solidarity in the face of death, were sitting in a corner of the room, pretending to chat cheerfully about Quenby. The booming voices of the Crawleys continued to rise and fall.

'. . . a meah fawmah's wife, my dear Emmah, not at all our class,' Harriet was saying.

'I presume the municipality will be present, as our poor Uncle was mayah,' said Ada to Miss Milburn.

'So I said to her,' continued Harriet, 'I am sorry, Mrs. Timms, but I could *hawdly* do that. Do not you think I was right?'

'Yes, I do think you were so right,' agreed Emma soothingly.

Mr. Ponsonby Stanfield and Mrs. Stanfield were shewn in. Ponsonby was a red-faced, bald little man of about sixty, with one of those fierce military moustaches which used to be found in Christmas crackers. Blanche was even redder in the face, and her rising bosom strained against her ill-fitting mourning; wisps of hair escaped from under her enormous hat, on to which crape had been pinned haphazardly, and a discerning eye could distinguish the huge roses which were hidden by it.

'Ah, howdy doo, howdy doo, hope we're not late,' exclaimed Ponsonby.

'Deah Ponsonby, deah Blanche, such a pleasure,' ejaculated the Crawleys.

'Just 'ad time for a quick one before we came here,' whispered Blanche to Harriet, whom she delighted in shocking.

Harriet drew herself up and flinched. 'This is a very sad occasion,' she said reproachfully.

'Yes, I'm sorry the poor old boy's snuffed out,' said Blanche with great cheerfulnesss.

'Luncheon is ready,' said Miss Milburn hastily.

Mrs. Graves gave Andrew a conspiratorial smile, and began to distribute the cousins in their proper places; they were very tiresome. Harriet said affectionately: 'May I sit next to deah Andrew,' and Ada wanted to talk to Aubrey. Everyone wanted to avoid Ponsonby and Blanche. 'Will you sit by me, Blanche?' said Mrs. Graves heroically, 'and Ponsonby, will you sit there by Margaret?'

'You must be so nervous of air-raids at Eastbourne,' said Harriet to Ponsonby; 'how fortunate that you have a good large cellah, into which you can always retire.'

'It don't take an air-raid to send Ponsonby to the cellar,' said Blanche jocosely.

'H'm, ah,' said Ponsonby nervously, 'I mean to say, er, what I mean is — that is what I was going to say — it's a very singular thing that you've been so free from air-raids at Handborough Regis.'

'A big bomb fell in Albemarle Terrace last week and killed a telegraph boy,' Andrew corrected him.

'And are you going to be a soldier, darling, when you grow up, and fight those horrid Germans?' asked Harriet fatuously.

'No, Cousin Harriet,' said Andrew distantly.

'Perhaps you would rather go into the Church,' said Ada gently.

'What's that?' asked Andrew.

'Cousin Ada means perhaps you'd like to be a clergyman, like the Vicar,' explained Mrs. Graves.

'I should be horrified at the idea,' exclaimed Andrew.

'I think your Vicah at Handborough such a fine type of clargyman,' remarked Harriet acidly.

A plum pudding, a trifle, and some jam tartlets were brought in.

'Ha, *embarras de richesse!*' cried Ponsonby.

'Three puddings in war-time!' remarked Emma. 'We never have more than one at Quenby.'

'One never knows what everyone will like,' said Mrs. Graves, rather nettled.

'You don't get such a choice at school I expect,' said Harriet severely to Andrew.

'No,' he answered crossly.

'The last time I went to a funeral, was poor Lord Lamberfield's at Harrogate,' said Ada importantly.

Blanche began:

'There was a young curate of Harrogate,
Who said: "There's a strait and a narrow gate". . .'

'Hush, Blanche, *please* — not at a funeral,' implored Ponsonby.

'You must tell me the rest some other time, Blanche,' said Aubrey with great good nature, and incurred a disdainful glance from Harriet Crawley.

'You'd better run upstairs now, dear,' said Mrs. Graves to Andrew. 'Say good-bye to everyone.'

'May I go up and see Stephen?' said Cynthia, tired of the company downstairs.

'Do, my dear,' said Mrs. Graves sympathetically.

Soon the cousins had to be sorted into carriages: in the first were the Crawleys, and the Quenby party; in the second the Aunts and the Stanfields. Blanche was very loquacious indeed; and at close quarters the Aunts were sorry to find that she smelt strongly of whisky.

'Nothing like a little spot,' she was saying, 'to keep the cold out; and it ain't altogether amusing to stand about in the cemetery planting Uncle William on a day like this. I bet the Vicar has taken a spot too.'

They were met by the stately figure of the Vicar, flanked by a shivering curate on either side. A melancholy grocer's assistant carried the cross; he was in his element. He had looked forward to this through a whole morning of weighing butter and slicing bacon.

'I am the resurrection and the life,' said the Vicar.

Mrs. Pulker had refused to come to the funeral; she said the family would think she was presuming; besides, she had to get tea ready for them when they came back. When the 'poor gentleman' was carried away, she went down to her kitchen and sat in front of the fire with her old hands folded, staring into the red coals. Presently she was roused by a bell-ring; it could not be any of the family, she hoped; surely they were all at the churchyard. It was Mrs. Marshall from next door. Mrs. Marshall was now a lady and kept servants of her own, but once she had been in service under Mrs. Pulker.

Mrs. Marshall kissed her. 'Yes, it's me, Mother Pulker,' she said, 'and I've come to sit with you a bit. I knew you'd be feeling low.' Mrs. Marshall found the little brown tea-pot and made tea. 'There, I've made you a nice cup of tea, dearie,' she said; 'drink it up, there's a lamb, and you'll feel better.'

Old Mrs. Pulker drank her cup of tea. 'You're very kind to me, Martha,' she said, and started to whimper.

'You have a good cry, dearie,' said Mrs. Marshall.

Mrs. Pulker had a good cry, and then Mrs. Marshall made her drink another cup of tea.

'Now I must be getting tea for the family,' said Mrs. Pulker anxiously.

'I'll help you cut bread and butter,' said Mrs. Marshall; 'and I've brought you in a lovely jam sandwich I baked this morning: I expect you haven't much in the house.'

'You're a good friend to me, Martha,' said the poor old soul; 'many's a one would have become stuck up in your position.'

'Nonsense, Mother Pulker,' said Mrs. Marshall, 'and when everything is over here, you're coming straight to me, d'you see?'

The morning-room was arranged for the reading of the will; the heavy chairs were placed in a semicircle ready for the family to sit and hear what Uncle William had left them. Mrs. Marshall left just as the family were coming in. They were already whispering and speculating; Emma was in an exuberant state of excitement, and was avoided with considerable coldness by everyone except her husband and daughter.

They took up their seats, staring self-consciously in front of them at the black marble clock, which no one had wound up since Uncle William had died. Ponsonby, who was an executor, stood up in the middle and pompously spluttered through the will.

Uncle William had made a will very satisfactory to

his heirs. He had not left all his property to Emma, but all the same he had left her an equal share with his nephews and nieces; whereas, being only a relation by marriage, she ought to have had nothing at all. The relatives had therefore their grievance against Emma, without being obliged to pay for it too dearly, and they went into dining-room tea in a very comfortable state of indignation.

'Deah Emmah,' said Harriet, 'you were always *so* attentive to poor Uncle William. How nice that you have your reward.'

Ponsonby was fidgeting nervously. 'I say, Anne,' he whispered, 'I can't take tea, you know. Poison to me. Forbidden by the doctor on account of nerves. Do you think we could possibly ask Mrs. Pulker . . .'

Blanche said to Miss Milburn in a penetrating whisper: 'I say, Margaret, do you think the old girl could find us a drop of whisky?'

Mrs. Pulker was standing nervously at the door. 'Is there anything . . . ?' she asked.

'I wonder if you can find some whisky for Mr. and Mrs. Stanfield; they don't take tea,' said Miss Milburn.

'Would brandy do?' she answered. 'I'm afraid there's no whisky.'

'Perfectly, Mrs. Pulker, perfectly,' said Ponsonby with strained cheerfulness, pretending not to notice Harriet's freezing glance.

'Disgusting tea,' said Emma with a grimace.

'Ha, Emma, you'd better join us in a glass of brandy when it comes,' said Ponsonby.

'I think I shall,' said Emma exuberantly; 'the tea is filthy — like seaweed.'

Mrs. Pulker brought in a bottle of brandy and two glasses. 'One for me too,' said Emma, 'please Mrs. Pulker. I'm having a day out.'

'Certainly, madam,' said Mrs. Pulker coldly. ('And the poor gentleman not two hours in his grave,' she was thinking. 'And Mrs. Milburn, as was always so devoted to him.')

'Here's how!' said Blanche, seizing her glass of brandy.

Ada made a diversion: 'Who was that person who left just as we came into the house?'

'The woman next door,' replied Miss Milburn, 'Mrs. Marshall.'

'Do you mean the ownah of the house next door?' said Ada. 'She hawdly looked like a lady.'

'Oh, she's risen in the world,' answered Miss Milburn; 'she was once in service as a housemaid, and Mrs. Pulker was cook at the same place. They're great friends. Mrs. Marshall is a good kind creature.'

'Deah me, you don't mean to say so,' said Harriet. 'How this neighbahhood has gone down. Formahly such nice people used to live in Tredegar Park. I nevah knew it had come to this. Could not Uncle William, as an ex-magistrate, have done something to preserve the amenities of the neighbahhood?'

Emma rose: 'I'm going to find Mrs. Pulker, to get her to help me look for a ring which Uncle William left to Gladys. If it isn't found at once, it's sure to get into the sale; and then it will be gone for ever.'

Aubrey protested: 'I shouldn't bother the poor old thing to-day; she's very upset, and she's had a lot to do.'

Emma said firmly: 'I certainly mean to find that ring at once, or it will be muddled away.'

'Emma, please leave it now,' said Miss Milburn. 'I will see Mrs. Pulker about it to-morrow when she has less to do.'

'Kindly don't interfere, Margaret,' said Mrs. Milburn angrily and rang the bell. 'Mrs. Pulker,' she said, 'I want you to help me to find a sapphire ring which Mr.

163

Stanfield left to Miss Gladys. It was her great-grandmother's.'

'Perhaps you'll come to the safe, ma'am,' said Mrs. Pulker, 'if Mr. Ponsonby will lend us the key.'

'Emmah is remarkably prompt in claiming her inheritance,' said Harriet, as Emma left the room.

'She's a bit nervous to-day,' said Aubrey apologetically; 'she's been very much upset, of course. She was so *very* fond of Uncle William.'

'*Ça se voit,*' said Blanche.

Harriet drew herself up: she did not understand French, and thought that anything said in that language was improper, or at best too frivolous for a funeral.

Emma burst in: 'I've found the ring, so we've nothing to wait for, Aubrey.

'Well, good-bye,' Aubrey began saying nervously.

'Good-bye,' said Emma; 'I shall see you, Anne and Margaret, at the sale, I expect.'

There was a moment's silence after Emma and Aubrey and Cynthia had gone. Harriet broke it. 'Reahlly!' she exclaimed.

'Emma has been behaving in a most extraordinary way,' said Ponsonby eagerly. He was almost grateful to her for being the scapegoat; at most family gatherings all the odium fell on Blanche. 'Very extraordinary indeed; remarkably bad taste, I consider.'

'Of course she was wildly excited about the will,' said Miss Milburn. 'She hoped that she and Aubrey were going to get everything.'

'She was lucky to get anything at all,' said Harriet; 'she was no real relation. Uncle William might as well have left something to Blanche.'

'*I* never toadied the poor old boy,' said Blanche.

'Emma was over here *constantly*,' remarked Mrs. Graves.

'Harriet, have you brought the yawd-measure?' asked Ada after a short silence.

'What do you mean, Adah?' said Harriet, who had a small business transaction in mind, but intended to outstay Anne and Margaret, who might be shocked.

'Surely you can hawdly have forgotten,' continued Ada, 'we meant to measure the settee here, to see if it would fit in our hall?'

'We could hawdly do that . . .' demurred Harriet.

'You had far better take the measurements while you are here,' said Miss Milburn sensibly. 'Otherwise you would only have to write, and that is never so satisfactory.'

'Of course, if you reahlly will not think it heartless . . .' began Harriet, taking a tape measure from her bag. 'And perhaps while we are here we might look at some othah things. We shall have no othah opportunity, I expect.'

Ponsonby and Blanche left, followed by Mrs. Graves and Miss Milburn, who left Ada and Harriet in possession, measuring the furniture and the pictures and taking copious notes.

THE Summer Term was Andrew's last at Selborne. At Michaelmas he was going to preparatory school in Handborough as a weekly boarder, and would only spend his week-ends at home. The Aunts made him try on a great many clothes, which he loathed, and tried to convince him that he would be very happy at Holmlea. Mrs. Stephens, the headmaster's wife, was so very nice, they said; and the garden was so very pretty; and one of the boys had just won a scholarship at Winchester. Andrew pretended to be interested; he even read the prospectus on glossy paper, illustrated with photographs, and tied with a green and white ribbon. He said cheerfully enough that the garden looked pretty. He did not say that the pit of his stomach felt cold whenever he thought of Holmlea, and that to talk to him of the prettiness of the garden was only insulting. It was so obviously unimportant in comparison with the fact that he was going to be plunged into a new and hostile world; Selborne had sometimes been bad enough, but at least he could always go home to tea.

He lived through his last weeks at Selborne with an emotional intensity, because they were the end of a period in his life. He was now unmolested by the other boys and was a favourite with the mistresses, and his last term was happy. He set himself to enjoy it passionately, being convinced that he would never be happy again. He even loved the clothes which he wore at school; they were considered babyish by the other boys, who laughed at his white blouse, and the little silk tasselled cord which tied at the neck. He had sometimes been ashamed of his tassels; now he loved them because he

166

would soon have to give them up, and would be made to wear a green and white tie.

There was no crocodile in the summer term; at the end of morning school the children ran along Northumberland Avenue to 'the Field'. This was a recent purchase of which the Miss Lows were very proud. In this small recreation ground the children were allowed to amuse themselves as they pleased, under the tolerant supervision of Miss Clements. The boys played 'Red Indians', or were sometimes persuaded by Miss Clements to get up a game of cricket. Andrew did not care for their games. He made friends with a lonely girl called Millicent, who was not amused by tennis, and with whom no girls wanted to talk secrets. They used to make mud-pies; often for the sake of privacy they carried their mud into the summer-house, and made their pies on a pretty little inlaid table which the Miss Lows foolishly kept there. Millicent was exceedingly good-natured, and allowed Andrew to order her about as much as he pleased.

As the last days came, Andrew felt that Selborne was slipping away from him, that he would leave and take nothing with him but himself, just as he had brought nothing but himself when he came. He did not love Selborne, but it seemed so wasteful to bring nothing away. Sometimes he tried to make time stand still, so that he might keep some moment for ever. He felt with the strong solipsism of childhood that the external world, the class-room where he was sitting, the maps and the black-board, the other children and Miss Clements herself, were only day-dreams dependent on his consciousness. If he did not think about them, they would not be there. Conversely, if he thought about them hard enough, they would be preserved by his thought, and would last for ever. He would therefore choose some moment to keep for ever; not any moment of extreme happiness or excitement, but some moment at which his mind was particularly clear and prepared for concentration. He would fix his attention on every sound, and let his eye travel along the wall in front of him, embracing every detail in its keen observation. Under this examination faces would take on fresh expressions, and even an ink-stain on the wall would leap into life, acquiring a significant relation to everything else, within a whole system of mysterious and vivid reality.

'I've caught it,' he would think; then gradually the tension of his mind would relax, and the moment would slip from his grasp, flowing like countless other moments down the ineluctable stream of time. Another day he would try to bring the moment back again. If the classroom and the other children and Miss Clements depended on his consciousness for reality, he thought that if he concentrated hard enough on some remembered detail, on the ink-stain on the wall, or on a hole in the oil-cloth on the table, he could bring back everything into being again. Sometimes in bed he would clench his fists, and strain as if with the effort of pulling the past back into life; often it would seem to tremble on the brink of reality, and then would suddenly sink like Eurydice to death again.

At the end of the term he did his first examination; nearly every paper revealed to him the power and quickness of his opening intelligence, and he answered the history paper with brilliance. Throughout the examination his energies and interests were completely absorbed in his work; he was hardly conscious of the others fidgeting or biting their pens and sighing; he wrote with single-minded vigour. On the last day he went to prize-giving, and was not at all surprised to receive the prize for the Boys' Class from Miss Low. She said: 'I am sure you will all be glad that Andrew Faringdon has won the prize for the Boys' Class, because he is leaving.' Andrew went back to his place blushing furiously; all the school clapped, and Denys clapped him on the back. Miss Low and Miss Fanny kissed him when he left with Nandy and Stephen, and they said they hoped he would come to see them some time. Denys called after him: 'Good-bye, Andrew, so glad you got the prize.'

PART III

1917

I

THE relations between Emma Milburn and her husband's family had never been friendly, and when she had the misfortune or the indiscretion to become involved in an unpleasant scandal a few years after her marriage, it was not surprising that they took the most uncharitable view of her conduct. Emma's dislike of her sisters-in-law turned to an active resentment, and feeling that they had injured her, she in her turn took every possible occasion to do them mischief. In the past twenty years she had paid off old scores with such generous interest that she no longer hated Anne and Margaret for the grievance that she had against them; she hated them with a far deeper hatred because of the mean and spiteful tricks which she had so often used in revenge.

When Andrew and Stephen came to Quenby after their mother's death, it at once occurred to Emma that if she could secure their guardianship it would be an excellent way of spiting her sisters-in-law. This scheme also appealed to a side of her character on which she could dwell with more self-satisfaction. A love of managing the affairs of as many people as possible was even more firmly rooted in her nature than hatred of her husband's family. She regarded herself as a universal benefactress, and had little doubt but that Andrew and Stephen, or indeed anyone else, would be better off under her care; it was therefore almost a duty to get hold of them.

From the first Emma had made an ally of Nandy, whom she had treated with great consideration at Quenby, and to whom she had made a few surreptitious visits in the nursery at Handborough Regis. It was openly agreed between them that Andrew and Stephen would be better off at Quenby, where they would have the advantages of a country life and of the companionship of their cousins; and Nandy was made to feel that her own position would there be free from the many embarrassments of which she complained at the Aunts' house.

Emma had also shewn what attention she could to the second Mrs. Faringdon, who fancied, not without reason, that she had been slighted by the rest of the Milburn family. At the same time that she had invited Oswald and Elsa to Quenby, Emma had taken the opportunity of putting Anne and Margaret further in the wrong with them. She had invited them to come over to lunch, without telling them that the Faringdons were there and expecting to meet them; and when they refused (as she knew they would), she was able to give the impression that they were deliberately refusing to meet Elsa.

With Nandy and Elsa on her side, it was not very difficult to work upon Oswald until he too was convinced that his children would be better off at Quenby than at Handborough. He would even so have hesitated to make a change so painful to the feelings of his sisters-in-law, if Emma had not worked up his indignation against them by representing them as deliberately trying to set the children against Elsa. Various incidents were reported to him: that Andrew dared not put up her photograph at Handborough; that once in the nursery he had let slip 'that German woman', no doubt the name that was given to her in the drawing-room. In anger he wrote to Emma that the children should go straight to Quenby from the Isle of Wight, where they were at that time spending their summer holidays with

174

their Aunt Mary and Frank; and he sent a telegram to the Aunts to inform them of his decision.

The children were rather surprised to be taken to Quenby when they left the Isle of Wight; but there were still some days left before Andrew's term at Holmlea began, and they were well enough content to pass them in the garden there. The elder cousins had not yet gone back to school, and were very kind to them. That summer the gold-fish in the pond were suffering from disease; the children used to go down and count the number of fish they could see swimming about feebly, and growing paler in colour. Then their silver-white bodies began to float to the surface. Tom landed a large corpse with a butterfly net, and deposited it in a herbaceous border. The fish was visited as a curiosity for several days, but it soon became extremely unsavoury. Philip suggested that they should have a grand funeral. 'Do let's,' cried Andrew, enchanted to hear him propose a game after his own heart. Flora, more modern and up-to-date, said that the fish ought to be cremated.

As the result of his extreme enthusiasm, Andrew succeeded in being appointed to direct the *pompes funèbres*. The funeral was fixed for the next morning at eleven o'clock, and in the intervening time the dead fish was the only object of his thoughts and conversation. Everyone else was intensely bored by his energy and his countless new ideas for the funeral ceremony.

All the cousins came to the funeral. Andrew had built a pyre with sticks and fir-cones, and had well sprinkled it with lavender to drown the smell of the deceased. Cynthia had consented to be the widow of the fish and the chief mourner, and appeared in an old black veil, thoughtfully carrying a bottle of methylated spirit in case her late husband should not prove easily inflammable. The ashes were carried on a spade in procession to the other side of the garden, to a group of fir-trees which the cousins called 'the church'; there Philip conducted a short burial service, and they left the fish in a grave strewn with flowers.

Andrew had thoroughly enjoyed the game and now looked everywhere for dead birds or mice; he looked forward to having a neat cemetery of animals, all ceremoniously interred. He thought perhaps he would be an undertaker when he grew up, instead of writing history books.

He asked Miss Hunt one day: 'Have you seen anything to bury?'

'No, I haven't,' she answered shortly in her gruff voice — somehow or other she seemed very disagreeable nowadays. 'A nasty morbid game,' she said.

Andrew was hurt; playing funerals was as good as any other game, and if she did not happen to care for it herself, she need not be so snappy.

There was a small island in the pond; the children used to cross on to it by a plank. There was little enough to do when one was there; half the island was occupied by a large bamboo, and there was barely room for four children to stand on the other half. Andrew was lured on to the island by Tom one afternoon, and marooned there; it was very easy to take the plank away. He screamed and called, but no one came; there was no one in sight. He was afraid he should be late for tea; perhaps he might even be left out all night. He flung himself down on the grass and cried, and beat the ground with his fists, but no one came. He remembered that he had once thought it would be fun to be shipwrecked on a desert island, and nearly revised his opinion. But that would not be the same thing, he thought; on a desert island there would be room to walk about, and things to do; such as killing wild birds and beasts, and building a hut, and in other ways making the island suitable for a prolonged stay. It was merely exasperating to be marooned within sight of the house, and to have to waste an hour or two waiting for a deliverer. He stood up again, and screamed till he was hoarse.

Miss Hunt and Nandy came down the path with Stephen, and delivered him. 'What's this, Andrew?' said Miss Hunt crossly.

'Tom put me here, and took the plank away,' said Andrew.

'Poor child, did you have to stay here a *long* time,' asked Nandy.

'Yes,' he said.

Miss Hunt was very much annoyed: she knew that she would have to punish Tom for behaving badly to Andrew; that meant that Nandy was one up on her. She could not wipe out the score by saying that Andrew had been a tell-tale; Tom had left him in obvious distress, from which she herself had been obliged to rescue him.

Philip and Arthur went back to school, and Andrew began to be surprised that there was still no talk of their return to Handborough Regis. Nandy evaded questions with the vague statement: 'You were looking a little off colour, dear; and we don't think you're quite strong enough to go to a boarding-school just yet. Surely you aren't anxious to leave Quenby and go to school?'

It was Tom who let the bombshell fall. Andrew was sitting on a garden seat reading *Coral Island*, when Tom rode up to him on a tricycle. 'You're coming to live with us,' said Tom, in the tone of one who is proud to be first with the news.

'I don't believe you,' said Andrew; 'who told you?'

'Mother told me, you can ask her yourself.'

Andrew went straight indoors to find Nandy; she was sewing in the nursery, an upstairs sitting-room still used by the Milburn children, though all of them had now come to school-room age. Aunt Emma was there talking to her.

'Nandy,' he cried, 'Tom says we've come to live here; have we?'

Nandy looked enquiringly at Mrs. Milburn, who smiled and said: 'Perhaps it was as well that it should come out that way.'

'Aren't you pleased?' asked Nandy enthusiastically.

'Am I going to school?' enquired Andrew, still puzzled and feeling his way.

'No, dear,' said Aunt Emma, 'your father doesn't think you're quite ready for school, so you're going to stay here, and do lessons with Tom and Mabel.'

'*Won't* that be lovely?' said Nandy.

Andrew felt a vast relief; he was not going to wear that green and white tie and that school suit, which the Aunts had bought him. He did not think about Tom and Mabel and Miss Hunt; he could only think of his reprieve from Holmlea.

'That will be lovely,' he said, adding with unconscious dishonesty: 'I always wondered why we never came to live here before.'

Nandy and Aunt Emma were very pleased with Andrew for making such a quotable remark. On the first opportunity Nandy said to Miss Hunt: 'Miss Hunt, *do* you know what Andrew said when he heard that we were coming to live here now? He said: "I always wondered why we never came to live here before!" '

'H'm,' said Miss Hunt, 'and I wonder very much why yer've come to live here now.'

Andrew was puzzled and hurt; Miss Hunt did not

178

seem to want them. He had a cold feeling inside; he had escaped from Holmlea and from those horrible school clothes only to be sent to the school-room with Tom and Mabel, whom he thoroughly disliked; and now Miss Hunt seemed to have taken a sudden dislike to him. If he had been at Handborough Regis he would always have had the Aunts to come back to at week-ends, there would have been an escape from Holmlea. At Quenby there would be no escape from Miss Hunt and Tom and Mabel.

When he went to bed that night in the store-room, he thought of his bed at Handborough in Aunt Margaret's room. 'Poor little bed!' he thought. Aunt Margaret would be sorry too; there would be no one to talk to while she was dressing for dinner, or when she got up in the mornings. Perhaps his bed would be taken away, and put in the lumber-room with the best dinner service. He cried himself to sleep, and refused to tell Nandy why he was crying.

A few days later Mrs. Milburn went into Handborough
Regis to do some shopping, and nearly ran into her
sisters-in-law in the High Street; with a terrified glance
in their direction, she fled for sanctuary into the first
shop, which happened to be a monumental mason's.
She came back to Quenby with a most amusing story of
how a persistent salesman had tried to sell her a Celtic
cross.

At Quenby the Aunts were now regarded as an oppo-
sition party in the family. Mrs. Milburn started this by
little jests at their expense. In her stories the Aunts
were represented as suspicious and rather ridiculous old
women, eaten up with malice against herself. Of course
she was very fond of them really — they were dears in
their way — and their attitude to herself was at once
pathetic and amusing.

This delicately insinuated hostility to the Aunts was
expressed more openly and rudely by the younger Milburns. One wet afternoon Cynthia and a friend under-
took to amuse the younger children, and fetched them
into the drawing-room to sing popular songs. Cynthia
said she would teach them *What d'you want to make
those eyes at me for?* She laughed and said: 'It will be
useful to sing to Aunt Anne if you meet her in Handborough Regis one day.' Turning to her friend, she
explained: 'We have some aunts with whom we aren't
exactly on good terms.'

'My dear, aunts are frightful,' said her friend. '*None*
of ours can endure us, which is just as well because
they're *too* poisonous.'

Andrew looked out of the window dolefully, and

watched the rain fall. He thought how much he would like to see Aunt Anne coming towards him; she would understand how wretchedly unhappy he was. Or perhaps she would not, and it would not matter, because his unhappiness would vanish at her coming. He wanted to run away for comfort; he would have liked to bury his head in Nandy's apron and cry. But if he told Nandy he was crying because he was at Quenby, Nandy would tell him that it was wrong and wicked, and ungrateful to God, who had so kindly brought him there from Handborough Regis. It was so terrible to be unhappy, and to suspect that one was wicked in being unhappy. One would certainly be punished for it by God, and made more unhappy still. He tried to sing Cynthia's dreadful songs, but his voice caught; he decided that it was safer not to sing, and stood at the back of the others.

Cynthia and her friend started singing patriotic songs. With unbearable persistence they sang a song with the refrain:

> Berlin, Berlin,
> We never shall give in,
> We never shall be satisfied
> Until we reach Berlin!

Andrew slipped silently out of the room; they thought he had gone to the lavatory, and so he had. He sat there and cried, burying his face in his hands. 'They can't find me here!' he thought.

Nandy went into Handborough Regis to fetch some of the children's things, an errand which she performed without much consideration for the Aunts' feelings. She returned to Quenby annoyed with them for giving her so little help. They had tried to keep behind anything that the children especially valued, for two excellent reasons; they hoped that Oswald might repent and give them back the children, and they were afraid that any books or toys which once went to Duckwold would never leave it.

Andrew had naturally been looking forward to Nandy's return with all the Boches and the Teddy bears and the other children, and his toy fire-engine, and his favourite kite. Nandy came back with very few of these things, and when Andrew said indignantly: 'But, Nandy, you *promised* to bring them,' she answered: 'I'm sorry, dear, but your Aunt Anne had put them away somewhere, and I couldn't.'

They were having tea in the school-room. Mabel said: 'The Aunts seem to be keeping all your toys. Perhaps they want to give them away to some children in Handborough Regis.'

Andrew was furious; his faith in the Aunts was suddenly shaken. They were keeping all his toys from him. Perhaps they had stolen them to give to horrid little Hutton, the doctor's son, of whom they were so fond. He could now quite understand why Aunt Emma talked about them in that facetious way, and why Cynthia did not like them. The people at Quenby were right; and he would be on their side against the Aunts.

'It's horrid of the Aunts to keep all your things,' said Tom; 'after all, they're yours.'

'It's too bad of them to steal my fire-engine,' lamented Andrew.

'Andrew,' said Miss Hunt crossly, 'yer mustn't say that about yer Aunts. Of course they wouldn't steal anything. Yer Aunt Emma wouldn't like to hear yer say that, *I* know.'

Andrew was sadly perplexed; here was everyone at Quenby saying all manner of things against the Aunts, and directly he joined in Miss Hunt seemed to find it necessary to snap his head off.

'But Tom said . . .' he began to protest angrily.

' 'Sh, dear,' said Nandy.

After tea she said to him: 'You know, Andrew, you mustn't say anything rude about the Aunts; after all, they are your Uncle Aubrey's sisters, and your Aunt Emma's sisters-in-law.'

Andrew was unhappy and puzzled; he had been rude about the Aunts because everyone at Quenby was rude about them, and because his own faith in them had begun to waver. Then he was scolded, and told that the people at Quenby did not like what he had said, and that he must be polite about the Aunts for Aunt Emma's sake. That was ridiculous, because she hated them. Andrew was the only person at Quenby, except Stephen, who was ever really fond of them; and now he was uncertain whether to be on their side, or to side with the Milburns against them.

For the moment he sided with the Milburns; he did not like them, and he was not convinced at heart that the Aunts were wrong in the quarrel, but he could not yet feel his way. In the meanwhile it was easier to acquiesce in anything that the cousins or Nandy said, than to defend the Aunts who were absent.

He was given a longer holiday than the other children. Nandy told him that it was good for him 'to rest his little brain', and the doctor said so too. Andrew was taken into Handborough to see the cousin's doctor, Dr. Waring; he disliked his consultations. Aunt Emma and Nandy used to whisper to the doctor too much; and once or twice they sent Andrew into the drawing-room to talk to Mrs. Waring, while they had a long talk with the doctor behind his back. He used to become frightened and uneasy; sometimes he was afraid that they were plotting unpleasant cures for him, perhaps they were going to operate on him, or perhaps they were going to shut him up in a dark room and forbid him to read. Sometimes he began to be afraid that he had a serious illness, but a great many delightful people had wasted away and died young, and he did not altogether dislike the idea. There was not really very much to live for. Stephen would miss him, of course, but he was young enough to get over it very quickly. Henceforward he would not bother to think what he should do when he was grown-up; he would die young.

Dr. Waring was very cheerful and silly; he evidently did not intend that Andrew should die just yet, but it did not seem likely that he could do much to prevent it, if he were sufficiently ill. He invariably called him 'dear boy', and spoke of him to Aunt Emma as 'dear Andwew'. When Nandy forgot to bring a prescription with her he told her that she was 'a vewy wicked woman'. Andrew drank a few bottles of a green concoction prescribed for him by Dr. Waring; and then his visits ceased. Mrs. Milburn wrote to the Aunts that Dr. Waring was *so* pleased with his improvement in health during his stay at Quenby.

Andrew was now allowed to do a few lessons with Miss Hunt and Mabel and Tom. He sat with them for an hour every morning, learning reading, writing and arithmetic; but directly they had a history lesson or anything else that was interesting he had to go away. Miss Hunt would say crossly: 'Yer Aunt Emma and yer Nuss say yer so well up in history that yer needn't do it with us. Yer can run away and play with yer little brother.'

'Oh, but mayn't I stay, Miss Hunt?' Andrew begged the first time; 'I *love* history!'

Tom and Mabel stared at him in astonishment.

184

'No, yer've heard what I said,' answered Miss Hunt; 'run away, there's a good bawy.'

One day Miss Hunt did not let Andrew out at the proper time. Nandy burst into the school-room and said: 'Andrew, why are you still here? You know you're supposed to come out at eleven with me and Stephen.'

'Andrew will come to yer when *I*'ve finished with him, Nuss,' said Miss Hunt, furious at Nandy's trespass into her school-room.

'Miss Hunt, you *know* Andrew is supposed to come out at eleven,' replied Nandy, furious at Miss Hunt's detention of her charge.

'Mrs. Milburn said he was to do our first lesson with us, and we haven't finished yet,' said Miss Hunt.

'Mrs. Milburn and the doctor said he wasn't to do more than one hour with you. Come at once, Andrew, put your books away.'

'Go on with yer work, Andrew,' said Miss Hunt, 'I'll send yer to yer Nuss when I'm ready.'

Tom and Mabel began to giggle. 'It isn't funny, children,' said Miss Hunt angrily; 'get on with yer lessons.'

Nandy went out. 'I shall tell Mrs. Milburn,' she said.

'And *I* shall tell Mrs. Milburn too,' said Miss Hunt.

Andrew spent another very uncomfortable five minutes in the school-room. 'Now yer can go to yer Nuss,' said Miss Hunt, dismissing him, 'though why yer can't do more than an hour's lessons is more than *I* can make out.'

Nandy was rather vexed. 'You know you must always come out at eleven, dear,' she said.

'But, Nandy, I couldn't help it, really I couldn't. Miss Hunt wouldn't let me go.'

'It doesn't matter what Miss Hunt says, your Aunt Emma wants you to come out at eleven.'

III

THE Aunts, meanwhile, were unremitting in their efforts to see the children. They wrote to Mrs. Milburn sending invitations for Andrew and Stephen; but each time she replied with an excuse. The children twice had previous engagements, and twice had colds; finally Emma wrote that they were settling down so nicely at Quenby that it would be a pity to risk upsetting them by a visit to Handborough Regis. The ladies of Handborough all agreed that Emma was behaving most unkindly; Mrs. Tomlinson, Mrs. Poltimore-Robinson, and Miss Low all wrote to ask the children to tea, in order that the Aunts might be able to see them.

'You don't want to go to tea with Mrs. Poltimore-Robinson (or with Mrs. Tomlinson, or Miss Low), do you, dear?' asked Aunt Emma.

'No, thank you, Aunt Emma,' said Andrew.

'Well, you shan't, dear; I'll make some excuse for you,' she replied.

Andrew thought how very kind Aunt Emma was; most grown-up people would have simply accepted invitations for him and Stephen, and would have announced: 'You're going to tea to-morrow with Mrs. Poltimore-Robinson (or Mrs. Tomlinson or Miss Low),' and that would have been the end of the matter.

The Aunts in desperation wrote to Colonel Faringdon to enquire whether he really wished the children to be kept permanently away from them; and they appended to their letter a list of the excuses furnished by Emma during the last few weeks. At the same time they wrote to his sister Mrs. Thompson, begging her to use her influence with him on their behalf.

When Andrew's ninth birthday came, Aunt Margaret rang him up on the telephone to wish him many happy returns of the day. He went to answer the telephone in mingled terror and delight. He thought Aunt Margaret sounded very kind on the telephone, and he wished he knew whether the Aunts or Aunt Emma were really kind. He was daily becoming more sorrowfully certain that both sides could not be right. He was unwilling to believe in the villainy of Aunt Emma, because she now had charge of him and was hand in glove with Nandy. If she were a villain, he would be in a very bad way indeed.

The Aunts wrung from Colonel Faringdon an admission that he had no wish to prevent them from seeing the children; they enclosed his letter in a brief note asking Andrew and Stephen over to lunch and tea. Mrs. Milburn was obliged to reply that she would send them; Berthe the Swiss maid should leave .them with the Aunts in the morning, and would meet them at the station after tea, and bring them back to Duckwold.

On the day before the children went to see the Aunts, Aunt Emma scored an important point against them. Andrew received a telegram from his father informing him that he had a sister. Aunt Emma and Nandy were delighted, and even Miss Hunt offered congratulations. The children were both wildly excited. 'I wonder when we shall see her,' they said over and over again. 'I wonder what she will be called.' 'Do you think she will be called Margaret, after Aunt Margaret?' suggested Andrew.

'I don't expect so, dear,' said Nandy. 'Perhaps she'll be called Elsa, after Mummy.'

This suggestion cooled Andrew's enthusiasm: he had forgotten that Miss Blankenheim was his new sister's mother. The Aunts, he felt, would therefore not approve of her. He was very much pleased to have a sister; but she was a guilty pleasure, as the wedding-cake had been. He felt a little aggrieved with the Aunts, because their disapproval clouded his pleasure. They would concentrate on the one aspect which he wished to forget; they would not think how delightful it was for him to have a baby sister, they would think of her primarily as the child of 'that German woman', and they would dislike her.

'If you hadn't had a new Mummy, you couldn't have had a new sister,' observed Nandy, in the tone in which grown-up people say: 'Bread and butter first, and *then* jam.' Grown-up people are not often logical, and when they are there is usually a sting in it somewhere. It is hardly worth while eating all that bread and butter in order to be allowed bread and jam. Andrew began to wonder whether the pleasure of having a new sister outweighed the anxiety of having a stepmother.

Soon Miss Blankenheim faded from the picture; they only talked about the baby. Andrew and Stephen went out with Nandy in Duckwold, telling the news to the grocer's boy and to the woman at the post-office, and to anyone else with whom they had the slightest acquaintance. They spent the rest of the day longing for Cynthia to come back from the hospital where she worked, and for Flora to return from her day-school in Handborough. Everyone else had heard the news, and even Tom and Mabel were interested in it. Andrew began to think of the Aunts as wicked fairies, liable to turn up late at the baby's christening, and to curse her with a hundred years' sleep, or something of the kind. The baby was certainly an important victory for the allied forces of Miss Blankenheim, Nandy, and Aunt Emma.

Next morning Andrew was told that he and Stephen

were going to spend a day with the Aunts. He was seized with shyness; it would be so difficult to meet them now he was living at Quenby. If they were really in the wrong in the confused family quarrel of which he was aware, though he did not quite understand it, and if he had really been removed from them for his good, it seemed dangerous to go back to them. On the other hand, he was afraid of discovering that they were really right, and that he had been led into captivity at Quenby through Aunt Emma's wickedness. He was nervous also because he would have to tell them that he had a baby sister, and that would annoy them.

'Must I go?' he asked.

'Yes, of course yer must go,' said Miss Hunt firmly. 'Yer Aunt Emma said it would be very nice for yer to go.'

'Can't Tom or Mabel go with me?' he asked. He felt that some of the awkward moments of which he was in dread could not arise if a representative from Quenby went with him.

'No, they're not asked,' said Miss Hunt shortly. 'Get yer boots on, and don't make a fuss.'

Andrew and Stephen went in by train with Berthe, the grim and silent Swiss maid. As they approached Handborough Regis, Andrew could not help feeling thrilled; after all, Handborough was such a delightful place that it was impossible not to feel some pleasure in going there, no matter on what errand. Even if one were being taken to Handborough to be beheaded, one's heart would surely leap up with momentary joy at the sight of its trees and spires, and of the sea-green cupola of the Opera House.

Andrew flattened his nose against the window; there was the recreation-ground, and a few children were playing on the swings; there was the dingy red-brick church of Saint Simon Zelotes; there were the Saw Mills. The train plunged into a tunnel. Andrew stood up and put on his hat; his heart beat hard for joy. They came out of the tunnel into the station. 'Handborough Regis,' cried the guard.

Aunt Margaret and Aunt Anne stood on the platform with Nigger. The children broke away from Berthe, and ran up to kiss them. All their doubts had vanished in the delight at being back at Handborough again with the Aunts. They took no notice of Berthe, as she gave their tickets to Aunt Margaret and went away.

'We've got a new little sister,' shouted Stephen.

'How *lovely!*' said Aunt Anne.

ANDREW and Stephen went back tearfully to Quenby.

'I wish we could keep you here,' said the Aunts.

'Can't we stay?' said Stephen.

'I'm afraid not, dear,' answered Aunt Anne. 'Berthe will be waiting for you at the station.'

'But suppose Berthe didn't come?' said Andrew.

'Well, then, of course, you would have to stay,' replied Aunt Margaret. 'How nice if she was too late!'

'I want Berthe to be run over by a bus,' said Stephen. 'A big red bus.'

'And made into a mess like raspberry jam!' added Andrew vindictively.

Aunt Margaret laughed. 'Poor Berthe!' she said. 'It's not her fault.'

'But I don't like her,' said Stephen.

'Well, anyway, there's Miss Hunt at Quenby, she's nice to you,' said Aunt Anne.

Andrew did not like to point out that Miss Hunt was the worst of his troubles there. He walked to the station with Stephen and the Aunts, hoping against hope and praying furiously under his breath: 'Please God *squash* Berthe.' They went on to the platform; Berthe was not yet there.

'I don't believe she's coming!' said Andrew.

'She's been run over by a bus, I expect,' said Stephen in a quiet tone of satisfaction.

Even the Aunts had begun to believe that Berthe was not going to appear in time to catch the train, when at the last moment she came on to the platform.

'Oh, Berthe,' said Stephen, with immense disappointment in his voice, 'we thought you had been run over by a bus.'

Nandy and Aunt Emma were sitting in the nursery sewing when Berthe brought the children back. 'Well, what sort of a day did you have, dears?' asked Aunt Emma.

'Lovely, thank you, Aunt Emma,' answered Andrew demurely.

A new edict from Egypt made Andrew still more discontented with his lot at Quenby. 'Yer father says,' said Miss Hunt, 'that he wants yer to be with yer cousins as much as possible; so yer to come out with Tom and Bell and me in the mornings, instead of with yer Nuss. And yer Aunt Emma says it will be very nice for yer.'

Andrew was still released from the school-room at eleven o'clock, but he now had only three quarters of an hour's liberty to walk about with Nandy and Stephen, or to play in the garden. Punctually at a quarter to twelve Miss Hunt came out of the house and began to scream: 'Hoo-hoo! Cuckoo! Hoo-hoo! Cuckoo!' in every direction, until Andrew came to her call.

'Manntenong mes enfangs,' said Miss Hunt, who had formerly been companion to an old lady during her travels in France, 'alley vous ong!'

Their walk was always to the village, where they did commissions for Mrs. Milburn in a dreary grocer's shop that smelt of cardboard and coarse soap, and in a draper's shop full of cheap and heart-breakingly ugly dress materials and furnishing fabrics. The grocer was a pathetic little man with a drooping moustache; his wife was very ill indeed, and he answered Miss Hunt's kind enquiries with deep melancholy.

'I'm afraid the end is not far off,' he would say,

shaking his silly little head. Andrew dreaded the visit to the grocer's; he daily expected to be told that 'Mrs. Porter had passed away'. Poor little Mr. Porter would be so unhappy, he would shake his head faster and faster, and cry into the castor sugar as he weighed it.

Mr. Jones the draper was a widower, a stern man and a nonconformist. He was unhappy too, because his daughter was very ill; after having a baby which she had no business to have, though of course the children did not know this.

'How's yer darter?' Miss Hunt would enquire, and she and Mr. Jones would whisper dismally across the counter, and shake their heads over poor Minnie Jones's misfortune. Then the impatient children would be relieved to hear Miss Hunt raise her voice and buy a reel of black cotton.

Duckwold always seemed to Andrew a village of the dead and dying; whenever they went out they met an empty hearse wandering about in search of its prey. Old Major Barton's house had bulletins pinned on the front door. Hay was spread in the road in front of Mrs. Middleton's house, and her door-knocker was covered with an old glove to deaden the sound. Mrs. Milburn knew all the invalids, and Miss Hunt brought back their latest news every day.

'Major Barton's better,' she said one morning.

'But he'll never get well again,' said Aunt Emma.

'Oh, I don't know, Mother,' answered Miss Hunt; 'I don't know why he shouldn't.'

'Don't be absurd, Ferdinand! I bet you he's gone before this nail comes off,' said Mrs. Milburn, shewing her a broken finger-nail.

After that Andrew watched Aunt Emma's finger-nail anxiously every day, as if Major Barton's life depended on it by sympathetic magic. Whenever he passed the little red-brick house with a white bow-window he thought: 'The nail *can't* stay on much longer; I wonder if old Major Barton *knows*.'

The finger-nail fell first, and Aunt Emma had to give Miss Hunt sixpence in payment of her debt. A few days later the blinds were drawn in the windows of the little house, and they met Berthe's fiancé, the undertaker, on his way there. 'Morning, Miss Hunt,' he said cheerfully; 'morning, Master Tom, Master Andrew, Miss Mabel. Just going to run the tape over Major Barton. Died early this morning, poor gentleman.'

'So you only just won your sixpence, Miss Hunt,' said Andrew.

' 'Sh,' she said angrily. 'I didn't think yer'd be so tactless,' she scolded, when Berthe's fiancé, the undertaker, had left them.

'But what have I said?' asked Andrew, who was always open to correction, if grown-ups would explain themselves, instead of scolding.

'Yer a tiresome little bawy, and yer know it,' said Miss Hunt, to the infinite delight of Tom and Mabel. They were pleased that Andrew had got into trouble, though they had no more notion than himself why Miss Hunt should be angry with him.

Miss Hunt was soon deep in conversation with Mrs. MacCorquodale, the doctor's wife. Tom and Mabel took advantage of this to push Andrew against a railing and pinch him.

'Ow, you pigs,' he cried.

'We're not pigs,' said Tom.

'And even if we were,' said Mabel, 'you oughtn't to say so now you're staying with us.'

'I wish I wasn't,' he moaned.

Mabel kicked him hard. Miss Hunt turned her head in time to see Andrew giving her a kick in retaliation.

'Yer a nasty quarrelsome little bawy,' she said. 'Fancy kicking a girl! What would yer father say?'

'I don't care what he would say,' said Andrew defiantly; 'and, anyway, she kicked me first.'

'Don't yer start arguing,' said Miss Hunt, and gripped his hand for the rest of a miserable walk, while Tom and Mabel walked behind, treading on his heels.

The walk into Duckwold became more and more of a nightmare. Every day the same shops were visited, and the same invalids were enquired after; and they were never any better. Andrew had to admit that there was little reason for the inhabitants of Duckwold to cling to life very tenaciously. Their surroundings were repellently hideous, and their relations and friends were dismal company. If Mrs. Middleton recovered, and the hay were removed in front of her house, and she came out again, there were only the three dirty streets which formed Duckwold, for her to walk in. She would perhaps do better to die; and then Berthe's fiancé would run a tape over her, and she would be carried out in a brown coffin with brass handles, and put into the expectant hearse.

One morning when Andrew was in the school-room writing his weekly letter to his father, he had a brilliant idea. He would hide somewhere until Miss Hunt and the cousins had gone into Duckwold, and then he would go out with Nandy instead.

'It's very jolly being here with the cousins,' Miss Hunt was dictating; 'I go out with them and Miss Hunt every morning.'

'Well, I shan't this morning,' he thought defiantly.

'Get on with yer letter,' said Miss Hunt. 'What are yer going to say to yer father now?'

'What shall I say?' asked Andrew.

'Who's writing yer letter, you or I?' asked Miss Hunt

rhetorically. 'Yer can ask after yer mother and yer sister, and then yer can stop. I can see yer want to get away to yer Nuss.'

Andrew told Nandy that he was going exploring. With great deliberation he went down the drive, letting himself be seen by Mabel, who was staring at him enviously out of the school-room window. When he had passed the magnolia tree, and was safely hidden from view, he slipped into the bushes at the end of the garden, and worked his way round to the back of the house. The stable-yard was empty, he was glad to see, and he was able unnoticed to climb up the stairs into a hayloft.

He lay down in the hay, throbbing with excitement and delight. The stable clock struck the three quarters. 'I'll count a thousand with my eyes shut,' he thought, 'and if I don't open them till I've done it, Miss Hunt won't find me.'

He counted conscientiously; when he had slurred some numbers in haste, he went back and counted them again. Then he opened his eyes. He doubted whether it was all clear yet; Miss Hunt might not yet have given up the search. He lay down in the hay. It was very dull just lying still and counting; another time he would bring a book. He supposed it would not be safe to hide every day, they would be sure to find out and prevent him. Miss Hunt would nag at him, and would demand: 'What would yer father say?'

The clock struck twelve, and Andrew came down the stairs. He wandered through the garden in case he could find Nandy and Stephen.

'Wherever have you been, dear?' asked Nandy. 'Miss Hunt has been looking for you everywhere.'

'Oh, I was just exploring,' said Andrew vaguely; 'where's Miss Hunt?'

196

'She's gone now,' said Nandy; 'you'd better come with us instead. You wouldn't be able to catch her up now.'

Andrew knew Nandy was pleased, but he did not venture to confide in her; she might feel bound to give him away. Grown-up people were not good at keeping secrets.

'I couldn't find yer,' said Miss Hunt afterwards; 'I called everywhere, and Tom and Bell called too. Didn't yer hear us?'

'No, Miss Hunt.'

'I hope yer weren't in the bushes playing tombstones,' said Miss Hunt accusingly.

'Why?' asked Andrew, delighted that Miss Hunt's suspicions were so wide of the mark.

'It's not a *manly* game,' said Miss Hunt fatuously.

'Well, I wasn't,' said Andrew; 'I was exploring.'

'It's very tiresome of yer to explore so far away,' said Miss Hunt, who had never suspected that Andrew had attempted to dodge her. He was very demure; and though she disliked him for coming to live at Quenby, for having Nandy as his nurse, and for being more intelligent than Tom and Mabel, she was obliged to admit that he was obedient.

Next morning Andrew came running up to her call, and the walk to Duckwold seemed drearier than ever after his liberty of the previous day. He began to think out other hiding-places; if he had a different one every day, he need never be found. It would be marvellous if he never had to go out with Miss Hunt and the cousins again. Every day he left the school-room before the others, and was free to wander in the garden alone, or with Nandy and Stephen, until Miss Hunt called. If he did not hear her, naturally he need not go. It was not very difficult to arrange not to hear Miss Hunt.

One day he walked into the garden carrying under his arm *Stories from the Canterbury Tales*, which Aunt Margaret had sent him for his birthday. He made his way to a sheltered summer-house, where it was still warm enough to sit and read. If he could become sufficiently absorbed in his book, he would not hear Miss Hunt calling. The summer-house was not far away, and her voice was far-reaching. He was afraid that anxiety not to hear Miss Hunt might prevent his complete absorption in the *Canterbury Tales*. It had never occurred to him to tell Miss Hunt a lie, and say that he had not heard her, if he really had.

Andrew read ϙbooks with a concentration and intensity which made him deaf and blind to the outside world. Grown-up people (who tend to think that a child must necessarily be doing mischief to itself or to others, whenever its whole energy is happily occupied and it has forgotten their existence) were always annoyed when they saw Andrew reading. They tried every means of plaguing him; they took his books away, or told him that his eyes were tired, or that he must go out. Sometimes they just sat and talked, and were angry if he did not answer. In spite of their persecution, he generally managed to read four or five books every week. They would never believe that he read them properly, or that he remembered anything about them. They themselves were fond of boasting that they never had any time for reading. This never convinced Andrew, who knew that reading was a necessity of life, and that grown-up people wasted hours of valuable time in uninteresting conversation.

After a few minutes he lost himself completely in the story of Palamon and Arcite, from which he was roused by a shout in his ear. Tom stood beside him. 'Come on, Andrew,' he said; 'Miss Hunt sent me to find you.'

Andrew decided that it was useless to appeal to Tom to help him; Tom would have the greatest pleasure in betraying him to Miss Hunt.

'Didn't yer hear me call?' said Miss Hunt; 'I suppose yer were buried in yer book. What would happen if we were all buried in our books, and took no notice of other people?'

Another morning Andrew found a little dead bird on one of the garden paths; it was an opportunity to play the game that Miss Hunt called 'tombstones'. He laid it in a large green leaf, and picked a spray of berries to lay on its grave. He went into the shrubs at the end of the garden, and hollowed out a grave for the bird near the fish's last resting-place. While occupied in this act of piety he heard shouts: 'Cuckoo! Hoo-hoo! Cuckoo!' and Tom and Mabel crying: 'Andrew! An-drew!' On the bird's grave he made a solemn vow: 'I *shan't* go out with them to-day.'

He came back from his walk with Nandy and Stephen, half timid, half defiant. He hoped that Miss Hunt would not ask if he had heard her calling. She might be content with scolding him for wandering so far away. If she did not ask a direct question, he would be safe. If she asked him straight out, he would own that he had deliberately played truant.

'Well, Andrew,' she said, 'what were yer up to to-day? Where were yer?'

'In the bushes.'

'Yer've been playing tombstones,' she cried triumphantly.

'Yes, Miss Hunt.'

'Why can't yer find a nicer game?' she demanded. 'Didn't yer hear when I called?'

'Yes, Miss Hunt.'

'Don't say "yes, Miss Hunt" to everything I say. Yer

mean "no", don't yer? Why can't yer attend to what I'm saying?'

'But I *did* hear you,' said Andrew, enjoying the role of George Washington.

'Why didn't yer come, then?' she asked, angrily.

'Because I wanted to go out with Nandy and Stephen,' he said timidly.

'Yer a very disobedient, rude little bawy,' she said; 'I don't know what yer father and yer Aunt Emma will say. Fancy leaving a *lady* to go out with a common Nuss!'

THE year drew towards its close. If you went out of doors, the dampness underneath your feet seemed to rush upwards and strike you in the heart. When he dressed in the morning Andrew looked out of the store-room window on to the fir-trees by the drive, and the rhododendron bushes, whose hideous dark leaves shone here and there with faint lustre like tarnished silver. When he came downstairs and pressed his face for a moment against the french windows of the school-room, he gazed across the vast grey lawn where a gigantic wellingtonia towered like a black spire against the sky. Only the white skeleton of an old thunder-struck acacia was bare, it would never more have any leaves. Every-where else there were trees and shrubs, dismal in their evergreen foliage, now that there was no ray of sun to justify it.

'Quenby's not a place for visitors in winter,' said Miss Hunt with grim satisfaction. Three years before they had gone back earlier than this to Handborough Regis, to find old Wace sweeping up the leaves on the Aunts' dry gravel paths. Beyond the croquet-lawn, flanked by its bare medlar and mulberry trees, there was a comfortable distant view of the town. In winter it was warm and reassuring to feel that other human habitation was near at hand.

A year ago Andrew had come over to Quenby with his father one winter's day. He remembered the long cheerful evening round the school-room table, when they played Prince's Quest to amuse him, because he was a visitor. Now he was no longer a visitor; he was living at Quenby, and could not expect them to put themselves out on his account. The evenings were now more serious. After tea, when the school-room table had been cleared, Nandy and Miss Hunt sat down with their knitting, and all the children had wooden rings on which they were making scarves 'for the soldiers'. They sang as they worked, and Miss Hunt led the chorus of *Keep the home fires burning*. Then, as the evenings grew yet longer and darker, the soldiers' scarves were put aside, and everyone set to work on Christmas presents. Mabel, who was engaged upon an indeterminate piece of knitting, and Tom who was pasting coloured paper on to cardboard boxes, were very scornful of Andrew's raffia basket, an extremely lop-sided and fragile piece of work which he was painfully executing under Miss Hunt's direction, without any expectation of being able to finish it.

But the mail to Egypt took a long time, and something better suited than this basket to bear the brunt of the journey had to be despatched to Mrs. Faringdon 'with love and best wishes from Andrew and Stephen'. Aunt Emma produced one and sixpence for this present, and Andrew naturally wanted to go with Stephen and Nandy to buy it, but this was very difficult to arrange. How was he to talk about *her* present, when he still did not know what to call her? In some ways this was just as well, because it prevented him from thinking much about her, and she was not a pleasant subject for thought. Real connected thought about someone without a name was impossible, because he thought chiefly in words. Thinking was telling things to himself. He could not tell himself anything about someone who was nameless; he could only see a dark face under a green hat, and then feel a shuddering sensation of unhappiness. The Aunts could not speak her name, but they had given up calling her 'that German woman'.

Lately in a letter to Andrew Aunt Anne had mentioned 'Joan's mother'; but 'Joan's mother' was only a description, not a name. You could not really think about 'Joan's mother' as a person, any more than you could think that Miss Hunt had 'a hard durable stone' in her brooch, which was the copybook description of an agate.

It was Nandy's one fault that she would always talk so glibly of 'Mummy'. Mummy was someone kind and pretty, who long ago had sat brushing her hair at a dressing-table, while she and Andrew talked and talked. Nandy had pulled him up short when he had spoken of his stepmother as 'Miss Blankenheim'. 'Miss Blankenham is your Aunt Bessie now, my dear,' she explained. It was all so confusing; and apparently there were lots more Blankenham uncles and aunts and cousins whom Andrew had never seen. It seemed only too likely that they would be a fresh source of trouble; there were already quite enough quarrels in the Milburn and Faringdon families, without a whole family of new relations, to make things worse.

He could write 'My dear Daddy and Mummy' in his weekly letters, and he could mention them in his prayers; that was different, and seemed to have no connection with real life. His prayers were an evening duty paid to God, and his letters were exercises in handwriting and composition set by Miss Hunt. 'Daddy and Mummy' were merely words that in either case were a necessary part of the formula, but they had nothing at all to do with Miss Blankenheim and her green hat.

Miss Hunt soon put an end to Andrew's embarrassment. 'Yer coming with Tom and Bell and me to buy yer mother's present this afternoon,' she said. 'Yer Aunt Emma said that would be very nice.'

'Oh, but I wanted to go and choose with Stephen and Nandy,' said Andrew.

'Oh, hang yer Nuss!' said Miss Hunt. 'Yer know what yer father said. Yer can choose quite well without yer little brother. Yer coming with us, and I don't want to hear any more about it.'

With great satisfaction Miss Hunt led the three children off again on the same walk that they had made that morning. To her urban taste the lanes could offer no attraction to compare with the three streets of Duckwold, and she would gladly have gone to the village twice every day. The lanes were now almost bare, but for a few red berries, while the Duckwold shop windows were rather fuller than usual. There were the regular displays of tins of salmon and pots of jam in Porter's stores, there were tobacconists with little piles of packets of Gold Flake, a baker's shop with a few melancholy buns decorated with coco-nut, and Mr. Jones's window full of savage-looking corsets. There were also some shiny Christmas cards at the news-agent's, and Miss Stevenson had a display of *lingerie* labelled 'Xmas gifts'.

This last shop was their objective. Miss Stevenson, with a sharp nose and a drop at the end of it, presided genteelly over this little chamber of horrors, and battled ineffectively with a large tabby-cat.

'Why, you're quaite a stranger, Miss Hunt!' she cried. 'Pussy, how often have I asked you not to sit on the peppermint creams!'

Miss Hunt explained the purpose of their visit.

'I daresay Mrs. Faringdon would laike this hair-taidy. It's quaite elegant. The warm claimate must make the hair fall dreadfully,' said Miss Stevenson, patting her own untidy bun, and pressing in a falling hair-pin.

'I had some naice handkerchiefs,' she continued, 'but I declare I can't faind them anywhere,' and she peered distractedly into biscuit tins and sweet bottles. The cat sprang from the counter and alighted on her bent back. Its mistress gave a wail of pain: 'Oh, Tibby, you naughty cat, what sharp claws you have!'

Miss Hunt picked up a velvet pincushion and thrust it at Andrew. 'Here, look at this. Would yer like to give yer mother this? Yer not looking at anything.'

'There was a naice lavender sachet, Master Andrew,' said Miss Stevenson, 'reely high-class, but I declare Pussy is sitting on it. He's so quiet now, I don't laike to upset him.'

'Oh no, don't move him!' said Andrew.

Tom and Mabel started to fidget by the door, when Miss Stevenson gave a little cry of triumph and held up a lace collar.

'Now this is quaite *the thing*,' she exclaimed. 'Don't you think it's allüring, Miss Hunt?'

'Very nice indeed, very nice,' replied Miss Hunt; 'how much?'

'Now I reely couldn't say,' answered Miss Stevenson, and peered shortsightedly at an undecipherable ticket. 'What do you say to one eleven three?'

'Too much,' said Miss Hunt.

'Well, I daresay it is; one and threepence to *you*, then.'

'Here, come along, Andrew, where's yer money? Are yer quite asleep?' said Miss Hunt.

He found his three sixpences, and the lace collar was his, but he wondered uneasily whether Nandy would think it a suitable present.

They made the round of the village for the sake of the walk; no one had yet stopped them to gossip with Miss Hunt, and there was still some time to kill before tea. The Church Schools had a notice of an entertainment at which Miss Cynthia Milburn was going to sing; they stopped for a few minutes to admire Cynthia's name in print, and while they were thus occupied the Vicar, returning from a funeral, alighted from his bicycle beside them.

'Christmas shopping already?' exclaimed Mr. Fielding archly. 'You early worms!'

'My cousin Andrew's mother is in Egypt,' explained Tom pompously, 'and the post takes a considerable time.'

Mr. Fielding beamed sympathetically. 'Our loved ones now far absent,' he quoted.

'My stepmother,' Andrew coldly corrected him.

'And how happy they must be, in spite of their absence,' preached Mr. Fielding with undamped ardour, 'when they think of the happy home where they have left you and your little brother. Cared for by your kind uncle and aunt and good Miss Hunt, romping about with your little playmates . . .'

'I think we must be getting along, Vicar,' said Miss Hunt bluntly. 'Tea-time, children! Come along.'

As they walked home, Miss Hunt improved the occasion. 'I hope yer listened to what the Vicar said. It's very good of yer Aunt Emma to have yer at Quenby, and I don't think yer quite realize it. I'm afraid yer an ungrateful and selfish little bawy.'

'I suppose my father pays,' said Andrew.

'That's no way to talk, as if yer Aunt Emma kept a lodging-house,' said Miss Hunt with indignation. 'It's the nasty common way yer have of looking at things ; just like yer Nuss. I wish yer could look at things more nicely, like Tom and Mabel. Yer may think yerself very clever, but one day yer'll find perhaps that yer not so clever as yer think. Anyhow, brains aren't the real things that matter. Yer wait till yer get to school.'

Andrew walked on in silent misery, feeling very wicked indeed. He must, he thought, be very far from grace when so far from having 'the real things that mattered', he did not even know what they were. He had no notion what 'nice way of looking at things' was possessed by Tom and Mabel, but denied to himself. Mabel was certainly looking very well pleased with herself at the moment, very conscious of having chosen the better part. Andrew did not think much of Mabel; it was most humiliating to have to look up to her and Tom as his spiritual superiors. He began to wonder if Miss Hunt were not merely being horrid. She knew that it would be no good trying to make out that he was not cleverer than Tom and Mabel, and therefore she was trying to pretend that they were better and nicer, which was much less easy to measure. However, he did not need Miss Hunt to tell him that brains did not go far towards making one happy at school; he knew that by experience.

Nandy did not think much of Miss Stevenson's lace collar. 'I think a little pincushion might have been nicer, dear,' she said.

'Well, I couldn't really help it,' said Andrew. 'Miss Hunt more or less made me buy the collar.'

Nandy did not like to disappoint him. She put it against her coat for a moment. 'Look,' she said, 'it's not too bad. It goes quite nicely with my coat, you see.'

Miss Hunt wanted to know what Nandy had to say. 'She said something sarcastic, I suppose? It's not so easy to go shopping in Duckwold, you know.'

'Oh no,' said Andrew, 'Nandy said it wasn't bad. She said it went quite nicely with her coat.'

'Fancy asking for yer mother's present!' said Miss Hunt angrily. 'That's a nice way to talk! I don't know what yer mother would say. I hope yer didn't give it to her?'

'Oh no, Miss Hunt, she didn't mean that.'

'H'm, I know yer Nuss,' said Miss Hunt grimly. 'Asking for yer mother's present indeed!'

'She wasn't!' cried Andrew.

'Yer a rude little bawy to contradict a lady,' said Miss Hunt. 'You and yer Nuss are a nice example for yer cousins to have in the house! Yer Aunt Emma was far too good.'

'I don't see that the cousins are any better,' said Andrew hotly.

'Yer wouldn't,' replied Miss Hunt, 'I never expected it.'

The cousins did nothing to raise themselves in Andrew's estimation. Next day they were together in the garden before their walk, sitting inside the wellingtonia, swinging on its branches. Andrew began sociably to make conversation about the character and attainments of Richard II, of whom he happened to be thinking at the moment. He had just read an historical novel.

'We're sick of your shewing off,' said Mabel.

'I'm not,' protested Andrew.

'Oh yes, you are,' said Tom.

'You think yourself so clever,' went on Mabel, 'but it's very kind of us to talk to you at all, when you're so rude about Mother.'

'I'm not!'

'You called her a lodging-house keeper.'

'Oh, Mabel, you know that's a lie!'

'Well then, do you call Miss Hunt a liar?' asked Mabel.

'No, I don't.'

'But she said you said Mother was a lodging-house keeper. If you say that's a lie, that means you call Miss Hunt a liar,' said Mabel triumphantly.

'Oh, don't torment!' cried Andrew, giving her an impatient push.

In an instant Mabel had upset him from his branch, and he was sprawling in the dirt at the bottom of the tree. She and Tom leapt on top of him and kept him with his face in the dust, wriggling in vain attempts to throw them off, and screaming himself hoarse at them.

Miss Hunt's voice was heard, calling them to their walk. Mabel scampered off, to be first with her story. It was hardly necessary, for Andrew knew that it was useless to appeal to Miss Hunt for sympathy or protection. He went in search of Nandy and Stephen.

'Come here, Andrew,' called Miss Hunt. 'Oh no, yer not going off with yer Nuss this afternoon, yer coming with us.'

'But Nandy said . . .' began Andrew.

'Oh, Nanny said, did she? Well, I say yer coming with me.'

'Oh, but she'll wonder where I am,' he protested.

'She ought to know yer father likes yer to be with us,' said Miss Hunt. 'She'll know I've got yer; yer needn't worry about her.'

Andrew went with Miss Hunt with an ill grace.

'What's this Mabel tells me?' she asked grimly. 'She says yer've been calling yer cousins beasts. Yer've no idea how yer ought to talk. Yer in yer cousins' home, and at least yer should be civil.'

'Well, they were sitting on me and pinching me,' explained Andrew.

Miss Hunt held up her hand. 'No tales out of school,' she said firmly.

'Well, you asked,' Andrew protested.

'I've no doubt yer deserved it,' said Miss Hunt with finality. 'Yer a very quarrelsome little bawy.'

Andrew despaired of any justice at Quenby now, and in his gloomier moments he began to wonder whether he did not deserve all his misfortunes. He could appreciate enough of his cousins' point of view to realize how intensely they must dislike having him and Stephen foisted in amongst them. It was all very well for Aunt Emma, who was paid for having them at Quenby, no matter what Miss Hunt might say. She seldom saw the children except at meals, and there were so many people in the house that a few more could not make much difference to her. But Miss Hunt and Tom and Mabel were all the time unable to forget the change in the household; they constantly had Andrew with them, and saw him using their things, but they had no compensation for his presence. It was not his fault; but he recognized that circumstances were all in favour of their disliking him. He felt that he was in the schoolroom on sufferance; he had been quartered upon Miss Hunt and the cousins, just as soldiers had been quartered upon some unfortunate people at Handborough Regis. He would have kept his place, content to be the humblest, and only anxious not to obtrude himself upon them; but that was not allowed. They took a savage delight in insisting on his father's wish that he should be with them; and although they did not wish for his company, and lost no occasion of being unpleasant when he was with them, they behaved as if they were hurt and offended when he avoided them.

Even Nandy made things more difficult. One day she said: 'Andrew, you know you oughtn't to let Miss Hunt hector you like that. You've as much right here as Tom and Mabel; otherwise Daddy wouldn't let you be here. I am sure he would want you to stick up for your rights, and you ought to do it for his sake.' Andrew had felt that by an effort he could keep his temper and lie down like a door-mat in front of Miss Hunt, but it seemed that this was wrong. But the only other thing he could do was to flare up into a rage, and he was certain that that was worse.

Another day Nandy said: 'Aunt Emma wishes you could get on better with Tom and Mabel. She wanted me to speak to you about it. I was very grieved to hear about you calling them names. You must never do that, dear. It's all right. It's all forgotten and forgiven. But if you find that you rub each other up the wrong way, you must remember, dear, that it's a sacrifice for them to have other children in their home. You wouldn't have been altogether pleased if Daddy and Mummy had had Frank to live with us in Cairo, would you?'

'But I don't want to live in their home!' Andrew protested.

'Hush, dear!' said Nandy firmly. 'It isn't right to talk like that. You know the hymn says:

> Can a child presume to choose
> Where or how to live?

You can be quite certain that Daddy and Mummy wouldn't have sent you to live here if it wasn't what they were sure was the best for you and Stephen. You ought to be very thankful to live in this beautiful house with this lovely big garden, and if you aren't grateful, you ought to ask God to make you. I'm sure Stephen is.'

Stephen might be. He led a sheltered enough life. But he knew quite well, whenever he came downstairs, that he was surrounded by Nandy's enemies and Andrew's enemies. They had not much to say to him, but they seemed not to wish to be unkind; however, if he found himself alone among them he usually burst out crying, and had to be fetched away.

ANDREW had never been so unhappy as he was at Quenby; even the worst days at Selborne had not been so bad. There he had been supported by a vivid home-life, quite unconnected with school; here he and Nandy and Stephen were thwarted at every turn if they tried to establish a home-circle of their own. At Selborne the lessons gave him food for his growing intellect and imagination; at Quenby everyone did their best to 'keep him back'. He was forced to withdraw more and more into himself, for only from within could he find the strength to resist the pressure that other people put upon him. He felt that they wanted to change him, to make him into a different person; this he passionately resented, and was determined to resist. They had no right to change him, and to rob him of himself; whatever else they might take away from him, this one thing he could save from them. He would fight against them while he had any courage left. He knew that he would have a happier and an easier time if he gave way, and conformed to their wishes. They would probably be kind when they had won. He was sustained in his battle by scorn of their world, which was tedious, irrational and unimaginative, and by loyalty to himself, in spite of growing doubts. Miss Hunt frequently told him that she did not know how he would get on at school, unless he became more like other children; and he remembered his loneliness at Selborne. He wondered if he were really less nice than other children. At school or at parties he could never talk to another child without the impression that the other child would rather be talking to someone else. He never felt that he was wanted, as Denys had been so obviously wanted by the other boys at Selborne.

There was another doubt which he never dared to formulate even to himself. Grown-up people thought he was so very peculiar; perhaps they doubted if he were quite right in his mind. He once overheard Aunt Emma saying to Mrs. Fielding, the vicar's wife: 'Poor Andrew! He *is* so unlike other children; we *do* think it so sad!' And she put a finger to her forehead, and nodded significantly. He could speak to himself when he was alone, and prove that he was not going deaf or dumb. Even at night he could see enough to be fairly certain that he had not suddenly been struck blind, and the morning would confirm this. How could he find a test to prove that he was not going mad?

His affection for Nandy was as strong as ever, and she was always ready to comfort him as far as she could; but she was not much help. She could only console him after the knocks he had received in the school-room; she could not protect him from receiving the same knocks again the next day. He longed to write to his father to say that he was miserable at Quenby, and would like to go back to the Aunts; but it was worse than useless to ask Nandy to help him in this. She was fond of Aunt Emma, and she had quarrelled with the Aunts. His official weekly letter was written under Miss Hunt's eye, and it was impossible to send any private message in it. He made plans to steal a piece of paper and an envelope; but he did not know how to get a stamp, or how to put his letter in the post without being observed. Worst of all, he did not really believe that his father would take any notice of it.

When he went out with Miss Hunt in the morning, or with Nandy in the afternoon, he used to look long and earnestly at the sign-post at the cross-roads where they turned into Duckwold. On the left he read: 'Duckwold ¼ M. Cranfield 6 M.', on the right: 'Brench-ford 2 M. Culverbridge 6 M. Handborough Regis 10 M.' The road that ran across the Handborough road went nowhere, that is to say nowhere that they knew. They often walked along the roads towards Tidbrook or Andhurst Saint Mary, but they never arrived at either of these places. Andrew wondered if he could ever walk the ten miles into Handborough. He would go to the Aunts and say: 'I've run away from Quenby.' If he made such a heroic effort to escape, they would surely not have the heart to send him back again. But what exactly could he say to them? They might expect him to have stripes to shew them, like Sextus in the Roman History book. No one had ever beaten him. The most he had to shew were a few bruises on his leg where Mabel had kicked him.

Aunt Emma would be furious that he had run away from her 'happy home'; but outwardly she would be all kindness. Berthe or Nandy would be sent over to Handborough to fetch him; and they would be very angry indeed. Perhaps the Aunts would not dare to keep him; and he would be sent back with Berthe, who would be stiff and hard and silent; or with Nandy, who would be more 'grieved' than she had ever been before, and would torture him with mute reproaches. When he was back at Quenby he would be exposed to the jeers of the cousins, and to the voluble scolding of Miss Hunt. Aunt Emma would kiss him, and would say that she was *so* sorry that he had not been happy at Quenby; why had he not told *her* at once, instead of running away to Aunt Margaret and Aunt Anne? *Why* was he not happy at Quenby?

Andrew continued to brood over plans of escape, until they ceased to be a means to an end, but became instead a part of his dream world: they were in themselves a temporary escape from the world in which the cousins nagged at him and bullied him, and Miss Hunt sniffed and scolded.

The Egyptian mail, which had hitherto only brought unpleasant commands from Colonel Faringdon, at last brought orders that he was to do more lessons. His father was beginning to feel that one hour's work with Miss Hunt every day was an inadequate preparation for school next September. He was still to leave Miss Hunt at eleven o'clock, which was as well for him, since he received much bad temper from her, and little instruction. But on two afternoons a week a Belgian Mademoiselle was to come over from Brenchford and take him for a walk, and make French conversation; and on two other afternoons a tutor was to come from Handborough to teach him and Mabel Arithmetic and Latin.

'Yer father says that yer to learn French and Latin,' said Miss Hunt, 'and yer Aunt Emma has very kindly found yer a Mam'zelle to go for walks with yer on Wednesdays and Fridays; and Mr. Scrymgeour is coming from Handborough on Tuesdays and Thursdays to teach you and Bell Arithmetic and Latin. And yer Aunt Emma says it will be very nice for yer.'

At first Andrew was rather overwhelmed and frightened, particularly at the prospect of going for walks with Mademoiselle de la Sablonnière. She arrived for the first time on a damp Friday afternoon.

'Bon jaw, Mam'zelle,' said Miss Hunt grimly, and pushed Andrew towards her, adding: 'Here, talk French to her, can't yer?'

'And this is André, yes?' asked Mademoiselle.

'Oui, Mademoiselle,' he said shyly.

'Ah, you talk French already?' she said encouragingly. 'Nous allons faire beaucoup de progrès, n'est-ce pas? Au revoir, Mees Hunt.'

Andrew was sorry to see that Mademoiselle de la Sablonnière was so prim and neat, and that her lips were carefully coloured a deep carmine. She was not his idea of a governess; Miss Low would certainly have never employed her to teach at Selborne.

He soon changed his mind about her; Mademoiselle was very amusing and vivacious, and the only person at Duckwold who ever spoke to him intelligently. Their walk began with a short circular tour of the farm, with conventional French conversation about the animals.

'Comment s'appelle t'elle cette bête?'

'Elle est une vache.'

'À quoi sert la vache?'

'La vache donne du lait.'

When this formality had been accomplished, they took a brisk walk in the direction of Andhurst Saint Mary, and carried on a far more lively conversation in English. For conscience' and convenience' sake, Mademoiselle interspersed an occasional French phrase or word; and their walk was not without instruction as well as pleasure.

'Dites-moi, mon petit André,' she asked, 'what is this Miss Hunt like? I think she is not a very clever teacher, n'est-ce pas?'

Andrew was delighted, and for two miles he told Mademoiselle what Miss Hunt was like; he did not omit the story of the 'common Nuss'.

'But it was not very polite, mon petit,' said Mademoiselle, laughing, 'to say that you had been hiding from Miss Hunt. You could have said you had not heard her; she would never have known.'

He was profoundly shocked. 'But that would have been a lie!' he said.

'It is better, perhaps, not to speak quite true but not to be rude, mon ami,' said Mademoiselle.

He saw that Mademoiselle seriously held this perverse point of view; he was no longer shocked, but only interested. Mademoiselle was not unprincipled; it was only that she had different principles. She did not think that lies did not matter; she only thought that politeness was more important than strict truthfulness. He was pleased; they now had a fruitful topic for endless ethical discussion.

'But, Mademoiselle, I don't think it matters nearly as much about being polite,' he said.

'Petit Ours!'

'What's that?' he asked suspiciously.

'Little Bear,' she said, smiling.

When they reached the gate at Quenby, Andrew and Mademoiselle walked up the drive chanting French grammar in unison, in case they met anyone.

'Il a un très bon accent, cet enfant,' said Mademoiselle to Cynthia.

The next week brought Mr. Scrymgeour from Handborough. He was a tall, sallow, disappointed man with thinning hair and an extraordinary hole in his cheek; it was large enough to hold the stump of chalk with which he wrote on the blackboard. Andrew's eyes were irresistibly focussed upon this unpleasant deformity of Mr. Scrymgeour's. He could not think how it had come about: perhaps Mr. Scrymgeour had fallen against an iron paling, and a spike had pushed his cheek in; or perhaps someone had done it with a red-hot poker. He regretfully decided that Mr. Scrymgeour might prefer not to be asked why he had a hole in his face.

Andrew was rather excited at the prospect of learning Latin: it was the language in which spells and legends were written, according to the story-books, and holy monks and hermits sang Latin hymns. It was a romantic language, even when it occurred on bottles at the chemist's shop. He was determined to be good at it, and was pleased to find that he made far more rapid progress than Mabel.

After an hour's Latin, Mr. Scrymgeour and the children took a ten minutes' airing in the garden, and Mr. Scrymgeour gazed at the gold-fish in the pond. He was a fisherman, as befitted his melancholy nature.

'I should like them for bait,' he said dismally; 'I wonder if Mrs. Milburn could spare me some? I could give her some nice Egyptian beans from my garden in exchange; very nice beans.'

1918

THE holidays came at last. They came suddenly, as a surprise; Andrew had not asked when they would begin. In the monotonous unpleasantness of life at Quenby he could only look forward to immediate pleasures — to Sunday mornings with Nandy, or to the next walk with Mademoiselle de la Sablonnière. One afternoon in December he had walked dismally to the end of the garden by himself; he leant on the railings for a few minutes, and stared into the sodden fields beyond, then, shivering with the damp cold, he went back reluctantly to the house. To his joy and surprise he found that Philip and Arthur had come back from their school at Brenchford.

Andrew was now able to spend most of his time with Nandy and Stephen and Old Bun. When he was obliged to go out with Miss Hunt, he need not walk with Mabel and Tom. His other cousins were kind to him, and had far more conversation. Flora could still tell interesting stories about dragons; and Arthur told him about school. Andrew liked to make him reconstruct a whole day at school from the moment he was called, until the lights were put out. Arthur asked about Mr. Scrymgeour's lessons, and regretted that he taught the old pronunciation of Latin.

One day Philip lagged with Andrew behind the others, and told him in solemn whispers how kittens were born. Andrew was incredulous; he had always imagined that God put them there suddenly in the night. They certainly did seem to come as a surprise; Mops the cat had frequently been discovered in a drawer or a cupboard, sitting comfortably in Miss

Hunt's hat or on Cynthia's handkerchiefs, surrounded by small blind kittens. Philip explained that one could always tell if Mops were going to have kittens. 'You feel next time,' he said.

Andrew had always thought that Mops herself did not know, and that it must have been a lovely surprise for her to wake up one morning and find four or five little kittens beside her; just as it must have been a lovely surprise for Miss Hunt to find her hat full of kittens. Sometimes he wondered if she had not chosen Miss Hunt's hat by design. An Angel of the Lord was hardly likely to appear unto Mops, and tell her that she was about to have a family; but she might have been driven by some premonition into Miss Hunt's hat, a wonderful instance of the way in which God guides His creatures.

Philip explained to him that it was far less wonderful.

'But how do the kittens *grow* there?' asked Andrew.

'God puts them there, of course,' said Philip.

Andrew secretly thought it was rather wasteful of God to make Mops have about twelve kittens every year, out of which they usually drowned eleven; but he supposed that it must give her pleasure.

The holidays ran their usual course; even though it was war-time, Christmas brought the usual excitement and over-eating, and was followed by the usual bilious attacks. During the rueful period of recovery Mrs. Milburn instituted a sugar-saving device. After a proportion of the family's sugar ration had been deducted for cooking purposes, the remainder was doled out separately every week. Each member of the household had a large bottle labelled with his name, in which he kept his weekly ration; and everyone was encouraged to save, and to contribute to a store which was being collected for jam-making in the summer. The device was

successful; the children never ceased to be amused by
the bottles of sugar arranged all round the table, and
loved explaining them to visitors.

Before the end of the week Miss Hunt was always
out of sugar, and wanting to borrow. Andrew enjoyed
lending to her from his own plenty; he never took more
than one lump of sugar in his tea. Miss Hunt stuck her
hand into his jar, and fumbled about with the sugar,
and then rattled the lumps into her cup with a promise
to repay them next week.

Though a termagant in the school-room, when Miss
Hunt was out of her own kingdom her lot was full of
mortification. Mrs. Milburn was always setting disagreeable duties upon her; and the elder Milburns
openly mocked her, now that they were free from her
rule, or at best treated her with patronizing affection.
In daring moments of emancipation her pupils copied
them. Tom was once heard to refer to her as 'a delicious little person', an expression which he had picked
up from Gladys; but Miss Hunt generally kept her
children well in subjection. Andrew, who suffered
more from her in the school-room than any of the others,
secretly rejoiced to see her humiliated in the dining-
room. She knew it and hated him all the more, and re-
venged upon the unfortunate child every slight on herself, and every kindness done by the Milburns to Nandy.

Miss Hunt's irritating habits asked for rough treatment. She would come down to breakfast clutching
her ear-rings in her hand, and would lay one on each
side of her plate, waiting for an opportunity to screw
them on in the course of the meal. One morning Mr.
Milburn caught her. 'Is that your horrible ear-rings
again, Ferdinand?' he demanded.

She tried to smuggle them into her napkin, mur-
muring: 'No, Father, it's nothing.'

The children, who had detected her in a lie, stared at each other and giggled; when they were alone with her again, she turned on Andrew and said: 'Why did yer laugh like that?'

'But everyone else was laughing,' he protested.

'No, they weren't laughing in the same way,' she said. 'Yer were laughing in a nasty sarcastic way, just like yer Nuss.'

In January Philip and Arthur went back to school at Brenchford; and Flora again went in every day to school at Handborough Regis. Andrew returned to the dreary routine of the school-room, and the daily walk to Duckwold with the cousins. Mr. Scrymgeour resumed his visits, and taught the third conjugation and long division. Andrew still wrote in his weekly letter to Egypt: 'I went for a walk with Mademoiselle, and we talked about the farm,' until Miss Hunt asked if they had not begun to be bored with it. Colonel and Mrs. Faringdon wrote back about the baby, and enclosed a new snapshot nearly every week. Then the children had colds, and Mrs. Milburn had bronchitis; and when they recovered they found that spring had come.

The spring seemed to have roused the maternal instincts in Mops the cat; Andrew observed that she was about to have a family, and in his pride at his new knowledge he told everyone the news. 'Mops is going to have a lot of kittens, five I shouldn't wonder; I felt them,' was his remark to Stephen, in the full hearing of several grown-up people.

Next morning Andrew and Stephen were playing a curious game, in which Stephen was an unfortunate young lady called Miss Smith, who had so many children that she did not know what to do, and kept on having more. Stephen had to ride on his tricycle to call on Andrew, who represented a friend named Miss Jones, to announce the birth of yet another baby. Then the two friends would lament, and wonder where the money could be found to feed and clothe so many infants.

In the middle of the game, before the dramatic situation had been properly developed, Nandy called Andrew and said she wanted to talk to him. He was very much annoyed, because Stephen was playing up to him satisfactorily: often he needed too much prompting when they were pretending things.

'Andrew, dear,' she said, 'I didn't quite like to hear you talk about Mops going to have kittens; Aunt Emma didn't like to hear you say that. One doesn't *talk* about these things. Do you see, my dear?'

Her voice made him feel uncomfortable. He blushed and said: 'But she *is* going to have kittens. I felt them, and so did Mabel.'

'Of course, dear, we all know that *animals* are born in *that way*,' said Nandy in a resigned tone of voice; 'it has to be, because God makes them like that. It's all very holy and beautiful and wonderful, like everything He does. We're "fearfully and wonderfully made", as it says in the Psalms. But one doesn't *talk* about it; it isn't *nice*. One "ponders it in one's heart", like Mary did, when the Angel told her that she was going to have a little child.'

Andrew felt acutely miserable. 'What a funny word "ponder" is,' he remarked irrelevantly, trying to make a distraction.

'Well, you see, dear, don't you? And you won't talk about kittens before they're born another time, will you? No, nobody's vexed, dear; it's only that I wanted you to know. And of course if Mops has some kittens it will be delightful,' Nandy concluded, brightening.

Andrew was annoyed with her for speaking as if there

227

were any doubt about the matter. 'Mops *is* going to have some kittens,' he said.

'Well, it will be very nice if she does, dear,' said Nandy weakly, and sent him back to play with Stephen.

Andrew *knew* that Mops was going to have some kittens; but he was tired of the subject, and ran away. Stephen rode up on his bicycle, still impersonating the fruitful Miss Smith.

'I've just had another baby,' he said; 'isn't it awful?'

Andrew now rather disliked the subject of births, and suggested that they should play something else.

In a few minutes he had to go out with Miss Hunt, who reopened the subject of Mops. 'We're tired of hearing yer talk about cats and kittens,' she said; 'can't yer find something healthier and more *manly* to occupy yer mind? It's not nice to talk about kittens before they're born.'

'Yes, Miss Hunt,' said Andrew submissively.

'Very well, then,' said Miss Hunt more pleasantly, 'I'll tell yer a secret; Mops has had four kittens this morning. Yer'll see them in good time, and now yer needn't say any more about it.'

'I knew all the time that she was going to have kittens,' thought Andrew.

The children also began to feel a maternal impulse. Mabel borrowed a large vegetable marrow from the gardener, who kept a number of marrows in the greenhouse until Mrs. Milburn had time to make them into jam. She carved a face upon her marrow and made it into a baby, which she nursed all day, and wheeled about the garden in an old perambulator. One afternoon it was taken to the gap in the trees, which they called 'the Church', and was solemnly baptized by Tom, under the name of 'Mary Rosina'. 'The Church' was fitted up for the occasion with an old wooden bench

228

for a pew, and a bell was tied to one of the branches of the tree.

Andrew was devoted to Mary Rosina. He kept taking the marrow-baby in his arms and nursing it, until its parent asked angrily: 'Why can't you go and get a baby for yourself?'

He wandered about the garden next day in search of a marrow. The gardener said that there were no more in the green-house; Mrs. Milburn had asked for some to be sent to the canteen in the village, to be made into marrow-and-ginger jam for the school-children and the troops.

Andrew's heart sank; he so badly wanted a thick yellow marrow to make into a nice fat baby. It would be such a comfort, he thought; he could play so many games with it, and he could tell it things. After all, it would understand quite as well as a real baby. He walked down the garden path resolved to get possession of a marrow by fair means or foul. There was a glint of purpose in his eyes, and he muttered like a spell the proverb of which Nandy was so fond: 'Where there's a will there's a way.' It had just occurred to him that when people wanted something very much, they usually got it; and he was anxious to see if this were really the case. He was determined not to lose his marrow-baby simply because he had weakly given up wanting it.

He looked into a potting-shed to see if any marrows were lying about there, overlooked in the general conscription. He was delighted to find three, out of which he selected a pale little marrow with a smooth surface for carving the mouth and eyes. It was just the right shape for rocking to sleep in his arms. That shewed that if one wanted something badly enough, one usually got it.

He decided that it might be as well to take it without

asking the gardener; and he carried it off to the house, clasping it to his bosom. It was not yet a baby, because he had not yet cut a face on it with Tom's pocket knife, but already he loved it far more than Mary Rosina or than any real baby; more even than his half-sister Joan in Egypt, of whom he received a snapshot nearly every week.

He decided to call his baby 'Peter Joseph', and went up to the nursery to find Tom, and to borrow his knife. Mabel was there.

'I'll make your baby for you,' she said.

'No, I want to,' said Andrew; and he made a horrible gash in the marrow to represent Peter Joseph's mouth, before Mabel could seize the knife.

'You'd much better have left it to me,' said Mabel; 'Mary Rosina's mouth is *far* better.'

'No, I *like* Peter Joseph's mouth,' said Andrew, kissing it passionately; 'but you can do the eyes if you like, Mabel,' he added.

When Peter Joseph had been made, Mabel declared that he must now be born: she did not offer to bear him, as Andrew was his parent. Since he was going to have a baby, the first stage was that he should be ill. He lay down on an ottoman, and Mabel arranged a barricade of chairs round him, and hung them with rugs to screen him from the light and from the observation of Nandy, who was working at the sewing-machine.

Mabel now firmly inserted the marrow between Andrew's jersey and his shirt, making an enormous and uncomfortable protuberance on his stomach. She told him to groan, and so he did. Then with Mabel as his mid-wife, Andrew was slowly delivered of his marrow-baby. Nandy turned her head from the sewing-machine. 'Dears, what *are* you playing at?' she asked.

ANDREW and Stephen no longer pretended to dislike going in to Handborough to see the Aunts. They were taken in again by Berthe one Monday; Mrs. Milburn had been able to use Mademoiselle de la Sablonnière as an excuse for refusing an invitation for the previous Wednesday. 'Andrew goes out every Wednesday,' she wrote, 'with a Belgian girl from Brenchford; his father is so anxious that he should speak French well, and we do think it so important to keep to a definite routine, to prepare him for the discipline of school. I am sure you will agree.'

To leave Quenby for the Aunts' house was like leaving school for home. They walked through the streets of Handborough comparing them with the bleakness of Duckwold. Handborough seemed full of pretty things; there were shops full of new books in bright fresh paper covers, silver-smiths with shining windows, and Art shops with coloured pictures and engravings. The streets were full of cheerful animation; ladies passed with children clinging to their arms, or with dogs on a lead. Mysterious people whom they did not know nodded to the Aunts, and Aunt Anne whispered to Andrew: 'That's Mrs. Selby-Jones — mad as a hatter!' or: 'There's that awful little Miss Willoughby.' These unknown ladies flitted by, and were swallowed up by the other people in the street, or they disappeared into the most unlikely-looking shops.

When they used to live in Handborough Regis, they seldom went into the town with the Aunts; shopping with them had still the pleasure of novelty. It was very different from shopping with Miss Hunt in Duckwold;

the girls in the shop served them quietly, without chattering about their home lives, and the shops did not smell so distressingly of cardboard and cheap soap. Aunt Anne took them into a tea-shop, and they sat in a warm corner at a green-tiled table and drank coffee; Aunt Margaret disapproved gently of this custom and said that other people could do what they liked, but she for her part was not going to spoil her luncheon.

When they went to the fish-shop, two delightful occupations were open to them; Andrew could not decide which to choose. He could wait on the pavement outside the next shop, where second-hand books were exposed on a tray; there was an assortment of old sermons, guide-books and natural histories, which it was a joy to turn over. On the other hand, if he went into the shop with Aunt Anne, he could find out what other people were having for luncheon. On a table at the side there lay trussed chickens and neat little piles of filleted fish labelled with their destination. Some of them were going to quite uninteresting people whom they did not know, but Mrs. Poltimore-Robinson had ordered six herrings and a rabbit. Andrew told Aunt Anne. 'How very nasty!' she said; 'but Mrs. Poltimore-Robinson always was a gross feeder!'

The Aunts' house was so much more attractive than Quenby: the children felt this even when they came in, and were sent to wash their hands. The water fell in the thinnest trickle into a round blue and white basin; and when you pulled the plug, it went out with a loud sucking noise, like a vulgar person drinking soup.

Fragrant smells came from the Aunts' kitchen, and lingered about their dining-room. Other people's food was too often merely 'food', prepared and eaten without thought. The Aunts' mint sauce had plenty of sugar in it, there were just enough cloves in their apple tarts,

232

and their custards were delicately flavoured with bay-leaf. They never ate fruit out of tins, and never made puddings out of powders.

After lunch the children sat quietly round the fire and looked at books, while Aunt Anne and Aunt Margaret knitted. They passed the afternoon peacefully, as if there were going to be many more like it; as if they would not have to go back to Quenby after tea. At twenty minutes to three the Aunts went upstairs, and at three o'clock they came downstairs dressed for walking. The children were hastily bundled into their coats and scarves and gloves, and there was the usual desperate search for the dog's lead.

'We'll go for a brisk walk,' said Aunt Margaret.

They walked fast against the wind; the damp and cold out of doors made them think cheerfully that the best of the day was coming. They would shut the wooden shutters and draw the curtains, and the dreary February evening would be shut out of the cheerful morning-room, together with everything unpleasant to think of. There would be china tea and hot scones, a wood fire and soft gas-light.

Nigger would lag behind, poking his nose into corners, sniffing and growling at other dogs; delaying Aunt Anne and Stephen, who loitered behind to drive him on.

'How they hang about,' said Aunt Margaret to Andrew; and Aunt Anne called after them: 'Wait for us little ones, you two!'

Aunt Anne had 'jobs' to be done; in her muff she carried a paper which was to be left at the Vicarage, and there were notes in Andrew's pocket which had to be delivered. Andrew could never believe that they were at all important: he fancied that Aunt Anne had brought them because she liked what she called 'an object for a walk'. He thought that it was a complicated game that she and Aunt Margaret played, instead of going for an ordinary walk. It was so pleasant and restful to pass the day with kind grown-ups and to take part in their games, and to forget your own unhappiness in listening to their cheerful conversation. They did not know half how bad it was at Quenby, and he could not bring himself to tell them. They talked instead of Handborough, or of remote things such as Egypt and the War.

Quenby seemed worse when they returned to it after a day in Handborough. Now that they knew the Aunts were in the right, and had always been in the right, it was so much more terrible to go back to the rule of Aunt Emma, who had been revealed to them for the wicked woman that she was. They now trembled at the thought of being kissed by her, because Aunt Anne said she was a serpent.

Andrew found that his one consolation at Quenby was threatened; more marrows were wanted at the canteen, and Peter Joseph was in great danger of being made into jam. Mary Rosina was carried off, and there was a voice in Rama — Rachel weeping for her children, and would not be comforted because they were not. Andrew was determined to be more resourceful than the bereaved Mabel; *his* baby should not be made into marrow-and-ginger-jam for the school-children and the troops. When he lived in Egypt, he had been particularly interested in the story of Moses in the bulrushes; Moses had been hidden by the edge of the Nile, and perhaps he had passed near the very place in one of his afternoon walks with Stephen and Nandy. He would hide Peter Joseph, as Miriam had hidden Moses, until the danger was overpast.

On reflection he decided that he would not hide Peter

234

Joseph in the rushes by the pond; anyone who found him there was not likely to be as kind to him as Pharaoh's daughter had been to Moses; and Andrew could not go there to play with his baby without being detected. Fortunately Quenby was full of hiding-places; there were stable-lofts where no one ever went, and there were several doors in the walls of the stable-yard opening into dark cupboard-like rooms which never seemed to be used for anything. In one of these Andrew hid Peter Joseph. 'Don't be frightened of the dark, baby,' he whispered; 'stay here and don't make a sound, and They shan't make you into jam.'

Nobody asked about Peter Joseph; it was assumed that he had perished with the other marrows. Mabel remarked sententiously that she and Andrew had sacrificed their children for their King and Country. 'Just like the Vicar at Handborough,' added Andrew.

He paid secret visits to Peter Joseph in the mornings, when Mabel and Tom were still safely out of the way in the school-room with Miss Hunt; and he nursed him with immense affection during the first days of his captivity. Then Peter Joseph was visited less regularly, and Andrew had to wrestle with a shameful feeling that perhaps after all he might as well have been made into jam like Mary Rosina. It was of course impossible to give him up now; it would be cruel after concealing him for so long; moreover he would find difficulty in explaining why he had not given him up before.

One day he went to pay a visit to his baby, more from duty than from affection, and found the door locked. At once his indifference vanished; he was seized with an access of parental love, and was torn with remorse for his past neglect. He could not get into the room, and he did not even know whether Peter Joseph were safely locked up inside, or whether he had been taken away to be made into jam. It was impossible to enquire, and impossible to ask for the key. When he went to bed and, as he always did, lay with his arms round his pillow, he pretended that he was holding his poor marrow-baby, which They had locked up all alone in the dark, or had made into jam for the troops; and he was very unhappy.

Peter Joseph perished as a victim of the War, like many others who attempted to escape it. He was not made into jam, but he rotted in his damp hiding-place. Andrew came frequently to try the door. After several weeks it yielded; it had been unlocked as mysteriously as it had been locked. The cupboard was heavy with a sweet and sickly smell of decay, and Peter Joseph was a green pulpy mess of putrefaction. Andrew felt no sorrow; you could not be sentimental over anything which smelt so unpleasant. He did not even think of giving his child Christian burial; but overcoming his revulsion he found a spade, and carried the corpse to the rubbish heap, covering it over so that it should not be detected.

PEOPLE now sometimes talked about 'when the War is over', and prophets had arisen who knew positively when it was going to end. To the children this was as remote from real life as the end of the World, which, after all, might occur at any time. 'Before the War' had become a golden age of luxury and freedom, which they dimly remembered and could hardly believe in. Now the cousins spent all the year at Quenby; before the War they used to go to the sea. They had paddled in Cardigan Bay, and they had seen old women in steeple-crowned hats, just like witches. 'Before the War' they used to act a play every Christmas, wearing the fancy-dresses out of the dressing-up cupboard; then they handed round cake and wine to the servants who had been called in to see them act. Once the cook had remarked that 'it was as good as a play', which was very silly, because of course it *was* a play.

'Before the War' Andrew and Stephen had lived in Egypt (though Stephen had forgotten it); their mother had been alive then, and they had never stayed at Quenby. Andrew felt that he was doomed to stay at Quenby until the end of the War; perhaps it would last for years, until he forgot that he had ever had a home and parents of his own, and began to call Aunt Emma 'Mummy'. When the War came to an end he would be delivered from his captivity, and would leave the cousins and Miss Hunt for ever. He hoped that the Allies would stop as soon as they possibly could, and would not bother to press on right to Berlin.

Grown-up people were still making efforts to win the

War; all the ladies of Duckwold were making jam and knitting socks and buying War Savings Certificates; and they tried to persuade other people to do so. In the end Duckwold bought so many War Savings Certificates that it was deemed to have presented the Government with the price of an aeroplane; and the Second Sunday before Easter was appointed to be observed as 'Aeroplane Sunday'.

The village was *en fête*; and this, as usual, required that Quenby should be in disorder. There was going to be a meeting on the lawn in the afternoon, and every available bench and chair and stool was brought out in readiness. The people of Duckwold assembled in the Church, and after a short prayer from the Vicar they set forth in procession towards Quenby; they were led by the Vicar and the Choir, and an amateur and uncertain brass band brought up the rear.

The whole procession appeared to be united by the same patriotic fervour; but while those in front were giving vent to it in hymns, those in the rear were becoming more and more secular. The Choir sang with unremitting perseverance out of Hymns Ancient and Modern, enlivened by the Vicar's light tenor and by the rich, fruity contralto which soared from the bosom of Mrs. MacCorquodale, the doctor's wife. They bellowed:

> 'O Lord, stretch forth thy mighty hand
> And guard and bless our Motherland!'

The brass band in the rear were certainly not accompanying this hymn; there was some doubt among themselves what they were playing, but those in their vicinity began to sing *There's a long, long trail a-winding*. Those in the middle of the procession, where the children from Quenby were walking, joined in with the hymn in front, or with the song behind, as they felt inclined; they knew the words of neither.

Just before they reached Quenby a diversion occurred which finally separated the more frivolous from the more earnest element in the procession. It had been arranged that an aeroplane should fly round the people of Duckwold during their patriotic celebrations. The conscientious aviator was not content with circling round the procession, but began to give an exhibition of 'stunts' over the field at the end of the Quenby garden, and finally shewed signs of coming down there. The tail end of the procession, including the brass band, promptly broke away from the rest, and ran into the field to watch the aeroplane. Andrew, wedged between Nandy and Miss Hunt, had no chance of escape, and was given no option but to go with the respectable part of the procession, and listen to patriotic speeches on the lawn.

The Vicar said a few words first:

'Dear Friends, we are all engaged on a great adventure. We are all taking our part, humble though it be, in the War that is to end War. Yes, even we at Duckwold, we also serve. All of us have helped in our little ways. We put by our pennies, we buy our War Savings Certificates, and then the Government can buy more aeroplanes, can it not? Dear friends, is it not an inspiring thought, that the lives of each and all of us can become of national, nay, of world-wide importance? We must all fight tooth and nail for the Truth and the Right, for the Victory of the Powers of Light over the Powers of Darkness, for the Triumph of Justice over the Oppressor, for God and Country. . . . Are we downhearted? I venture to think not.'

Mr. Jones, the solemn nonconformist draper, was next invited to speak, and astonishingly revealed himself

239

as a humorous speaker. Some people, he said, were tired of the War; for his part he was not. It brought out all the best in all of us; and it was so delightful to discover how really good and unselfish and brave our neighbours were, that it would be a pity if we did not sometimes have a little trouble, such as a War, to reveal it to us. But for those who were tired of the War he had only one word, PERSEVERANCE.

Perseverance was not an easy word, and it was not only the younger members of his audience who were likely to find it difficult. He would like, he said, to illustrate the meaning of Perseverance by a little fable. 'Once upon a time there were two flies called Jimmy and Johnny who fell into a pan of cream, and they were very frightened. Now these two flies were different in character; one had Perseverance, and the other had not. Well, Jimmy, he was the one who had no Perseverance, said: "We're lost"; and sure enough he was drowned. But Johnny said: "I'm not going to give in, I'm not going to give in" — he had Perseverance, you see. So Johnny flapped and he flapped, and he skipped and he jumped' — and Mr. Jones the draper went through all these motions, vigorously flapping and flopping and skipping and jumping — 'and in the end Johnny found he had churned the cream to butter, and was standing safe on dry land,' concluded the draper; and he added that this spirit of Perseverance had always characterized little Britain and little Duckwold, and there was more need of it at the present than there ever had been.

Mr. Milburn ended the proceedings with a dull speech. He praised the eloquence of the Vicar and of Mr. Jones the draper, and said that he and Mrs. Milburn were glad to welcome the people of Duckwold at Quenby, and that he hoped that they would soon meet there to celebrate Victory. After one or two phrases about 'our men in France' he suggested that they should sing the National Anthem.

Andrew sang vigorously, but forgot to take his hat off. Miss Hunt scolded him till he cried, and then scolded him for crying.

IV

In the Easter holidays Quenby was fuller and more cheerful. Tom and Mabel were not entirely pleased at having their brothers and sister home from school, for they had now to take a back place. But Andrew, who had no position to lose, was very glad to have a change of society; he even rose in the world with the return of Flora and Philip and Arthur, who were inclined to patronize him, and who preferred his conversation to that of Tom and Mabel.

Miss Hunt was not pleased at Andrew's rise in the world, and did her best to counteract it. She decided to teach him 'manners' during the holidays from other lessons, and while the elder children were about. One day she came into the school-room carrying a plate and a knife and fork. 'Here, Andrew,' she called.

Andrew turned away from the dolls' house where he and Flora were making up a story about its inhabitants.

'Come here,' said Miss Hunt, 'and don't bother Flora. I've got something for yer to do. I'm going to teach yer how to eat.'

The cousins burst out laughing.

'One does it with one's teeth,' observed Arthur.

'Yer know what I meant, I'm going to teach Andrew to eat properly,' said Miss Hunt crossly. 'Here, sit down here. Sit up straight and don't draw yer chair away from the table like that.'

Andrew was pushed and pulled into the right attitude. 'Now what would yer do if there was a piece of meat on that plate?' asked Miss Hunt.

'Eat it!' said Arthur.

'Be quiet, Arthur!' ordered Miss Hunt. 'It's not at all

242

funny that yer cousin can't eat nicely yet, though he's only a year younger than you. Don't fidget, Andrew, yer've got to learn to sit still. These things are quite as important as yer Latin, and they've got to be learned thoroughly. Now take the knife in yer right hand and the fork in yer left.'

Andrew dutifully cut and ate the air for a few minutes, and then put down his knife and fork.

'I've not finished with yer yet,' said Miss Hunt, 'I'm going to teach yer to open and shut doors.'

Miss Hunt went in and out of the school-room door, and Andrew had to open and shut it for her. At the third repetition of the ceremony Philip and Arthur and Flora lined up and made sweeping bows as she sailed into the school-room with all the dignity of her four foot eight, and Andrew was spared any further lessons in decorum.

Miss Hunt had failed in her attempt to humiliate him, and the leaders of opinion at Quenby were unexpectedly on his side. Andrew was therefore much pleased with himself for the moment, but his pride came before a fall.

At the top of a cedar tree in the garden one of the gardeners had rigged up a kind of platform, where the elder cousins were fond of sitting. They called it 'the aeroplane'. Andrew was invited to come up there one afternoon by Flora, which was a great mark of condescension. There was not very much room on the aeroplane, and Tom and Mabel were not asked.

'Yer won't be able to get up there,' croaked Miss Hunt at the foot of the tree; 'yer not used to the country like the others. Yer can't climb trees.'

'Oh, Miss Hunt, you know I can,' protested Andrew, who sometimes clambered up a few branches on an easy fir tree.

'Very well,' said Miss Hunt.

He began well enough, but a few branches up he came to an awkward gap. 'I'm stuck,' he wailed.

Flora shouted down encouragement: 'It's all right, you can do it easily if you stretch.'

But Andrew did not at all want to stretch. He was secure, if unhappy, on a firm bough, and in front of him there was a yawning gap between him and the slippery knot in the tree which was his next possible foothold; and he had every reason to have little confidence in his own agility.

'I can't do it,' he cried.

'I'll come and give you a hand,' offered Flora.

'No, it's no use, I can't,' said Andrew.

'Yer frightened, I knew yer would be,' said Miss Hunt.

Andrew made a half-hearted lurch forwards, and then recoiled on to his bough, having effected nothing except a tear in his jersey.

'Yer'd better come down,' said Miss Hunt, 'it's no sense tearing yer good clothes.'

'It's no good standing there if you can't get any further,' said Flora coldly.

Andrew shamefacedly climbed down to the ground and gave himself up to Miss Hunt. 'I told yer yer couldn't manage it,' she said.

'Well, I thought it would be easier,' he said.

'Yer'll often find that there are more things yer can't do than yer think,' said Miss Hunt, and with small regard for logic she went on to tell him that he very well *could* have climbed up to the aeroplane if he had possessed average courage and agility.

'Yer stand there quite pleased with yerself,' she remarked indignantly, 'and let yerself be beaten by a tree.'

244

This was needlessly unkind; Andrew was not pleased with himself, nor was he standing talking to Miss Hunt from choice.

'Well, what does it matter if I do go up the silly old tree or not?' he said. It mattered to no one but him, and he did not want Miss Hunt to see how much it mattered that he could hear the Olympians talking and laughing up at the top of the tree, and knew that if he had been more venturesome he might be there with them, instead of being cast down to the company of Miss Hunt and Tom and Mabel.

Miss Hunt had to admit that it did not matter very much. 'It's the principle of the thing,' she scolded. Grown-up people always saved up their principles like that, and brought them out unfairly at the last moment, when they were already beaten by rights. 'Yer must learn to be able to do things yerself and not get frightened because yer can't always have yer Nuss there to hold yer hand,' continued Miss Hunt. 'Fancy being afraid of climbing a tree, and yer father a soldier too!'

One after another Miss Hunt was coming out with the meanest of grown-up taunts. Andrew, however, was well aware that he had not chosen his father's profession, and that, had the choice been his, he would certainly have chosen anything else rather than the army.

'I don't know how yer going to follow in yer father's footsteps,' ended Miss Hunt with triumph.

Andrew said that he was not going to attempt to do anything of the sort; however, during the course of a walk in which Miss Hunt and Tom led the way, Mabel argued with unusual ingenuity, and almost convinced Andrew that as the elder son of a soldier he would have to be a soldier too.

'But at that rate Daddy would have been a sailor,'

he said, 'because I know that Grandad was in the navy.'

'That's all the same thing,' replied Mabel, 'and I daresay you could go into the navy if you would rather, or even the air force.'

Andrew had a moment of dismay at these horrifying alternatives. The army was certainly by far the least evil of the three; one was on dry ground, and Daddy at any rate never had to do anything really dangerous.

'But Paul's in the army and Uncle Aubrey isn't,' said Andrew.

Mabel argued that the army was so distinguished a profession that Paul was allowed to follow it, instead of going into an office like his father. Therefore as Colonel Faringdon was in the army, he would be sure to make Andrew go into the army too. It was what everyone would expect, and even if Andrew managed to get out of it (which was extremely unlikely) everyone would certainly despise him, and he would wish that he had done the proper thing.

In front of Andrew stretched an appalling future: Quenby, then school, and then the parade ground. Life was certainly not worth living. Some months ago, when he used to see Dr. Waring, he had made up his mind that he was going to die young, but now nothing seemed likely to come of that. He was doomed to live, and in front of him there lay a series of transmigrations of soul into different selves. Already he had caught a glimpse of an older self whom he did not like very much. The older self was awkward and had not very good taste. He had a tendency to talk loud and to make rather cheap jokes, for which Andrew had to blush afterwards. With infinite distaste he contemplated a gallery of possible future selves who wore long trousers, who greased their hair, who had to shave. Surely, he thought, God would spare him the shame of reaching the extraordinarily unattractive age of seventeen; but he had heard someone say that it was not right to pray that one might die, so there was nothing to do but to leave it to the Will of God.

V

AFTER Easter Miss Hunt bought a rabbit, a large, yellow lop-eared doe which she called 'Myrtle'; and she had a hutch made for it and set up in the aviary. She also bought a little book called *Rabbit-keeping for Profit* which everyone at Quenby read; it persuaded them all that rabbit-keeping was an extremely agreeable and profitable pastime. A rabbit cost very little and a hutch could be made for nothing; in due course it would have a litter and the young rabbits could be sold very advantageously. It seemed, however, that young rabbits were difficult to rear, because on the slightest provocation their mothers ate them; the other chief danger in rabbit-keeping was that one might give the creatures too many cabbage or lettuce leaves and that they would swell up to a great size and burst.

Myrtle was installed in the aviary, and the children industriously hunted for plantain leaves and sow-thistle and meadowsweet, and brought them to Miss Hunt for Myrtle's supper in quantities sufficient to feed five rabbits. In the morning Myrtle's hutch was 'done out', and she was persuaded to waddle round the aviary while her bed was being made. She was a great success with the children, but they were not satisfied; Tom and Mabel clamoured to have rabbits of their own, and Andrew wanted to have one far more than they, but was too shy to ask. He hoped Miss Hunt would enquire whether he did not want one too.

Miss Hunt had said nothing about it to Andrew; but one day when he came back from a walk with Mademoiselle de la Sablonnière, Mabel told him that she and

Tom had gone with Miss Hunt into Duckwold, and had each bought a Belgian hare.

'I want a rabbit too,' said Andrew.

'You're just copycatting us,' said Mabel scornfully and appealed to Miss Hunt. 'Isn't Andrew a copycat? He wants to have a rabbit now just because we've got them.'

'So yer want a rabbit, do yer?' said Miss Hunt. 'Well, who's going to look after it when yer go to school, *I* should like to know? And who's going to look after it when yer get tired of it? Yer don't stick to things like Tom and Mabel; when yer tired of anything yer just leave it to yer Nuss. If yer have a rabbit yer'll soon be whimpering: "Oo, Nanny, feed my rabbit, because I don't want to, boo-hoo." ' And Miss Hunt gave a not very convincing impression of Andrew crying.

Andrew was very angry and unhappy. 'No, I shan't,' he said; 'I want to have a rabbit; and why shouldn't I have one as much as Tom and Mabel?'

'Bee-caws,' said Miss Hunt indignantly, 'it's yer cousins' home, and it's not yours, though yer seem to think yer can do what yer like here because yer Aunt Emma is so kind as to have yer at Quenby. Why should yer have a rabbit indeed, when yer only staying here? And not for very long now, we all hope.'

'But can't I have one while I'm here, Miss Hunt?' Andrew pleaded.

'Yer a very tiresome little bawy,' said Miss Hunt; 'that's enough about rabbits. Run away to yer Nuss.'

Andrew ran up to the store-room, but there was no one there. He flung himself into Nandy's rocking-chair and cried so hard that he soon had cried away the worst of his misery; and the motion of the rocking-chair turned his sobs into little hiccupping gulps. It would be a pity, he thought, if he were not still crying when Nandy

came; it was better to cry secretly and never to be discovered at all, or else to be found crying. It was annoying when They came in and said: 'You've been crying.'
When They found you still in tears, They were capable
of being sympathetic, because They wanted you to stop.
When They discovered that you had been crying, but
had recovered, They were often hard-hearted enough
to scold and say: 'It's not *manly* to cry.' Why should
any child want to be manly?

Andrew's eyes were sure to be red when Nandy came
in, and he was sure to sniff as if he had a cold in his
nose. He thought he would try if he could cry a little
more till Nandy came. This was not very difficult to
do. After all, he had badly wanted a rabbit, and if Tom
and Mabel each had one, it was a shame that he should
be left out of it.

Nandy's sympathy would have been easily won, even
if Andrew had not been in tears. She thought that he
was being unfairly treated, and that Miss Hunt had no
authority to forbid him to keep a rabbit. 'Let's go and
find Aunt Emma, dear,' she suggested; 'and we'll see
what she says. I'm sure she'll let you have a rabbit, if
she knows you really want one. And if Aunt Emma says
you can, it doesn't matter what Miss Hunt says.'

They found Mrs. Milburn. 'Oh, Mrs. Milburn,' said
Nandy, 'I found Andrew in the store-room, crying as if
his heart would break; and it seems he wanted to have a
rabbit like the others, but Miss Hunt didn't think he
had better have one. Do you think he might?'

'Do you really want one, dear?' asked Aunt Emma.

'Oh yes, please, Aunt Emma,' Andrew entreated.

'Well, you shouldn't have cried, dear, that's silly,'
she said; 'you should have told me, and then it would
have been quite all right. I don't see why you shouldn't
have a rabbit, but you must take care of it properly if

you do. And now you and Nandy can go and buy one whenever you like.'

Aunt Emma was so kind that Andrew found it hard to believe that she was a serpent; but she was, of course, he remembered. Perhaps even serpents had their better moments. People did have their better moments; Nandy had hers, when she would give in to Andrew over some little point or other, instead of being restrained by her conscience; but unhappily she called these her 'weak moments', and did not like him to use them as a precedent.

'Well, isn't that nice?' said Nandy as they left Mrs. Milburn; 'now to-morrow afternoon we can go and look for a rabbit.'

'But do you think Miss Hunt will mind?' asked Andrew anxiously.

'Now, Andrew,' said Nandy sharply, 'you're not to think any more about Miss Hunt. That's weak and silly. If your Aunt Emma lets you have a rabbit you can have one, and there's no need to worry any more about it.'

Next morning, after lessons, Andrew and Nandy went to order a rabbit hutch from the man at the farm, and in the afternoon they started to search for a rabbit. They had not much knowledge about rabbits; Andrew was only determined not to buy a lop-eared rabbit like Myrtle, nor a Belgian hare, because Tom and Mabel each had one. Stephen said the rabbit must be as much like Old Bun as possible, and Andrew politely agreed, but refused to buy a rabbit that had eczema.

Finally they chose a young doe of no pedigree, which a pleasant farmer's wife offered them for two shillings. It was not a good choice, but they were all pleased. They promised to fetch the rabbit as soon as a hutch was ready for it; and Andrew went home working out the immense profits he was sure to gain as soon as it had a litter. According to the rabbit-book he might expect this at any time after it was six or seven months old, and then on frequent occasions.

In due course his hutch came from the carpenter and was set up in the aviary. Miss Hunt found it when she went to feed Myrtle; Andrew had been too shy to mention it to her, and no one else had thought of telling her. She asked Mrs. Milburn what the meaning of it was, and heard that Andrew had been given permission to keep a rabbit. She was exceedingly angry, but kept it to herself until she next had him in the school-room.

When he came in to his lesson she said: 'So yer going to have a rabbit, I hear; why wasn't I told anything about it?'

Andrew felt confused; he could hardly say that he had felt too shy to mention it, and that Nandy had said that it was none of Miss Hunt's business.

'Aunt Emma said I could have a rabbit,' he replied timidly, knowing that he was not answering Miss Hunt's question.

'Well, if yer'd told us,' said Miss Hunt, 'we could have helped yer to find a rabbit; if yer hadn't gone off in that underhand way with yer Nuss. What sort of rabbit did yer buy?'

'Oh, I don't know; a brown one.'

'Well, I don't suppose yer know anything about rabbits, or that yer Nuss does. Yer'd have done much better to come with Tom and Mabel and me. I don't know why yer must always go with yer Nuss and yer little brother. Yer know what yer father said.'

'Yes, Miss Hunt,' said Andrew; and settled down to his preparation for Mr. Scrymgeour.

Stephen and Nandy went to fetch the rabbit, because Andrew was having lessons with Mr. Scrymgeour.

They brought it in a covered basket borrowed from the farm. Tom and Mabel and Miss Hunt were contemptuous of it, and said that it was a low-bred creature; and its subsequent conduct did not endear it to them. When it was let loose in a wired-in grass plot with the other rabbits, it proved to be spiteful and opinionated. It set its back up, and refused to play with Myrtle and the Belgian hares; it bit one of them, and kicked the other. Miss Hunt was able to say to Andrew with great satisfaction: 'If yer'd only come with Bell and Tom and me, instead of with yer Nuss, yer'd have got a much better rabbit than that wretched creature.'

'Doing the rabbits' continued to be a delightful occupation; even the dirty work of turning out the hutches was not unpleasant: rabbits had not the disagreeable smell of horses or cows. The collection of rabbit food was always amusing on a fine day; and if it were wet, they could raid the kitchen garden.

Andrew was anxious to try experiments, to see how much lettuce one could give a rabbit before it burst. He longed for one of the rabbits to have babies, to see if it would eat them; but only Myrtle was old enough. He asked Mabel impatiently why Myrtle did not have a litter, because according to the rabbit-book she was the right age. Mabel much disconcerted him by asking: 'Who do you suppose could be the father, if Myrtle had babies?'

'I don't know,' said Andrew; 'we could pretend your rabbit was.'

'Don't be silly,' said Mabel, 'it couldn't be; it's a she.'

'Need there be a father?' asked Andrew.

'Of course there must be,' said Mabel decisively.

'But why?'

'You're not old enough to understand,' answered Mabel pompously, and tossed her head.

Andrew was stung by this; he knew by experience from their lessons with Mr. Scrymgeour that he was far more intelligent than Mabel, and anything that she could understand, he could certainly understand quite as well, and probably a good deal better. But it would be unwise to be rude, as Mabel would not tell him then.

'I'm sure I could understand if you can,' he said. 'Do tell me, Mabel.'

'No, I wasn't to tell the other children,' said Mabel importantly.

'But how do you know yourself?' he asked.

'Flora told me; a girl at school told her, and she'd been told by her mother.'

Andrew was mystified: 'But why is it all so secret, why baby rabbits must have fathers?'

'Silly! It's not just rabbits,' exclaimed Mabel. 'It's how babies are born.'

'Oh, but I know that, you know I do,' protested Andrew.

'I bet you you don't,' said Mabel. And then of course she had to tell him.

Andrew was obliged to admit that Mabel's story was new to him; at first he thought it was a horrible invention of her own.

'I don't believe you,' he said. 'You made that up.'

'No, I didn't; you can ask Mother or Miss Hunt if you like. It's perfectly true.'

He could see that she was really in earnest, and her story had a horrible plausibility. It was too nasty, he thought, to be merely an invention of Mabel's.

'Well, I think it's perfectly disgusting,' he said with a shudder.

'It's very wrong to say that,' said Mabel priggishly. 'It's very holy and beautiful. At least the mother of the girl who told Flora said so.'

'Rubbish, you know it's horrid,' said Andrew.

'But if God made it like that, it must be right,' said Mabel, using the argument with which the mother of the girl at Flora's school had apologized for the crudeness of the 'facts of life'.

Andrew wondered why God could not find a way of doing these things more nicely. In a flash he understood a hundred grown-up mysteries and reticences. He knew now the reason why so many things were said to be 'not nice'. It was really remarkable that there were not more of them, since there was at the back of all life this incredibly dirty story that Mabel had just told him. It seemed to poison the whole world for him, and to blot out the sun.

'Well, I shan't ever marry and have children,' he said with decision. He had always thought that it must be very disagreeable to be married; there would be all the vulgar jokes people made, and there would be confetti and orange blossom. That would be unpleasant enough; but nothing like so unpleasant as to go away and live with someone who was not even a relation. His mother used to tell him that he was to marry when he was twenty-eight. Once he asked her whom he was to marry, but she said: 'Your wife isn't born yet, I hope. She must be younger than you.' That consoled him; it made everything so much more uncertain. Perhaps she would never be born at all. Still, he never failed to protest. He would be a bachelor, he said; he would try hard to have the button in the plum pudding at Christmas. But then he did not know the worst. Now nothing would ever induce him to marry; perhaps it was really as well that his mother was dead and could not make him.

'I think it would be rather fun to be married,' said Mabel. Andrew was inexpressibly shocked, and broke off the conversation.

He wandered away alone, thinking how very nasty the facts of life were. He wished that Mabel had not told him. He envied children like Stephen who did not yet know; he even envied himself a few minutes ago on his way down the path, before he met Mabel in the aviary. In two minutes everything had been changed: he had been changed, and was now a different person. He passed his hands over his face. He hoped he did not look so different that everyone would notice it; his face was hot and flushed, but otherwise everything seemed where it was before. He was dreadfully afraid that Nandy would notice that something was wrong, and would not leave him alone until she knew what it was.

He was oppressed with a feeling of guilt and misery, like that of Adam and Eve when they had tasted the tree of knowledge and were ashamed of their nakedness. He was frightened and ashamed because he knew a dirty secret; and he was told that it was wrong of him not to think it holy and beautiful. It was, he thought, obviously shameful and ugly; but he was forced to admit that Mabel's argument had considerable force. If God had arranged it, it certainly ought to be holy and beautiful. Perhaps after all it was Satan who had done it.

For days afterwards he was upset by Mabel's story. The Bible was so dreadfully explicit, and there was always the danger that the first lesson in Church would make him blush furiously; he had to turn his face away, or to look down at the floor and hope that the grown-up people would not see. If they saw, they would know that he *knew*. Sex was mentioned directly only in the Bible, but elsewhere it was implied in a thousand things. Andrew carefully circumvented these things; just as, when he was younger, he had avoided all reference to unhappiness or physical pain. He did not like, at first, to hear anyone speak of sons and daughters, or fathers and mothers; Mabel had given these words an obscene significance. If you came to look at it, it was as bad to think about brothers and sisters, cousins, or uncles and aunts; on working things out, he found that all relationship was based on IT. Even in innocent and everyday things IT was lurking grimly in the background; and you were always liable to run up against IT with a shock.

IT seemed to Andrew more horrible than any murder or cruelty, and it was appalling to think how often IT had happened. IT had to happen before anyone could be born; and there were millions of people in the world. A great many people were born every day; therefore IT must happen all over the world a great many times every day. It made one feel sick to think of it.

He felt that it was wrong to be haunted by these unpleasant thoughts, and violently tried to repel them. It seemed unfair that it should be wrong, because these thoughts were so unpleasant that no one could enjoy having them, but they would persistently return to torment him. The slightest thing was liable to start a train of thought which led inevitably to IT; and sometimes IT came spontaneously into his head without any preparation. If he saw IT coming he would try to head IT off; but usually IT was too quick for him. It was very awkward when IT attacked him during lessons, because his hands twitched uncomfortably and he could not hold his pen properly. He began to write even more vilely than usual, and was terrified that Miss Hunt or Mr. Scrymgeour would notice. They always went on dictating remorselessly, and he felt that he would scream if IT did not stop soon.

Mabel had been proud of knowing, because the smaller children did not know; and she felt older and superior. Andrew hated feeling older. It was not as if knowledge brought any advantage; the fictions in which small children believed were far more agreeable than the truth. Andrew used to believe that a beautiful angel had carried him down from Heaven, and had put him in his mother's bed while she was asleep. It was a pity to have to sacrifice this pretty story in favour of a grim reality. That sort of thing was constantly happening as you grew older; the good things vanished away, and bad things came in their place. The angel who had brought him into the world had gone, and a doctor had been called in instead. His last shreds of belief in Father Christmas were lost, and he already doubted the existence of Fairies.

However, Andrew was quite sure that grown-up people did not think he was old enough to *know*, and did not mean to tell him for a long time yet. Mabel had not yet been *told* by an authorized person, and she was more than four years older than him. It was therefore likely that for at least four more years he would have to bear the guilt of knowing what he ought not to know. His father would probably tell him, or perhaps Nandy would. He could imagine how extremely awkward that conversation would be, and he was very much afraid that Nandy or his father would discover then, if they had not previously done so, that he already knew. All the same he longed to be *told* properly, in order to be released from the burden of secret and illicit knowledge.

Worse than the illegality of his knowledge was the sinfulness of it. IT was always lurking in the background somewhere, and was an irresistible magnet to his thoughts; yet to think about IT filled him with misery and with a sense of sinfulness. It was God who forgave sins; but this was a sin which he could not confess into Nandy's apron in his evening prayers. There was some alleviation of his guilt in Duckwold church on Sundays when they said the general confession, and like Tom and Mabel and Miss Hunt he prayed: 'Spare Thou them, O God, which confess their faults, restore Thou them that are penitent'; but he needed a more direct and personal way of atonement. He returned to the private religion of his earlier childhood; hermits did not confine their activities to telling beads and gathering simples — they did penance.

Andrew regretfully abandoned the idea of scourging himself; he had nothing to do it with, and even if he succeeded in finding a way, he did not know how to explain away the stripes, which would certainly puzzle Nandy when he had his bath. A hair shirt was obviously unprocurable, but after giving some thought to the matter he was able to devise a similar means of mortification. It was easy to slip the cord from his dressing-gown and take it to bed with him, and once in bed there was no difficulty in passing it underneath his pyjamas and tying it very tightly round his waist, against the bare skin; at other times he would tie his ankles together. There were other penances for which no instrument was required. He could merely lie still in an uncomfortable position until he gave himself leave to move.

Andrew did not at all enjoy hurting himself, but he found in his voluntary acts of self-punishment a certain exaltation which effectively put all thoughts of IT out of his mind, and which generally left him so tired that he fell asleep before they could recur.

DURING the summer Aunt Mary and Frank came to stay for a few days at Quenby. Mabel and Andrew were sent into Duckwold to meet them, and as it was a fine day they decided to walk there and to come back in the car. They were both in a good humour that afternoon. They did not get on badly together when Miss Hunt and Tom were not there to set them against each other, and they even had a few tastes in common; they were both passionately fond of Aunt Emma's dolls' house, and if they had been left to themselves they would have played nothing but 'girls' games' in which it was considered 'babyish' for Mabel and 'unmanly' for Andrew to indulge.

'Of course I remember Uncle Oswald,' Mabel was saying, 'he's awfully nice. But I've only seen Aunt Elsa once when she came to lunch. Isn't she Scotch?'

Andrew blushed. 'She's German,' he said.

'Not really?' asked Mabel.

'Yes, Aunt Margaret told me.'

'What a pity,' said Mabel in a grown-up voice; 'but what's she *like*, Andrew?'

Andrew allowed himself the dangerous luxury of speaking out of the fullness of his heart. All his fear and distrust and dislike of the dark woman in the green hat came pouring out in long sentences that tumbled over each other in their breathless haste. He was saying things he could never have said to Nandy or Stephen or the Aunts, things which he had not even said to himself until this moment when he was thinking them aloud for the first time. He felt inspired; cold shudders ran down his back and tears came into his eyes, and he felt

260

his face stiffen as the skin tightened over his cheek-bones. Suddenly he stopped, breathless, and felt ashamed and frightened, because he had so completely exposed himself in front of Mabel, whom he had every reason not to trust with his confidence.

'Promise not to tell!' he urged.

Mabel was embarrassed and a little frightened by this outburst, and was ready enough to give her promise. Andrew saw that she was serious and friendly this afternoon, and he felt reassured for the moment. They finished their walk in silence.

Mrs. Thompson was paying a visit of inspection to Quenby and to her brother's children. She had felt doubtful of Oswald's wisdom in removing Andrew and Stephen from Handborough Regis, and had been in correspondence with their aunts on the subject. Mrs. Milburn took great pains to be as charming as possible to her, and to be most affectionate to Andrew and Stephen and Frank during her stay. She asked the Aunts over to meet Mrs. Thompson, to shew she had nothing to fear from them.

Aunt Mary had unwisely decided to employ Frank to question Andrew about his life at Quenby: she thought it would 'come more naturally' from him. Frank was no diplomatist; the first moment that he caught Andrew alone in the garden he asked him solemnly: 'Which do you like best, being here or at Handborough Regis?'

'Aunt Mary told you to ask me that,' said Andrew accusingly.

'Yes, she did,' admitted Frank.

'Well, if Aunt Mary had asked me herself I'd have told her,' said Andrew loftily.

'All right, you needn't be so huffy,' said Frank, 'and now I'm going to ask Tom and Mabel how they like you being here,' and he walked off with dignity on his mission.

Andrew stood still a moment, biting his lip with annoyance at Aunt Mary's ruse. It then occurred to him that Frank was likely to cause a good deal of mischief by further questions, and he ran after him to prevent him.

'Mummy told me to,' was all that Frank would reply to Andrew's protests, and before he could be brought to see reason silence was imposed by the sight of Aunt Emma approaching across the lawn between Aunt Margaret and Aunt Anne. The Aunts and Andrew greeted each other with some constraint under Aunt Emma's eye; they were rather cross, and he was extremely shy and uncomfortable.

Aunt Emma sent Andrew off with the Aunts to join Stephen and Nandy by the pond, and carried Frank off with her to look for his mother, an arrangement exasperating to Andrew, who was particularly anxious not to let Frank out of his sight, until he had forced him to promise not to question Tom and Mabel. He dragged along sullenly at the side of his aunts, shuffling his feet. He knew they thought he ought to seem pleased to see them, but after all Quenby was not the place for them, and he liked people to stay in their proper place — like Nigger, who always barked when Mrs. Simpkin came out of the kitchen. Besides, he was worried about Frank.

Nandy and the Aunts said good afternoon to each other very coldly, and Andrew felt more and more what a horrible day it was going to be. He talked very loud to Aunt Anne about Stephen's tricycle, and knew that he was being rather silly about it. Stephen smiled benevolently, and seemed glad to see the Aunts in his quiet way. Nandy and Aunt Margaret were talking very politely about the weather; they thought the rain would keep off until the hay had been brought in.

For once it was a relief to see Miss Hunt coming with Tom and Mabel. Her raucous voice was raised in welcome. 'Well, Aunt Margaret, well, Aunt Anne, I'm very glad to see yer,' she shouted. 'Here, Tom, here, Bell, kiss yer aunts.'

Mabel whispered to Andrew: 'Suppose I told Miss Hunt what you said yesterday?'

'What d'you mean?' he whispered uneasily.

'About Aunt Elsa.'

'You *mustn't*, you promised!' he cried.

'What's this, children?' asked Miss Hunt.

'Miss Hunt, Andrew said . . .'

'No, I didn't!'

'Oh, you story!'

'Yer a tiresome little bawy,' said Miss Hunt, 'and it's tea-time. Yer'd better go off with yer Nuss and wash.'

Again Andrew was dragged off in misery, leaving a potential mischief-maker in command of the situation. He rightly supposed that Mabel had threatened him out of the devilry of the moment, and that she had no deliberately laid plan of blackmail. He hoped that she would think no more of it if he left the subject, but it was so hard to leave the subject alone. She could get him into endless trouble by repeating his secrets, and until that moment it had not occurred to him that she was likely to betray him. He would now have to keep a watch on Mabel as well as Frank, and it would be particularly difficult this afternoon, when there were four aunts there to complicate things.

They had tea on the terrace, and it was an extremely unpleasant meal. Andrew was acutely conscious of the hostilities seething among the family group round the tea-table. The Aunts hated Nandy and Aunt Emma;

Nandy hated the Aunts and Miss Hunt; Miss Hunt hated Nandy and Stephen and him; he hated Aunt Emma, Miss Hunt, Tom and Mabel, and possibly Frank as well. Aunt Emma, who sat there offering sugar and milk, probably hated nearly all of them; and Aunt Mary was looking on and judging them; you could not blame her if she condemned the lot of them. He was on tenterhooks, waiting for the explosion; but they were well-bred people, and each ominous rumble soon grew quiet. It could hardly have been more terrible if they had come to blows.

The grown-ups and Stephen sat on after the tea-table had been carried away. Tom and Mabel and Andrew were ordered to play clock-golf with Frank; none of them wanted to play, and they were all very sulky, except Frank, who was on his best behaviour as a visitor. The sky was darkening, and it was growing hot and stuffy; it was very difficult to keep their tempers under control. Andrew was putting erratically, and Mabel was nagging at him because he was not really trying. Frank was looking down his nose in disapproval and preparing a report for his mother.

They were all called away from the game to say good-bye to the Aunts. Andrew badly wanted to cry; they were his only kind relations, and their visit to-day had been a miserable failure. He could not even be sorry that they were going back to Handborough Regis.

Mabel trod hard and viciously on his toe as they turned to go back to their game. 'Brute!' he cried, and kicked her hard on the shin. She burst into tears. 'Very well,' she screamed, 'I shall tell Frank all you said about Aunt Elsa, and I shall tell Miss Hunt, and I shall tell Mother.'

Frank looked extremely shocked. 'Mummy says . . .'' he began.

264

'Frank, Andrew hates Aunt Elsa, Andrew hates Aunt Elsa, Andrew hates Aunt Elsa,' chanted Mabel, dodging Andrew's onslaughts.

He gave up trying to stop it. His secret was out now, and it was quite useless to appeal to Mabel or to Frank. He would now receive cold glances from Aunt Emma, sermons from Nandy and Aunt Mary, and repeated scoldings from Miss Hunt. Worst of all, everyone would now *know* part of his private and secret thoughts; and having once got inside his private self, they were sure to go on prying and poking. Quenby was now intolerable.

'Yes, and I hate you all, and I hate Aunt Emma, and I hate Quenby,' he screamed.

He turned and ran blindly down the drive after the Aunts' car; tears were streaming down his face, and he screamed himself hoarse to make them stop. They saw him in time to stop before they reached the crossroads. He climbed panting on to the step of the car, and said they must take him away from Quenby for ever.

'What on earth is the meaning of this, Andrew?' asked Aunt Anne angrily. 'We're ashamed of you for making such a scene.'

'You had better go back at once,' said Aunt Margaret coldly.

They drove on, and Andrew walked back slowly and despairingly to Quenby. He knew that he was going to face universal disapproval from the grown-ups, with whom that little prig Frank would identify himself, and that Tom and Mabel would take every advantage of the situation.

Nandy was waiting for him. He longed to plunge his head into her apron and cry, but she was cold and grieved. Now that he was in disgrace her apron was not a comforting extension of his pocket-handkerchief; it was the stiff white surplice of a priest, waiting to reconcile a sinner, by the way of penance, with an offended God.

VII

At Michaelmas Andrew went to school. He did not go to Holmlea; Mrs. Milburn had chosen a school at Pippingford, some fifteen miles from Handborough Regis.

During the last days before he went, Andrew and Nandy were very busy going through all his clothes, and checking them against a printed list sent by the Matron of Saint Peter's School. At last there seemed to be the right number of everything, and they packed up his trunk carefully, beginning with boots and ending with a linen hold-all containing his shirts and handkerchiefs and underclothes. Beside his trunk Andrew had a little fat hand-bag; the school-list said this was to contain 'things necessary for the night', which it explained priggishly as 'Bible, pyjamas, sponge-bag, &c.'

Andrew was very unhappy at parting from Stephen; but he was delighted to leave Quenby and the cousins. Nandy went with him, so he did not yet begin to feel frightened of school. They left after lunch, and the car took them to Duckwold station, where they took the train into Handborough Regis.

At Handborough there are two stations; trains to Pippingford went from the Western station, in a different part of the town from the Southern station at which they arrived. Nandy engaged an outside porter to carry Andrew's box, and they walked beside him. The old man was evidently past his work, and tottered feebly under the weight, and more than once was obliged to rest. When they reached the Western station they found that they had just missed the connection, and that there was no train to Pippingford until seven.

Andrew felt immensely relieved. They sat down in

the waiting-room, and Nandy opened a large brown paper parcel which she was carrying. 'They're some books from your Daddy,' she said. 'They were to be given you when you got to school; but I expect you'd like one to read now.' There was a bound volume of the *Boys' Own Paper* and another of *Chums*. Nandy bought herself a paper, and they sat down and read quietly. Nandy was such a soothing person; Andrew sat close in to her side. She was smoother and more comforting when she had her apron on; but all the same it was a great blessing that they had missed the train, and he still had her with him.

At tea-time she went into the station, and brought back a bag of buns, and two cups of dark brown station tea. 'It looks dreadfully strong,' she said; 'but it will do us both good, my dear.' They had quite a cheerful picnic in the waiting-room; Andrew tried to forget that he would have his next meal at Saint Peter's School. Nandy talked a little too cheerfully about the Christmas holidays.

It was dark when they took their train; the journey was exciting, because they did not know when they were due to arrive at Pippingford. At the first stop there were tall pointed trees on either side of the station; they craned out of the window and learned from the guard that it was Langton. At the next station there were low spreading trees, and it was called Ashfield. The third station was Pippingford.

There was no one to meet them, and no cab at the station. At Nandy's request the station-master telephoned to Saint Peter's School. 'Yes, it's young Master Faringdon and his nurse,' he said. 'Can Mrs. Chapman send to fetch him from the station?' He told them that a dog-cart would be sent for them in a quarter of an hour. They sat in the corner of the waiting-room: Andrew propped his head against Nandy's shoulder; he was too tired now to mind about anything.

The dog-cart arrived, driven by a withered-looking old man with a yellow face which seemed to be kept in position by his high stiff collar. 'Is this the young gentleman for Saint Peter's School?' he asked.

They climbed up into the dog-cart. It was a fine starry night: Andrew thought it such a pity that there were no five-pointed stars set at proper intervals in an expanse of dark blue sky, like stars in pictures. The real sky was blurred and smeared, instead of being neatly pierced by little pin-points of light.

They drove about a mile along a hilly road; at first there were houses and lights, then there was a wood on one side of the road and on the other an occasional isolated house. They turned off the road on to a rough drive, which seemed to go round in circles. The man with the yellow face pointed out a dark clump of trees. 'That's where Saint Peter's School is,' he said; but they did not seem to come any nearer to it, the longer they drove. Then suddenly they turned a curve, and the clump of trees was straight in front of them. The man with the yellow face climbed down and fixed a gate open. They drove between the dark trees, and then out into the open again, and there the house stood.

The main part of the house was a square, grey Georgian building; in front there was a semicircular porch supported on fluted Ionic columns, at the back there were straggling wings of more recent date. The dog-cart's wheels crunched the gravel in front of the house. They climbed down and went into the porch; and Mrs. Chapman, the headmaster's wife, came towards them, a slim, pale and exceedingly handsome woman.

'How do you do, Nurse?' she said. 'This is Andrew, isn't it?' and she touched him lightly on the forehead,

269

with very tightly closed but not unfriendly lips. 'I'll shew you his room, Nurse,' she said; 'then you must come and have something to eat.'

They walked upstairs; the carpet was soft and thick. Overhead was an eighteenth-century painted ceiling. 'When you're in the School, you'll go up by the side stairs,' said Mrs. Chapman to Andrew.

Mrs. Chapman led them along a passage, and opened a door into a bedroom; there were four other boys already in bed. 'We call this the Blue Room,' she said, 'because it used to be blue.' It was now distempered a bright pink.

'This is Matron,' said Mrs. Chapman, and introduced a severe-looking woman in a nurse's uniform, wearing pince-nez. 'We'll leave Andrew with you now, Matron,' she said. Nandy kissed him good-bye. 'You must come here and pay Andrew a visit some day,' said Mrs. Chapman kindly.

'You must hurry up and get to bed,' said Matron; 'and then I'll bring you your supper. Put your clothes neatly in the basket under your bed; and no talking, mind, until you're undressed.' Matron went away. Andrew brushed his teeth, and said his prayers; and then he was in bed and could look about him.

Three of the other boys were lying down in bed and chattering volubly. The fourth, a fair boy called Tony, with prominent teeth, was talking in a low voice to his mother, who was sitting by his bed.

James, a red-faced boy, said: 'You're Andrew, aren't you?'

'Well, you're a good boy,' said Christopher, who slept in the next bed, 'because you've come late. If you hadn't, we shouldn't still be allowed to talk.' Christopher had already been a term in the school; everyone else in the room was new.

'What wonderful boys you are at Saint Peter's,' said Tony's mother brightly. 'They ring a bell, and then you all go to sleep! And then they ring another bell, and you all wake up! I wonder if you'll like that, Tony darling.'

Matron brought Andrew a cup of cocoa, and stood over him while he drank it. 'I am afraid you must come away now, Mrs. Le Mesurier,' she said to Tony's mother. 'Silence now, boys; good night.' And she turned out the light.

Andrew turned his face to the wall. He hoped that he would remember at once where he was, when he woke in the morning. It would be such a shock to wake up and find that he was at school, if he expected to wake in the store-room at Quenby with Stephen and Nandy. It was always unpleasant to wake in a new room; the window and the furniture were always in the wrong place. In the first moments of waking you tried to force them into their right places, so that it might become the same room in which you had woken yesterday; but they were always recalcitrant. You were obliged in the end to resign yourself to waking up elsewhere. He was tired, and soon fell asleep.

He was wakened by a maid bustling in at five minutes to seven: she drew up the blind and placed a mug of milk heavily on Andrew's wash-stand, and another on Christopher's.

'Why's she given us that?' asked Andrew.

'Because we're delicate,' said Christopher. 'At least I am, and you must be, I suppose. Filthy stuff!'

Andrew was flattered at being considered delicate; but it was very unpleasant to be called with a mug of milk, and it looked blue round the edges.

'The boys in the Brown Room pour theirs out of the window,' said Christopher. 'They're lucky; they can throw it into the bushes. We can't do it here because it would only go on the drive, and someone would see it, and we should be swished.'

At seven the bell rang, and they had to get up. At twenty-three minutes past Matron came in. 'What, aren't you ready, boys?' she cried. 'It's silence time by *my* watch. Hurry up. If it weren't the first day you would all have bad conduct marks.'

'Oh, but, Matron!' protested Christopher.

'Oh, it's no use telling me what the time is by *your* watch,' said Matron; 'when I'm here you go by mine. Get dressed all of you, and read your Scripture Unions.'

'What's that?' asked Ernest.

'Oh, of course, you new boys haven't got them. Mrs. Chapman will give them to you, I expect, and tell you what to do with them. I haven't time to see about it now.' And Matron stumped out of the room.

Mrs. Chapman glided into the room carrying a packet of cards. 'These are your Scripture Union cards, dears,' she said. 'They're a list of pieces from the Bible for you to read every day; and I've brought them so that you can begin this morning.'

Each new boy was given a card, and in addition a little book full of texts, one to be learnt each morning; and a book-marker with a picture of cherry blossom, inscribed *Be strong and of a good courage. Joshua i. 6.*

'Now put these in your Bibles, and you can begin at once, dears,' said Mrs. Chapman. 'It's the third chapter of Habakkuk for to-day — near the end of the Old Testament.'

'I haven't got a Bible unpacked; it's in my box,' said Ernest.

'Oh, dear child, I wish you'd *think*,' said Mrs. Chapman; 'it stands to reason that you put things that you'll want at once in your bag, doesn't it?'

She went away, and they all solemnly knelt down and said their prayers. Andrew had once read a school story in which the hero, a very good boy called Derek, was bullied by bad boys because he said his prayers. He was relieved to find that everyone else at Saint Peter's said prayers, just as he did.

A bell rang, and they went downstairs. As it was the first day of the term, the whole school collected in the play-room, and sat on benches against the wall. A few minutes later the headmaster, Mr. Chapman, came in; he walked all round the room shaking hands, and then sat down at a desk at the end of the room.

Mr. Chapman was a red-faced man with a Roman nose, who above all things resembled a turkey-cock. At present he seemed in a good mood, and he delivered his customary homily for the beginning of term.

'Well, we're very glad to see you back again. I don't suppose you're so pleased to be back, but the harder you work, the quicker the term will pass. But you must remember that it isn't what you learn that matters: you're not here to learn, but to learn to learn; to use your minds if you've got any. So you must not mind being taught what you may think a lot of rubbish. We shan't teach you much rubbish, but it wouldn't matter if we did. It doesn't matter what you learn, so long as you learn to use your minds properly. They say that Chinese is a splendid mental exercise, and it might be a good thing to make the whole school do nothing but Chinese for a whole term. I think I shall try it some time; but I shan't this term. I shall now take the names of boys who are going to learn Music, Dancing, Riding, or Carpentry.' When he came to Andrew's name he told him that his aunt had written that he was to learn dancing, but none of the other 'extras'.

Mrs. Chapman and the maids came in for prayers;

then they sang *O God our help in ages past* and went in to breakfast.

Andrew sat near the middle of a long table; on his left were boys younger than himself, descending to 'the babies' who sat by Mrs. Chapman. On his right were boys of his own age, and some of a few months older; most of them had already been one or two terms at Saint Peter's. Matron sat at that end of the table.

Everyone had to eat the same amount; and it was a great deal. It seemed to Andrew that it was almost impossible to eat so much in the twenty-five minutes allowed for breakfast. There was porridge, and then haddock, and two slices of bread and margarine and one of bread and marmalade. It was impossible to persuade Matron to let one off the second slice of bread and margarine. Andrew exerted all his energies in an attempt to finish in time; but he seemed at least one slice of bread and margarine behind everyone else. He had no time to waste in conversation.

Mr. Chapman stood up to say grace; they all scraped back their chairs and stood up. Andrew still had his bread and marmalade to eat and had to stay behind in the dining-room, standing at his place and eating, when the maids came in to clear away.

VIII

ANDREW had been placed in the Third Form, which
worked in the play-room under Miss Jenkyns, a rheumatic and elderly mistress. Brian was the head boy of the
form, and had the duty of collecting books, of filling
ink-pots, and of setting a good example. When he said
'O Lord' once, Miss Jenkyns was deeply pained.

'That is a very profane exclamation,' she said.

'May I say "good Heavens", Miss Jenkyns?' asked
Brian.

'Perhaps that is better,' she admitted.

'Please, Miss Jenkyns, may I say "gracious"?' demanded Christopher.

'And may I say "mercy"?' asked James.

'I had rather none of you exclaimed at all,' said Miss
Jenkyns.

Andrew enjoyed his work and did not mind football
as much as he had expected. The new boys played a
gentle little game under the supervision of Miss Jenkyns,
or of a kind old master, Mr. Glover. It did not last very
long, and there was time to read for a quarter of an hour
between games and afternoon school.

The dancing class was a worse ordeal. This was held
on Monday evenings. The boys had to wear Eton suits
and very tight white cotton gloves, and they walked
down to the dining-room each carrying a skipping-rope.
The dancing-mistress, Miss Falk, was a Jewess, who
added to her very considerable stature by wearing a
large comb in her hair, and shoes with very high heels.
The new boys were introduced to her and had to shake
hands.

'Not with the glove, Andrew,' said Miss Falk;

and he had to pull off his exceedingly tight white glove.

'Now you will all march round nicely, dears, and you must all smile at me nicely when you pass,' she said.

The music mistress played a march from *The Pirates of Penzance*. '*Smile*, boys,' entreated Miss Falk, 'don't frown like that, or I shall run away. Go round once more, and all smile this time.'

Brian obstinately put on a fixed frown.

'*That's* better,' said Miss Falk; 'but Brian hasn't smiled at me yet; and I'm afraid you must all go round once more until he does.'

Brian gave a hideous grin, with which she had to be content.

The children were then spaced out, so as to have room for skipping. This was very difficult. It was satisfying to hear the rope beat on the floor, and to feel it come through under one's feet; but this did not always happen. The elder boys did it quite easily, and more or less in time to the music; but the new boys were getting into terrible difficulties. Tony caught his rope in the electric light, and the lamp came whirring down within a few inches of the floor; Ernest dropped one end of his skipping-rope with a loud clatter, and James had lost his balance, and fallen on the slippery floor. Andrew did not want any such disasters to overtake him; he was pleased when his rope became entangled, and he managed to spend a long time unravelling it.

After they had done some curious exercises, described by Miss Falk as 'Scotch Reels', there was a short interval. They were allowed to sit on the floor and talk.

'Well, boys,' said Miss Falk, 'I hope you had *lovely* holidays. I wonder if any of you thought of *me* since last term? Hands up, who thought of me. Only ten of you thought of me? I *wonder* what you thought about me?'

Andrew thought she was a fool.

'Now if you're all rested, dears,' said Miss Falk, 'we'll go on to the second part of our programme, which is *real* dancing. If you'll find your partners, perhaps Miss Blackett will play us a nice Valse.'

An elder boy called Roger kindly asked Andrew to dance with him; Ernest was left over, and had to dance with Miss Falk. Talking was not allowed while they danced. 'One — two — three,' counted Miss Falk. 'One and, two and, three — on your toes more, Ernest. That's better; chassé, dear, like this. One — two — three.'

Andrew liked Roger, who steered him round safely without running into the other couples; but he thought dancing a tiring and giddy occupation. He wished he could take off his gloves. Roger's had split down the seam, and were damp with sweat.

They danced a polka, which was very strenuous, and then a foxtrot. Finally they danced the Lancers, which was restful. 'Thank goodness,' whispered Roger; 'that means it's nearly bed-time.'

They all had to file by Miss Falk and shake hands. 'Well, I shall look forward to seeing you all next Monday,' she said; 'I hope you won't forget me quite before then. Do you think you will, Andrew?'

'No, I shall never forget you, Miss Falk,' said Andrew.

Miss Falk did not come on the next Monday; she had fallen ill of Spanish influenza. Saint Peter's had also been attacked by this epidemic, which made a rapid progress through the school. The sick-room was filled in a day, and the bedrooms at the back of the house, where the elder boys slept, had to be converted into extra wards. The school had suddenly become very small; there were only two classes, and only one game of football. The head boy and one other boy had been carried off in ambulances; they were seriously ill, and were prayed for at school prayers. There were several hospital nurses in the matron's room, and Mrs. Chapman walked round the house twice a day spraying a strong-smelling disinfectant.

The term had started well in fine autumn weather; now it was becoming cold and grey. The staff was over-worked and often short-tempered, and the boys were depressed and frightened by the illness in the school. Often they saw nurses whispering together, and they wondered if someone were going to die. For a week the epidemic seemed to stand still, then again boys became ill with alarming suddenness, and more rooms had to be converted into sick-rooms. When boys went up to bed at night they often found that they had been moved into a different room, and that their own beds were being used for influenza patients. Boys were shifted from room to room; placed in beds next to others whom they would else have only known by sight, they formed rapid friendships and enmities, soon to be dissolved by another change.

Andrew escaped the epidemic for nearly three weeks. He was taken ill during a French lesson, a conversation class taken by old Monsieur Molinier, who came over from Handborough Regis. Andrew used to be a favourite pupil; thanks to Mademoiselle de la Sablonnière, he had a tolerable accent. That day, however, he could do nothing. 'Mais il est idiot, ce garçon,' said Monsieur Molinier; and Andrew wept.

At the end of the lesson he went to the Matron's room, and found one of the hospital nurses. 'I don't feel very well,' he said.

'Well, and what's the matter with you?' she asked.

'I've got a cough,' he said, 'and a sort of pain in my stomach. I think it's a stomach cough.'

She laughed. 'Well, I'll take your temperature,' she said.

It was 103°, and Andrew was promptly sent to bed in the Mauve Room.

IX

Stephen felt lost and lonely when Nandy took Andrew away to school. The unusual kindness of Miss Hunt and the cousins only made him feel more wretched. They were still strangers to him, and they frightened him. He was even more distressed when Nandy telephoned from Handborough that she had missed her connection, and could not return that night. Philip slept in the store-room to keep Stephen company. He was glad of this, because he knew that Andrew liked Philip better than any of the others; but he longed for Nandy to come back.

Nandy returned the following day, but not to stay. It had been decided that Stephen was too old to have a nurse any longer, and in future he was to be in Miss Hunt's charge. Nandy left one morning very early, while Stephen was still in bed. He had not been told anything beforehand, and was surprised to find her bending over him and kissing him good-bye. She told him not to cry, and said that she was sure that she would see him again one day. Then she was gone.

Stephen's life at Quenby underwent a complete change. Within a few days he lost both Andrew, his constant companion and counsellor, and Nandy, who had cared for him devotedly all his life. His new companion was Tom. He did lessons with Tom in the mornings; went with Miss Hunt and Tom to the village; played with Tom in the garden; and slept with him in a little room at the top of the house. He hated Tom.

Tom saw that Stephen was afraid of him, and was quick to take advantage of his size. He made Stephen fetch and carry for him, and he found unending pleasure in kicking and pinching him. On their walks he would make Stephen lag behind Miss Hunt, and then he would tread on his heels and kick his shins. Sometimes in their bedroom Tom pinched Stephen till he cried out. 'Stop it, you fool, she'll hear you,' Tom would hiss at him; and Stephen, though he only wished that Miss Hunt would hear, did not dare to make a sound.

One evening Tom broke Stephen's toy aeroplane. It was a stupid thing, and Stephen had been annoyed with it ever since the day when he had been given it off a Christmas tree at a party. Still, he managed to coax a few tears for it. He knew that Aunt Emma would be coming up in a minute, and he hoped that if she saw him crying she might understand how unhappy he was with Tom. It sounded silly when he told Aunt Emma that he was crying because Tom had broken his toy.

'Tom,' said Aunt Emma sharply, 'I'm ashamed of you. Look what you've done. You've made little Stephen cry. Say you're sorry at once.'

It was no use. Stephen could see that Aunt Emma thought him a baby for crying about nothing. He saw that he would have to put up with Tom as well as he could; no one was ever going to make things any better for him. Andrew would come back at Christmas, but that would not be for months and months.

Stephen had a short respite when the epidemic of influenza reached Quenby. He caught it and went to bed. Tom was removed from the infection to his father's dressing-room, and Stephen, who was not very ill, was left in peace. He enjoyed the visits of the doctor, who tickled him pleasantly with his stethoscope and used to allow him to choose the colour of his medicine.

Stephen's happiness did not last long. One day Tom, looking more than usually yellow, was brought into the room, supported by Miss Hunt and Aunt Emma. 'Here's company for you,' said Aunt Emma cheerfully.

Tom had influenza too, and he and Stephen were to be together even more closely than before, day and night.

X

ANDREW was very ill. The nurses did not like him, because he was clumsy and tiresome, and frequently upset his medicine or his food. The boys in the Mauve Room were not so ill as he was, and they used to laugh at him and tease him. He hardly cared, he was far too ill. His mind swam confusedly through the day. He was dimly aware of medicine and of cups of milk, of visits from Mrs. Chapman and the nurses, and of a pleasant suspension of all obligation to do anything or to make any effort. He disliked any interruption of this state of not-being. Once Mrs. Chapman stood over him and scolded him; the nurses had complained that he gave trouble. He soon sank back, and the protective waves of fever swept over him, coming between him and other people.

His temperature rose; one afternoon he babbled confusedly all through the two hours during which they had been ordered to rest in silence. Mrs. Chapman came in and told him to be quiet, and he whimpered and said that everyone was unkind to him. So the other boys told him afterwards; he remembered nothing about it.

The other boys were noisy and impatient at being kept in bed. Paul and Robin always poured their medicine away, and never stopped talking in silence time. Desmond, a little boy of only six, was wildly obstreperous in the morning, and in the evening was always whimpering. 'I want mother,' he wailed; 'I want to go home; I want some solid foo-oo-ood!'

One evening two nurses came into the room; the night-nurse was just taking over duty from the day-nurse. They stood by Andrew's bed, thinking he was asleep. 'That child Andrew,' said the day-nurse, 'he's been very ill, but to-day he was a good deal better. His temperature was down to ninety-nine this evening.'

He began to recover; soon he had a little fish for his lunch, and a thin slice of bread and butter for his tea. He began to read again with avidity all the old magazines he could find.

Towards the end of his convalescence, which was slow, Mrs. Chapman came into the Mauve Room one morning while he was sitting up in bed.

'What do you think, children?' she said. 'The War's over!'

They gasped. The War was over at last, the War which had lasted so long that they could hardly remember a time when it was not there.

'Your father and mother will be able to come back from Egypt now, Andrew,' said Mrs. Chapman kindly. 'Won't that be lovely?'

'Lovely!' said Andrew.

He thought: 'We shan't live at Quenby any more. There'll be no more walks into Duckwold with Miss Hunt; no more bullying from Tom and Mabel; no more hiding from them in the garden. We shan't have to live with Aunt Emma and pretend to like her; we shan't be kept away from Handborough Regis and the Aunts.' Now there was peace in the World, there would surely be peace at home. Soon Colonel Faringdon would come back from Egypt, and would take them away from the Milburns for ever.

Andrew felt uneasily that there was something unpleasant that he had forgotten, some lurking cause for disquiet, something that would prevent the realization of his dreams of escape, some further misfortune that would fall upon him when he had shaken off all the troubles that the War had brought upon him and Stephen. Suddenly he remembered. It was not his mother who was coming back with his father from Cairo. Before his mind's troubled vision there passed the green hat and the dark, disconcerting face of his stepmother.